SELECTED SHORT STORIES

DOVER THRIFT EDITIONS

Henry James

DOVER PUBLICATIONS, INC.
MINEOLA, NEW YORK

DOVER THRIFT EDITIONS

GENERAL EDITOR: SUSAN L. RATTINER
EDITOR OF THIS VOLUME: JANET B. KOPITO

Bibliographical Note

This Dover edition, first published in 2017, contains the unabridged texts of five short stories by Henry James. The original publication information for each story can be found in the Bibliography on page vii.

International Standard Book Number

ISBN-13: 978-0-486-81290-8
ISBN-10: 0-486-81290-1

Manufactured in the United States by LSC Communications
81290101   2017
www.doverpublications.com

Note

The author of twenty novels and more than one hundred short stories, as well as essays and reviews, plays, two autobiographies, and many other works, Henry James is one of the foremost authors of the mid-to-late nineteenth and early twentieth centuries. Born in New York City in 1843, he was one of five children in the well-to-do James family. His older brother, William James, contributed to and shaped the psychological and philosophical theories of the time; his sister, Alice James, revealed her troubled personal history in her famous *Diary*, first published in 1934 and revised and republished in 1964.

The James family moved often during Henry's youth, traveling to Europe in the late 1850s and living in Albany, Newport, Rhode Island, and Boston. In 1862, James began the study of law at Harvard, but withdrew in 1863, intending instead to write (James received an honorary degree from Harvard in 1911). While in his twenties, Henry embarked on the "Grand Tour," and the European locales he visited made a lasting impression on him, especially France and Italy. He moved to London in 1869, and by the late 1870s had become enmeshed in the city's social milieu.

Traveling back and forth to Europe and absorbing the varied cultures, James keenly observed the contrast between the traditional lifestyle of Europeans and the modern, "freer," habits of Americans. He drew upon this theme in his works *Daisy Miller* (1878), *The Europeans* (1878), and *The Ambassadors* (1903). In addition, James delved into the supernatural in the suspenseful stories "The Altar of the Dead" (1895), "The Beast in the Jungle" (1903), and his best-known work in the genre, "The Turn of the Screw" (1898). Other significant literary achievements of James's career are *Washington*

Square (1880), *The Portrait of a Lady* (1881), *The Wings of the Dove* (1902), and *The Golden Bowl* (1904). Many of James's works—including those in the present edition—appeared in journals before being published in book form.

The five short works comprising *Selected Short Stories* appeared in roughly a fifteen-year period: 1879 to 1893. Joining the three supernatural tales mentioned above, "Sir Edmond Orme" (1879) concerns the appearance of a "pale young man in black, with the air of a gentleman," who is invisible to all but the narrator and a woman whose daughter he admires. When the daughter is struck by the odd behavior of both her mother and the unnamed narrator, she exclaims, "One would think you had seen a ghost." Sir Edmund Orme is, indeed, a supernatural visitor, and the purpose of his visits eventually is revealed. "Georgina's Reasons" (1884) depicts a "singular girl" whose actions bring into question her true character; an acquaintance believes that her friend is, perhaps, lacking in shame (and, as the narrator adds, "conscience"). It is up to the reader to weigh Georgina's choices and ponder her motivations. "Lord Beaupré" (1892) demonstrates the outcome of a plot intended to manipulate the human heart—a daunting task that has unforeseen consequences. James includes some comparisons between British and American manners in this tale—a favorite theme. The predicament in "The Real Thing" (1892) involves the appearance of a destitute, but striking, married couple who hope to model for an artist whose "perversity" is "an innate preference for the represented subject over the real one"—he prefers to employ models who can be *transformed* into the subject to be portrayed, rather than the "real thing." "The Middle Years" (1893) shares its title with James's posthumously published autobiography (1917), as well as the masterwork of the protagonist, Dencombe, who, appraising the achievements of his career, regrets that at this late stage of his life, he will not be given the opportunity to "have another go." He is treated by a physician, Doctor Hugh, who, it turns out, is reading, and enjoying immensely, Dencombe's latest book. The two forge a bond that helps clarify the older man's understanding of life: "We work in the dark—we do what we can—we give what we have."

Henry James moved to England in 1876 and largely remained there for decades. In 1915, he became a naturalized British subject. After experiencing a series of illnesses in his late sixties, James died of a stroke in 1916.

Bibliography

"Sir Edward Orme"
First published in *Black and White*, December 1879.
Reprinted in *The Lesson of the Master* (London & New York: Macmillan, 1892).

"Georgina's Reasons"
First published as a serial in *The Sun,* a New York newspaper, July–August, 1884.
Reprinted in *Stories Revived* (London: Macmillan, 1885).

"Lord Beaupré"
First published in *Macmillan's Magazine,* April–June, 1892.
Reprinted in *The Private Life* (London: Osgood, McIlvaine, 1893).

"The Real Thing"
First published in *Black and White*, April 1892.
Reprinted in *The Real Thing and Other Tales* (London and New York: Macmillan, 1893).

"The Middle Years"
First published in *Scribner's Magazine,* May 1893.
Reprinted in *Terminations* (New York: Harper, 1895).

Contents

SELECTED SHORT STORIES

SIR EDMUND ORME

THE STATEMENT APPEARS to have been written, though the fragment is undated, long after the death of his wife, whom I take to have been one of the persons referred to. There is, however, nothing in the strange story to establish this point, which is, perhaps, not of importance. When I took possession of his effects I found these pages, in a locked drawer, among papers relating to the unfortunate lady's too brief career (she died in childbirth a year after her marriage), letters, memoranda, accounts, faded photographs, cards of invitation. That is the only connection I can point to, and you may easily and will probably say that the tale is too extravagant to have had a demonstrable origin. I cannot, I admit, vouch for his having intended it as a report of real occurrence—I can only vouch for his general veracity. In any case it was written for himself, not for others. I offer it to others—having full option—precisely because it is so singular. Let them, in respect to the form of the thing, bear in mind that it was written quite for himself. I have altered nothing but the names.

If there's a story in the matter I recognise the exact moment at which it began. This was on a soft, still Sunday noon in November, just after church, on the sunny Parade. Brighton was full of people; it was the height of the season, and the day was even more respectable than lovely—which helped to account for the multitude of walkers. The blue sea itself was decorous; it seemed to doze, with a gentle snore (if that be decorum), as if nature were preaching a sermon. After writing letters all the morning I had come out to take a look at it before luncheon. I was leaning over the rail which separates the King's Road from the beach, and I think I was smoking a cigarette, when I became conscious of an intended joke in the shape of a light walking-stick laid across my shoulders. The idea, I found, had been thrown off by Teddy Bostwick, of the Rifles and was intended as a contribution to talk. Our talk came off as we strolled together—he always took your arm to show you he forgave your obtuseness about his humour—and looked at the people, and bowed to some of them, and wondered who others were, and differed in opinion as to the prettiness of the girls. About Charlotte Marden we agreed, however, as we saw her coming toward us with her mother; and there surely could have been no one who wouldn't have agreed with us. The Brighton air, of old, used to make plain girls pretty and pretty girls prettier still—I don't know whether it works the spell now. The place, at any rate, was rare for complexions, and Miss Marden's was one that made people turn round. It made us stop, heaven knows—at least, it was one of the things, for we already knew the ladies.

We turned with them, we joined them, we went where they were going. They were only going to the end and back—they had just come out of church. It was another manifestation of Teddy's humour that he got immediate possession of Charlotte, leaving me to walk with her mother. However, I was not unhappy; the girl was before me and I had her to talk about. We prolonged our walk, Mrs. Marden kept me, and presently she said she was tired and must sit down. We found a place on a sheltered bench—we gossiped as the people passed. It had already struck me, in this pair, that the resemblance between the mother and the daughter was wonderful even among such resemblances—the more so that it took so little account of a difference of nature. One often hears mature mothers spoken of as warnings—signposts, more or less discouraging, of the way daughters may go. But there was nothing deterrent in the idea that Charlotte, at fifty-five, should be as beautiful, even though it were conditioned on her being as pale and preoccupied, as Mrs. Marden. At twenty-two she had a kind of rosy blankness and she was admirably handsome. Her head had the charming shape of her mother's, and her features the same fine order. Then there were looks and movements and tones (moments when you could scarcely say whether it were aspect or sound), which, between the two personalities, were a reflection, a recall.

These ladies had a small fortune and a cheerful little house at Brighton, full of portraits and tokens and trophies (stuffed animals on the top of bookcases, and sallow, varnished fish under glass), to which Mrs. Marden professed herself attached by pious memories. Her husband had been "ordered" there in ill-health, to spend the last years of his life, and she had already mentioned to me that it was a place in which she felt herself still under the protection of his goodness. His goodness appeared to have been great, and she sometimes had the air of defending it against mysterious imputations. Some sense of protection, of an influence invoked and cherished, was evidently necessary to her; she had a dim wistfulness, a longing for security. She wanted friends and she had a good many. She was kind to me on our first meeting, and I never suspected her of the vulgar purpose of "making up" to me—a suspicion, of course, unduly frequent in conceited young men. It never struck me that she wanted me for her daughter, nor yet, like some unnatural mammas, for herself. It was as if they had had a common deep, shy need and had been ready to say: "Oh, be friendly to us and be trustful! Don't be afraid, you won't be expected to marry us." "Of course there's something about mamma; that's really what makes her such a dear!" Charlotte said to me, confidentially, at an early stage of our acquaintance. She worshipped her mother's appearance. It was the only thing she was vain of; she accepted the raised eyebrows as a charming ultimate fact. "She looks as if she were waiting for the doctor, dear mamma," she said on another occasion. "Perhaps *you're* the doctor; do you think you are?" It appeared in the event that I had some healing power. At any rate when I learned, for she once dropped the remark, that Mrs. Marden also thought there was something "awfully strange" about Charlotte, the relation between the two ladies became extremely interesting. It was happy enough, at bottom; each had the other so much on her mind.

On the Parade the stream of strollers held its course, and Charlotte presently went by with Teddy Bostwick. She smiled and nodded and continued, but when she came back she stopped and spoke to us. Captain Bostwick positively declined to go in, he said the occasion was too jolly: might they therefore take another turn? Her mother dropped a "Do as you like," and the girl gave me an impertinent smile over her shoulder as they quitted us. Teddy looked at me with his glass in one eye; but I didn't mind that; it was only of Miss Marden I was thinking as I observed to my companion, laughing:

"She's a bit of a coquette, you know."

"Don't say that—don't say that!" Mrs. Marden murmured.

"The nicest girls always are—just a little," I was magnanimous enough to plead.

"Then why are they always punished?"

The intensity of the question startled me—it had come out in such a vivid flash. Therefore I had to think a moment before I inquired: "What do you know about it?"

"I was a bad girl myself."

"And were you punished?"

"I carry it through life," said Mrs. Marden, looking away from me. "Ah!" she suddenly panted, in the next breath, rising to her feet and staring at her daughter, who had reappeared again with Captain Bostwick. She stood a few seconds, with the queerest expression in her face; then she sank upon the seat again and I saw that she had blushed crimson. Charlotte, who had observed her movement, came straight up to her and, taking her hand with quick tenderness, seated herself on the other side of her. The girl had turned pale—she gave her mother a fixed, frightened look. Mrs. Marden, who had had some shock which escaped our detection, recovered herself; that is she sat quiet and inexpressive, gazing at the indifferent crowd, the sunny air, the slumbering sea. My eye happened to fall, however, on the interlocked hands of the two ladies, and I quickly guessed that the grasp of the elder one was violent. Bostwick stood before them, wondering what was the matter and asking me from his little vacant disk if I knew; which led Charlotte to say to him after a moment, with a certain irritation:

"Don't stand there that way, Captain Bostwick; go away—*please* go away."

I got up at this, hoping that Mrs. Marden wasn't ill; but she immediately begged that we would *not* go away, that we would particularly stay and that we would presently come home to lunch. She drew me down beside her and for a moment I felt her hand pressing my arm in a way that might have been an involuntary betrayal of distress and might have been a private signal. What she might have wished to point out to me I couldn't divine: perhaps she had seen somebody or something abnormal in the crowd. She explained to us in a few minutes that she was all right; that she was only liable to palpitations—they came as quickly as they went. It was time to move, and we moved. The incident was felt to be closed. Bostwick and I lunched with our sociable friends, and when

I walked away with him he declared that he had never seen such dear kind creatures.

Mrs. Marden had made us promise to come back the next day to tea, and had exhorted us in general to come as often as we could. Yet the next day, when at five o'clock I knocked at the door of the pretty house, it was to learn that the ladies had gone up to town. They had left a message for us with the butler: he was to say that they had suddenly been called—were very sorry. They would be absent a few days. This was all I could extract from the dumb domestic. I went again three days later, but they were still away; and it was not till the end of a week that I got a note from Mrs. Marden, saying "We are back; do come and forgive us." It was on this occasion, I remember (the occasion of my going just after getting the note), that she told me she had intuitions. I don't know how many people there were in England at that time in that predicament, but there were very few who would have mentioned it; so that the announcement struck me as original, especially as her point was that some of these uncanny promptings were connected with me. There were other people present—idle Brighton folk, old women with frightened eyes and irrelevant interjections—and I had but a few minutes' talk with Charlotte; but the day after this I met them both at dinner and had the satisfaction of sitting next to Miss Marden. I recall that hour as the hour on which it first completely came over me that she was a beautiful, liberal creature. I had seen her personality in patches and gleams, like a song sung in snatches, but now it was before me in a large rosy glow, as if it had been a full volume of sound—I heard the whole of the air. It was sweet, fresh music—I was often to hum it over.

After dinner I had a few words with Mrs. Marden; it was at the moment, late in the evening, when tea was handed about. A servant passed near us with a tray, I asked her if she would have a cup, and, on her assenting, took one and handed it to her. She put out her hand for it and I gave it to her, safely as I supposed; but as she was in the act of receiving it she started and faltered, so that the cup and saucer dropped with a crash of porcelain and without, on the part of my interlocutress, the usual woman's movement to save her dress. I stooped to pick up the fragments and when I raised myself Mrs. Marden was looking across the room at her daughter, who looked back at her smiling, but with an anxious light in her eyes. "Dear mamma, what on earth *is* the matter with you?" the silent question seemed to say. Mrs. Marden coloured, just as she had done after her strange movement on the Parade the other week, and I was therefore surprised when she said to me with unexpected assurance: "You should really have a steadier hand!" I had begun to stammer a defence of my hand when I became aware that she had fixed her eyes upon me with an intense appeal. It was ambiguous at first and only added to my confusion; then suddenly I understood, as plainly as if she had murmured "Make believe it was you—make believe it was you." The servant came back to take the morsels of the cup and wipe up the spilt tea, and while I was in the midst of making believe Mrs. Marden abruptly brushed away from me and from her daughter's attention and went into another room. I noticed that she gave no heed to the state of her dress.

I saw nothing more of either of them that evening, but the next morning, in the King's Road, I met Miss Marden with a roll of music in her muff. She told me she had been a little way alone, to practice duets with a friend, and I asked her if she would go a little way further in company. She gave me leave to attend her to her door, and as we stood before it I inquired if I might go in. "No, not to-day—I don't want you," she said, candidly, though not roughly; while the words caused me to direct a wistful, disconcerted gaze at one of the windows of the house. It fell upon the white face of Mrs. Marden, who was looking out at us from the drawing-room. She stood there long enough for me to see that it was she and not an apparition, as I had thought for a second, and then she vanished before her daughter had observed her. The girl, during our walk, had said nothing about her. As I had been told they didn't want me I left them alone a little, after which circumstances supervened that kept us still longer apart. I finally went up to London, and while there I received a pressing invitation to come immediately down to Tranton, a pretty old place in Sussex belonging to a couple whose acquaintance I had lately made.

I went to Tranton from town, and on arriving found the Mardens, with a dozen other people, in the house. The first thing Mrs. Marden said was: "Will you forgive me?" and when I asked what I had to forgive she answered: "My throwing my tea over you." I replied that it had gone over herself; whereupon she said: "At any rate I was very rude; but some day I think you'll understand, and then you'll make allowances for me." The first day I was there she dropped two or three of these references (she had already indulged in more than one), to the mystic initiation that was in store for me; so that I began, as the phrase is, to chaff her about it, to say I would rather it were less wonderful and take it out at once. She answered that when it should come to me I would have to take it out—there would be little enough option. That it *would* come was privately clear to her, a deep presentiment, which was the only reason she had ever mentioned the matter. Didn't I remember she had told me she had intuitions? From the first time of her seeing me she had been sure there were things I should not escape knowing. Meanwhile there was nothing to do but wait and keep cool, not to be precipitate. She particularly wished not to be any more nervous than she was. And I was above all not to be nervous myself—one got used to everything. I declared that though I couldn't make out what she was talking about I was terribly frightened; the absence of a clue gave such a range to one's imagination. I exaggerated on purpose; for if Mrs. Marden was mystifying I can scarcely say she was alarming. I couldn't imagine what she meant, but I wondered more than I shuddered. I might have said to myself that she was a little wrong in the upper story; but that never occurred to me. She struck me as hopelessly right.

There were other girls in the house, but Charlotte Marden was the most charming; which was so generally felt to be the case that she really interfered with the slaughter of ground game. There were two or three men, and I was of the number, who actually preferred her to the society of the beaters. In short she was recognised as a form of sport superior and exquisite. She was kind to all of us—she made us go out late and come in early. I don't know whether she flirted, but several other members of the party thought *they* did. Indeed, as regards himself, Teddy Bostwick, who had come over from Brighton, was visibly sure.

The third day I was at Tranton was a Sunday, and there was a very pretty walk to morning service over the fields. It was grey, windless weather, and the bell of the little old church that nestled in the hollow of the Sussex down sounded near and domestic. We were a straggling procession, in the mild damp air (which, as always at that season, gave one the feeling that after the trees were bare there was more of it—a larger sky), and I managed to fall a good way behind with Miss Marden. I remember entertaining, as we moved together over the turf, a strong impulse to say something intensely personal, something violent and important—important for *me*, such as that I had never seen her so lovely, or that that particular moment was the sweetest of my life. But always, in youth, such words have been on the lips many times before they are spoken; and I had the sense, not that I didn't know her well enough (I cared little for that), but that she didn't know *me* well enough. In the church, where there were old Tranton tombs and brasses, the big Tranton pew was full. Several of us were scattered, and I found a seat for Miss Marden, and another for myself beside it, at a distance from her mother and from most of our friends. There were two or three decent rustics on the bench, who moved in further to make room for us, and I took my place first, to cut off my companion from our neighbours. After she was seated there was still a space left, which remained empty till service was about half over.

This at least was the moment at which I became aware that another person had entered and had taken the seat. When I noticed him he had apparently been for some minutes in the pew, for he had settled himself and put down his hat beside him, and, with his hands crossed on the nob of his cane, was gazing before him at the altar. He was a pale young man in black, with the air of a gentleman. I was slightly startled on perceiving him, for Miss Marden had not attracted my attention to his entrance by moving to make room for him. After a few minutes, observing that he had no prayerbook, I reached across my neighbour and placed mine before him, on the ledge of the pew; a manœuvre the motive of which was not unconnected with the possibility that, in my own destitution, Miss Marden would give me one side of *her* velvet volume to hold. The pretext, however, was destined to fail, for at the moment I offered him the book the intruder—whose intrusion I had so condoned—rose from his place without thanking me, stepped noiselessly out of the pew (it had no door), and, so discreetly as to attract no attention, passed down the centre of the church. A few minutes had sufficed for his devotions. His behaviour was unbecoming, his early departure even more than his late arrival; but he managed so quietly that we were not incommoded, and I perceived, on turning a little to glance after him, that nobody was disturbed by his withdrawal. I only noticed, and with surprise, that Mrs. Marden had been so affected by it as to rise, involuntarily, an instant, in her place. She stared at him as he passed, but he passed very quickly, and she as quickly dropped down again, though not too soon to catch my eye across the church. Five minutes later I asked Miss Marden, in a low voice, if she would kindly pass me back my prayer-book—I had waited to see if she would spontaneously perform the act. She restored this aid to devotion, but had been so far from troubling herself about it that she could say to me as she did so: "Why on earth did you put it there?" I was on the point of answering her when she dropped on her knees, and I held my tongue. I had only been going to say: "To be decently civil."

After the benediction, as we were leaving our places, I was slightly surprised, again, to see that Mrs. Marden, instead of going out with her companions, had come up the aisle to join us, having apparently something to say to her daughter. She said it, but in an instant I observed that it was only a pretext—her real business was with me. She pushed Charlotte forward and suddenly murmured to me: "Did you see him?"

"The gentleman who sat down here? How could I help seeing him?"

"Hush!" she said, with the intensest excitement; "don't *speak* to her—don't tell her!" She slipped her hand into my arm, to keep me near her, to keep me, it seemed, away from her daughter. The precaution was unnecessary, for Teddy Bostwick had already taken possession of Miss Marden, and as they passed out of church in front of me I saw one of the other men close up on her other hand. It appeared to be considered that I had had my turn. Mrs. Marden withdrew her hand from my arm as soon as we got out, but not before I felt that she had really needed the support. "Don't speak to any one—don't tell any one!" she went on.

"I don't understand. Tell them what?"

"Why, that you saw him."

"Surely they saw him for themselves."

"Not one of them, not one of them." She spoke in a tone of such passionate decision that I glanced at her—she was staring straight before her. But she felt the challenge of my eyes and she stopped short, in the old brown timber porch of the church, with the others well in advance of us, and said, looking at me now and in a quite extraordinary manner: "You're the only person, the only person in the world."

"But *you*, dear madam?"

"Oh me—of course. That's my curse!" And with this she moved rapidly away from me to join the body of the party. I hovered on its outskirts on the way home, for I had food for rumination. Whom had I seen and why was the apparition—it rose before my mind's eye very vividly again—invisible to the others? If an exception had been made for Mrs. Marden, why did it constitute a curse, and why was I to share so questionable an advantage? This inquiry, carried on in my own locked breast, kept me doubtless silent enough during luncheon. After luncheon I went out on the old terrace to smoke a cigarette, but I had only taken a couple of turns when I perceived Mrs. Marden's moulded mask at the window of one of the rooms which opened on the crooked flags. It reminded me of the same flitting presence at the window at Brighton the day I met Charlotte and walked home with her. But this time my ambiguous friend didn't vanish; she tapped on the pane and motioned me to come in. She was in a queer little apartment, one of the many reception-rooms of which the ground-floor at Tranton consisted; it was known as the Indian room and had a decoration vaguely Oriental—bamboo lounges, lacquered screens, lanterns with long fringes and strange idols in cabinets, objects not held to conduce to sociability. The place was little used, and when I went round to her we had it to ourselves. As soon as I entered she said to me: "Please tell me this; are you in love with my daughter?"

I hesitated a moment. "Before I answer your question will you kindly tell me what gives you the idea? I don't consider that I have been very forward."

Mrs. Marden, contradicting me with her beautiful anxious eyes, gave me no satisfaction on the point I mentioned; she only went on strenuously:

"Did you say nothing to her on the way to church?"

"What makes you think I said anything?"

"The fact that you saw him."

"Saw whom, dear Mrs. Marden?"

"Oh, you know," she answered, gravely, even a little reproachfully, as if I were trying to humiliate her by making her phrase the unphraseable.

"Do you mean the gentleman who formed the subject of your strange statement in church—the one who came into the pew?"

"You saw him, you saw him!" Mrs. Marden panted, with a strange mixture of dismay and relief.

"Of course I saw him; and so did you."

"It didn't follow. Did you feel it to be inevitable?"

I was puzzled again. "Inevitable?"

"That you *should* see him?"

"Certainly, since I'm not blind."

"You might have been; every one else is." I was wonderfully at sea, and I frankly confessed it to my interlocutress; but the case was not made clearer by her presently exclaiming: "I knew you would, from the moment you should be really in love with her! I knew it would be the test—what do I mean?—the proof."

"Are there such strange bewilderments attached to that high state?" I asked, smiling.

"You perceive there are. You see him, you see him!" Mrs. Marden announced, with tremendous exaltation. "You'll see him again."

"I've no objection; but I shall take more interest in him if you'll kindly tell me who he is."

She hesitated, looking down a moment; then she said, raising her eyes: "I'll tell you if you'll tell me first what you said to her on the way to church."

"Has she told you I said anything?"

"Do I need that?" smiled Mrs. Marden.

"Oh yes, I remember—your intuitions! But I'm sorry to see they're at fault this time; because I really said nothing to your daughter that was the least out of the way."

"Are you very sure?"

"On my honour, Mrs. Marden."

"Then you consider that you're not in love with her?"

"That's another affair!" I laughed.

"You are—you *are*! You wouldn't have seen him if you hadn't been."

"Who the deuce *is* he, then, madam?" I inquired with some irritation.

She would still only answer me with another question. "Didn't you at least *want* to say something to her—didn't you come very near it?"

The question was much to the point; it justified the famous intuitions. "Very near it—it was the turn of a hair. I don't know what kept me quiet."

"That was quite enough," said Mrs. Marden. "It isn't what you say that determines it; it's what you feel. *That's* what he goes by."

I was annoyed, at last, by her reiterated reference to an identity yet to be established, and I clasped my hands with an air of supplication which covered much real impatience, a sharper curiosity and even the first short throbs of a certain sacred dread. "I entreat you to tell me whom you're talking about."

She threw up her arms, looking away from me, as if to shake off both reserve and responsibility. "Sir Edmund Orme."

"And who is Sir Edmund Orme?"

At the moment I spoke she gave a start. "Hush, here they come." Then as, following the direction of her eyes, I saw Charlotte Marden on the terrace, at the window, she added, with an intensity of warning: "Don't notice him—*never!*"

Charlotte, who had had her hands beside her eyes, peering into the room and smiling, made a sign that she was to be admitted, on which I went and opened the long window. Her mother turned away, and the girl came in with a laughing challenge: "What plot, in the world are you two hatching here?" Some plan—I forget what—was in prospect for the afternoon, as to which Mrs. Marden's participation or consent was solicited—*my* adhesion was taken for granted—and she had been half over the place in her quest. I was flurried, because I saw that Mrs. Marden was flurried (when she turned round to meet her daughter she covered it by a kind of extravagance, throwing herself on the girl's neck and embracing her), and to pass it off I said, fancifully, to Charlotte:

"I've been asking your mother for your hand."

"Oh, indeed, and has she given it?" Miss Marden answered, gayly.

"She was just going to when you appeared there."

"Well, it's only for a moment—I'll leave you free."

"Do you like him, Charlotte?" Mrs. Marden asked, with a candour I scarcely expected.

"It's difficult to say it *before* him isn't it?" the girl replied, entering into the humour of the thing, but looking at me as if she didn't like me.

She would have had to say it before another person as well, for at that moment there stepped into the room from the terrace (the window had been left open), a gentleman who had come into sight, at least into mine, only within the instant. Mrs. Marden had said "Here *they* come," but he appeared to have followed her daughter at a certain distance. I immediately recognised him as the personage who had sat beside us in church. This time I saw him better, saw that his face and his whole air were strange. I speak of him as a personage, because one felt, indescribably, as if a reigning prince had come into the room. He held himself with a kind of habitual majesty, as if he were different from us. Yet he looked fixedly and gravely at me, till I wondered what he expected of me. Did he consider that I should bend my knee or kiss his hand? He turned his eyes in the same way on Mrs. Marden, but she knew what to do. After the first agitation produced by his approach she took no notice of him whatever; it made me remember her passionate adjuration to me. I had to achieve a great effort to imitate her, for though I knew nothing about him but that he was Sir Edmund Orme I felt his presence as a strong appeal, almost as an oppression. He stood there without speaking—young, pale, handsome, clean-shaven, decorous, with extraordinary light blue eyes and something old-fashioned, like a portrait of years ago, in his head, his manner of wearing his hair. He was in complete mourning (one immediately felt that he was very well dressed), and he carried his hat in his hand. He looked again strangely hard at me, harder than any one in the world had ever looked before; and I remember feeling rather cold and wishing he would say something. No silence had ever seemed to me so soundless. All this was of course an impression intensely rapid; but that it had consumed some instants was proved to me suddenly by the aspect of Charlotte Marden, who stared from her mother to me and back again (he never looked at her, and she had no appearance of looking at him), and then broke out with: "What on earth is the matter with you? You've such odd faces!" I felt the colour come back to mine, and when she went on in the same tone: "One would think you had seen a ghost!" I was conscious that I had turned very red. Sir Edmund Orme never blushed, and I could see that he had no capacity for embarrassment. One had met people of that sort, but never any one with such a grand indifference.

"Don't be impertinent; and go and tell them all that I'll join them," said Mrs. Marden with much dignity, but with a quaver in her voice.

"And will you come—*you*?" the girl asked, turning away. I made no answer, taking the question, somehow, as meant for her companion. But he was more silent than I, and when she reached the door (she was going out that way), she stopped, with her hand on the knob, and looked at me, repeating it. I assented, springing forward to open the door for her, and as she passed out she exclaimed to me mockingly: "You haven't got your wits about you—you sha'n't have my hand!"

I closed the door and turned round to find that Sir Edmund Orme had during the moment my back was presented to him retired by the window. Mrs. Marden stood there and we looked at each other long. It had only then—as the girl flitted away—come home to me that her daughter was unconscious of what had happened. It was *that*, oddly enough, that gave me a sudden, sharp shake, and not my own perception of our visitor, which appeared perfectly natural. It made the fact vivid to me that she had been equally unaware of him in church, and the two facts together— now that they were over—set my heart more sensibly beating. I wiped my forehead, and Mrs. Marden broke out with a low distressful wail: "Now you know my life—now you know my life!"

"In God's name who is he—*what* is he?"

"He's a man I wronged."

"How did you wrong him?"

"Oh, awfully—years ago."

"Years ago? Why, he's very young."

"Young—young?" cried Mrs. Marden. "He was born before *I* was!"

"Then why does he look so?"

She came nearer to me, she laid her hand on my arm, and there was something in her face that made me shrink a little. "Don't you understand—don't you *feel*?" she murmured, reproachfully.

"I feel very queer!" I laughed; and I was conscious that my laugh betrayed it.

"He's dead!" said Mrs. Marden, from her white face.

"Dead?" I panted. "Then that gentleman was—?" I couldn't even say the word.

"Call him what you like—there are twenty vulgar names. He's a perfect presence."

"He's a splendid presence!" I cried. "The place is haunted— *haunted*!" I exulted in the word as if it represented the fulfilment of my dearest dream.

"It isn't the place—more's the pity! That has nothing to do with it!"

"Then it's you, dear lady?" I said, as if this were still better.

"No, nor me either—I wish it were!"

"Perhaps it's me," I suggested with a sickly smile.

"It's nobody but my child—my innocent, innocent child!" And with this Mrs. Marden broke down—she dropped into a chair and burst into tears. I stammered some question—I pressed on her some bewildered appeal, but she waved me off, unexpectedly and passionately. I persisted—couldn't I help her, couldn't I intervene? "You *have* intervened," she sobbed; "you're *in* it, you're *in* it."

"I'm very glad to be in anything so curious," I boldly declared.

"Glad or not, you can't get out of it."

"I don't want to get out of it—it's too interesting."

"I'm glad you like it. Go away."

"But I want to know more about it."

"You'll see all you want—go away!"

"But I want to understand what I see."

"How can you—when I don't understand myself?"

"We'll do so together—we'll make it out."

At this she got up, doing what she could to obliterate her tears. "Yes, it will be better together—that's why I've liked you."

"Oh, we'll see it through!" I declared.

"Then you must control yourself better."

"I will, I will—with practice."

"You'll get used to it," said Mrs. Marden, in a tone I never forgot. "But go and join them—I'll come in a moment."

I passed out to the terrace and I felt that I had a part to play. So far from dreading another encounter with the "perfect presence," as Mrs. Marden called it, I was filled with an excitement that was positively joyous. I desired a renewal of the sensation—I opened myself wide to the impression, I went round the house as quickly as if I expected to overtake Sir Edmund Orme. I didn't overtake him just then, but the day was not to close without my recognising that, as Mrs. Marden had said, I should see all I wanted of him.

We took, or most of us took, the collective sociable walk which, in the English country-house, is the consecrated pastime on Sunday afternoons. We were restricted to such a regulated ramble as the ladies were good for; the afternoons, moreover, were short, and by five o'clock we were restored to the fireside in the hall, with a sense, on my part at least, that we might have done a little more for our tea. Mrs. Marden had said she would join us, but she had not appeared; her daughter, who had seen her again before we went out, only explained that she was tired. She remained invisible all the afternoon, but this was a detail to which I gave as little heed as I had given to the circumstance of my not having Miss Marden to myself during all our walk. I was too much taken up with another emotion to care; I felt beneath my feet the threshold of the strange door, in my life, which had suddenly been thrown open and out of which unspeakable vibrations played up through me like a fountain. I had heard all my days of apparitions, but it was a different thing to have seen one and to know that I should in all probability see it familiarly, as it were, again. I was on the look-out for it, as a pilot for the flash of a revolving light, and I was ready to generalise on the sinister subject, to declare that ghosts were much less alarming and much more amusing than was commonly supposed. There is no doubt that I was extremely nervous. I couldn't get over the distinction conferred upon me—the exception (in the way of mystic enlargement of vision), made in my favour. At the same time I think I did justice to Mrs. Marden's absence; it was a commentary on what she had said to me—"Now you know my life." She had probably been seeing Sir Edmund Orme for years, and, not having my firm fibre, she had broken down under him. Her nerve was gone, though she had also been able to attest that, in a degree, one got used to him. She had got used to breaking down.

Afternoon tea, when the dusk fell early, was a friendly hour at Tranton; the firelight played into the wide, white last-century hall; sympathies almost confessed themselves, lingering together, before dressing, on deep sofas, in muddy boots, for last words, after walks; and even solitary absorption in the third volume of a novel that was wanted by some one else seemed a form of geniality. I watched my moment and went over to Charlotte Marden when I saw she was about to withdraw. The ladies had left the place one by one, and after I had addressed myself particularly to Miss Marden the three men who were near her gradually dispersed. We had a little vague talk—she appeared preoccupied, and heaven knows *I* was— after which she said she must go: she should be late for dinner. I proved to her by book that she had plenty of time, and she objected that she must at any rate go up to see her mother: she was afraid she was unwell.

"On the contrary, she's better than she has been for a long time—I'll guarantee that," I said. "She has found out that she can have confidence in me, and that has done her good." Miss Marden had dropped into her chair again. I was standing before her, and she looked up at me without a smile—with a dim distress in her beautiful eyes; not exactly as if I were hurting her, but as if she were no longer disposed to treat as a joke what had passed (whatever it was, it was at the same time difficult to be serious about it), between her mother and myself. But I could answer her inquiry in all kindness and candour, for I was really conscious that the poor lady had put off a part of her burden on me and was proportionately relieved and eased. "I'm sure she has slept all the afternoon as she hasn't slept for years," I went on. "You have only to ask her."

Charlotte got up again. "You make yourself out very useful."

"You've a good quarter of an hour," I said. "Haven't I a right to talk to you a little this way, alone, when your mother has given me your hand?"

"And is it *your* mother who has given me yours? I'm much obliged to her, but I don't want it. I think our hands are not our mothers'—they happen to be our own!" laughed the girl.

"Sit down, sit down and let me tell you!" I pleaded.

I still stood before her, urgently, to see if she wouldn't oblige me. She hesitated a moment, looking vaguely this way and that, as if under a compulsion that was slightly painful. The empty hall was quiet—we heard the loud ticking of the great clock. Then she slowly sank down and I drew a chair close to her. This made me face round to the fire again, and with the movement I perceived, disconcertedly, that we were not alone. The next instant, more strangely than I can say, my discomposure, instead of increasing, dropped, for the person before the fire was Sir Edmund Orme. He stood there as I had seen him in the Indian room, looking at me with the expressionless attention which borrowed its sternness from his sombre distinction. I knew so much more about him now that I had to check a movement of recognition, an acknowledgment of his presence. When once I was aware of it, and that it lasted, the sense that we had company, Charlotte and I, quitted me; it was impressed on me on the contrary that I was more intensely alone with Miss Marden. She evidently saw nothing to look at, and I made a tremendous and very nearly successful effort to conceal from her that my own situation was different. I say "very nearly," because she watched me an instant—while my words were arrested—in a way that made me fear she was going to say again, as she had said in the Indian room: "What on earth is the matter with you?"

What the matter with me was I quickly told her, for the full knowledge of it rolled over me with the touching spectacle of her unconsciousness. It was touching that she became, in the presence of this extraordinary portent. What was portended, danger or sorrow, bliss or bane, was a minor question; all I saw, as she sat there, was that, innocent and charming, she was close to a horror, as she might have thought it, that happened to be veiled from her but that might at any moment be disclosed. I didn't mind it now, as I found, but nothing was more possible than she should, and if it wasn't curious and interesting it might easily be very dreadful. If I didn't mind it for myself, as I afterwards saw, this was largely because I was so taken up with the idea of protecting *her*. My heart beat high with this idea, on the spot; I determined to do everything I could to keep her sense sealed. What I could do might have been very obscure to me if I had not, in all this, become more aware than of anything else that I loved her. The way to save her was to love her, and the way to love her was to tell her, now and here, that I did so. Sir Edmund Orme didn't prevent me, especially as after a moment he turned his back to us and stood looking discreetly at the fire. At the end of another moment he leaned his head on his arm, against the chimneypiece, with an air of gradual dejection, like a spirit still more weary than discreet. Charlotte Marden was startled by what I said to her, and she jumped up to escape it; but she took no offence—my tenderness was too real. She only moved about the room with a deprecating murmur, and I was so busy following up any little advantage that I might have obtained that I didn't notice in what manner Sir Edmund Orme disappeared. I only observed presently that he had gone. This made no difference—he had been so small a hindrance; I only remember being struck, suddenly, with something inexorable in the slow, sweet, sad headshake that Miss Marden gave me.

"I don't ask for an answer now," I said; "I only want you to be sure—to know how much depends on it."

"Oh, I don't want to give it to you, now or ever!" she replied. "I hate the subject, please—I wish one could be let alone." And then, as if I might have found something harsh in this irrepressible, artless cry of beauty beset, she added quickly, vaguely, kindly, as she left the room: "Thank you, thank you—thank you so much!"

At dinner I could be generous enough to be glad, for her, that I was placed on the same side of the table with her, where she couldn't see me. Her mother was nearly opposite to me, and just after we had sat down Mrs. Marden gave me one long, deep look, in which all our strange communion was expressed. It meant of course "She has told me," but it meant other things beside. At any rate I know what my answering look to her conveyed: "I've seen him again—I've seen him again!" This didn't prevent Mrs. Marden from treating her neighbours with her usual scrupulous blandness. After dinner, when, in the drawing-room, the men joined the ladies and I went straight up to her to tell her how I wished we could have some private conversation, she said immediately, in a low tone, looking down at her fan while she opened and shut it:

"He's here—he's here."

"Here?" I looked round the room, but I was disappointed.

"Look where *she* is," said Mrs. Marden, with just the faintest asperity. Charlotte was in fact not in the main saloon, but in an apartment into which it opened and which was known as the morning-room. I took a few steps and saw her, through a doorway, upright in the middle of the room, talking with three gentlemen whose backs were practically turned to me. For a moment my quest seemed vain; then I recognised that one of the gentlemen—the middle one—was Sir Edmund Orme. This time it *was* surprising that the others didn't see him. Charlotte seemed to be looking straight at him, addressing her conversation to him. She saw me after an instant, however, and immediately turned her eyes away. I went back to her mother with an annoyed sense that the girl would think I was watching *her*, which would be unjust. Mrs. Marden had found a small sofa—a little apart—and I sat down beside her. There were some questions I had so wanted to go into that I wished we were once more in the Indian room. I presently gathered, however, that our privacy was all-sufficient. We communicated so closely and completely now, and with such silent reciprocities, that it would in every circumstance be adequate.

"Oh, yes, he's there," I said; "and at about a quarter-past seven he was in the hall."

"I knew it at the time, and I was so glad!"

"So glad?"

"That it was your affair, this time, and not mine. It's a rest for me."

"Did you sleep all the afternoon?" I asked.

"As I haven't done for months. But how did you know that?"

"As *you* knew, I take it, that Sir Edmund was in the hall. We shall evidently each of us know things now—where the other is concerned."

"Where *he* is concerned," Mrs. Marden amended. "It's a blessing, the way you take it," she added, with a long, mild sigh.

"I take it as a man who's in love with your daughter."

"Of course—of course." Intense as I now felt my desire for the girl to be, I couldn't help laughing a little at the tone of these words; and it led my companion immediately to say: "Otherwise you wouldn't have seen him."

"But every one doesn't see him who's in love with her, or there would be dozens."

"They're not in love with her as you are."

"I can, of course, only speak for myself; and I found a moment, before dinner, to do so."

"She told me immediately."

"And have I any hope—any chance?"

"That's what *I* long for, what I pray for."

"Ah, how can I thank you enough?" I murmured.

"I believe it will all pass—if she loves you," Mrs. Marden continued.

"It will all pass?"

"We shall never see him again."

"Oh, if she loves me I don't care how often I see him!"

"Ah, you take it better than I could," said my companion. "You have the happiness not to know—not to understand."

"I don't indeed. What on earth does he want?"

"He wants to make me suffer." She turned her wan face upon me with this, and I saw now for the first time, fully, how perfectly, if this had been Sir Edmund Orme's purpose, he had succeeded. "For what I did to him," Mrs. Marden explained.

"And what did you do to him?"

She looked at me a moment. "I killed him." As I had seen him fifty yards away only five minutes before the words gave me a start. "Yes, I make you jump; be careful. He's there still, but he killed himself. I broke his heart—he thought me awfully bad. We were to have been married, but I broke it off—just at the last. I saw some one I liked better; I had no reason but that. It wasn't for interest, or money, or position, or anything of that sort. All *those* things were his. It was simply that I fell in love with Captain Marden. When I saw him I felt that I couldn't marry any one else. I wasn't in love with Edmund Orme—my mother, my elder sister had brought it about. But he did love me. I told him I didn't care—that I couldn't, that I *wouldn't*. I threw him over, and he took something, some abominable drug or draught that proved fatal. It was dreadful, it was horrible, he was found that way—he died in agony. I married Captain Marden, but not for five years. I was happy, perfectly happy; time obliterates. But when my husband died I began to see him."

I had listened intently, but I wondered. "To see your husband?"

"Never, never *that* way, thank God! To see *him*, with Chartie—always with Chartie. The first time it nearly killed me—about seven years ago, when she first came out. Never when I'm by myself—only with her. Sometimes not for months, then every day for a week. I've tried everything to break the spell—doctors and *régimes* and climates; I've prayed to God on my knees. That day at Brighton, on the Parade with you, when you thought I was ill, that was the first for an age. And then, in the evening, when I knocked my tea over you, and the day you were at the door with Charlotte and I saw you from the window—each time he was there."

"I see, I see." I was more thrilled than I could say.

"It's an apparition like another."

"Like another? Have you ever seen another?"

"No, I mean the sort of thing one has heard of. It's tremendously interesting to encounter a case."

"Do you call me a 'case'?" Mrs. Marden asked, with exquisite resentment.

"I mean myself."

"Oh, you're the right one!" she exclaimed. "I was right when I trusted you."

"I'm devoutly grateful you did; but what made you do it?"

"I had thought the whole thing out—I had had time to in those dreadful years, while he was punishing me in my daughter."

"Hardly that," I objected, "if she never knew."

"That has been my terror, that she *will*, from one occasion to another. I've an unspeakable dread of the effect on her."

"She sha'n't, she sha'n't!" I declared, so loud that several people looked round. Mrs. Marden made me get up, and I had no more talk with her that evening. The next day I told her I must take my departure from Tranton—it was neither comfortable nor considerate to remain as a rejected suitor. She was disconcerted, but she accepted my reasons, only saying to me out of her mournful eyes: "You'll leave me alone then with my burden?" It was of course understood between us that for many weeks to come there would be no discretion in "worrying poor Charlotte": such were the terms in which, with odd feminine and maternal inconsistency, she alluded to an attitude on my part that she favoured. I was prepared to be heroically considerate, but it seemed to me that even this delicacy permitted me to say a word to Miss Marden before I went. I begged her, after breakfast, to take a turn with me on the terrace, and as she hesitated, looking at me distantly, I informed her that it was only to ask her a question and to say good-bye—I was leaving Tranton for *her*.

She came out with me, and we passed slowly round the house three or four times. Nothing is finer than this great airy platform, from which every look is a sweep of the country, with the sea on the furthest edge. It might have been that as we passed the windows we were conspicuous to our friends in the house, who would divine, sarcastically, why I was so significantly bolting. But I didn't care; I only wondered whether they wouldn't really this time make out Sir Edmund Orme, who joined us on one of our turns and strolled slowly on the other side of my companion. Of what transcendent essence he was composed I knew not; I have no theory about him (leaving that to others), any more than I have one about such or such another of my fellow-mortals whom I have elbowed in life. He was as positive, as individual, as ultimate a fact as any of these. Above all he was as respectable, as sensitive a fact; so that I should no more have thought of taking a liberty, of practicing an experiment with him, of touching him, for instance, or speaking to him, since he set the example of silence, than I should have thought of committing any other social grossness. He had always, as I saw more fully later, the perfect propriety of his position—had always the appearance of being dressed and, in attitude and aspect, of comporting himself, as the occasion demanded. He looked strange, incontestably, but somehow he always looked *right*. I very soon came to attach an idea of beauty to his unmentionable presence, the beauty of an old story of love and pain. What I ended by feeling was that he was on my side, that he was watching over my interest, that he was looking to it that my heart shouldn't be broken. Oh, he had taken it seriously, his own catastrophe—he had certainly proved that in his day. If poor Mrs. Marden, as she told me, had thought it out, I also subjected the case to the finest analysis of which my intellect was capable. It was a case of retributive justice. The mother was to pay, in suffering, for the suffering she had inflicted, and as the disposition to jilt a lover might have been transmitted to the daughter, the daughter was to be watched, so that *she* might be made to suffer should she do an equal wrong. She might reproduce her mother in character as vividly as she did in face. On the day she should transgress, in other words, her eyes would be opened suddenly and unpitiedly to the "perfect presence," which she would have to work as she could into her conception of a young lady's universe. I had no great fear for her, because I didn't believe she was, in any cruel degree, a coquette. We should have a good deal of ground to get over before I, at least, should be in a position to be sacrificed by her. She couldn't throw me over before she had made a little more of me.

The question I asked her on the terrace that morning was whether I might continue, during the winter, to come to Mrs. Marden's house. I promised not to come too often and not to speak to her for three months of the question I had raised the day before. She replied that I might do as I liked, and on this we parted.

I carried out the vow I had made her; I held my tongue for my three months. Unexpectedly to myself there were moments of this time when she struck me as capable of playing with a man. I wanted so to make her like me that I became subtle and ingenious, wonderfully alert, patiently diplomatic. Sometimes I thought I had earned my reward, brought her to the point of saying: "Well, well, you're the best of them all—you may speak to me now." Then there was a greater blankness than ever in her beauty, and on certain days a mocking light in her eyes, of which the meaning seemed to be: "If you don't take care, I *will* accept you, to have done with you the more effectually." Mrs. Marden was a great help to me simply by believing in me, and I valued her faith all the more that it continued even though there was a sudden intermission of the miracle that had been wrought for me. After our visit to Tranton Sir Edmund Orme gave us a holiday, and I confess it was at first a disappointment to me. I felt less designated, less connected with Charlotte. "Oh, don't cry till you're out of the wood," her mother said; "he has let me off sometimes for six months. He'll break out

again when you least expect it—he knows what he's about." For
her these weeks were happy, and she was wise enough not to talk
about me to the girl. She was so good as to assure me that I was
taking the right way, that I looked as if I felt secure and that in the
long run women give way to that. She had known them do it even
when the man was a fool for looking so—or was a fool on any
terms. For herself she felt it to be a good time, a sort of St. Martin's
summer of the soul. She was better than she had been for years, and
she had me to thank for it. The sense of visitation was light upon
her—she wasn't in anguish every time she looked round. Charlotte
contradicted me very often, but she contradicted herself still more.
That winter was a wonder of mildness, and we often sat out in the
sun. I walked up and down with Charlotte, and Mrs. Marden, sometimes on a bench, sometimes in a bath-chair, waited for us and
smiled at us as we passed. I always looked out for a sign in her face—
"He's with you, he's with you" (she would see him before I should),
but nothing came; the season had brought us also a sort of spiritual
softness. Toward the end of April the air was so like June that, meeting my two friends one night at some Brighton sociability—an
evening party with amateur music—I drew Miss Marden unre-
sistingly out upon a balcony to which a window in one of the rooms
stood open. The night was close and thick, the stars were dim, and
below us, under the cliff, we heard the regular rumble of the sea. We
listened to it a little and we heard mixed with it, from within the
house, the sound of a violin accompanied by a piano—a performance which had been our pretext for passing out.

"Do you like me a little better?" I asked, abruptly, after a minute.
"Could you listen to me again?"

I had no sooner spoken than she laid her hand quickly, with a
certain force, on my arm. "Hush!—isn't there some one there?"
She was looking into the gloom of the far end of the balcony. This
balcony ran the whole width of the house, a width very great in the
best of the old houses at Brighton. We were lighted a little by the
open window behind us, but the other windows, curtained within,
left the darkness undiminished, so that I made out but dimly the
figure of a gentleman standing there and looking at us. He was in
evening dress, like a guest—I saw the vague shine of his white shirt
and the pale oval of his face—and he might perfectly have been a
guest who had stepped out in advance of us to take the air. Miss
Marden took him for one at first—then evidently, even in a few

seconds, she saw that the intensity of his gaze was unconventional. What else she saw I couldn't determine; I was too taken up with my own impression to do more than feel the quick contact of her uneasiness. My own impression was in fact the strongest of sensations, a sensation of horror; for what could the thing mean but that the girl at last *saw*? I heard her give a sudden, gasping "Ah!" and move quickly into the house. It was only afterwards that I knew that I myself had had a totally new emotion—my horror passing into anger, and my anger into a stride along the balcony with a gesture of reprobation. The case was simplified to the vision of a frightened girl whom I loved. I advanced to vindicate her security, but I found nothing there to meet me. It was either all a mistake or Sir Edmund Orme had vanished.

I followed Miss Marden immediately, but there were symptoms of confusion in the drawing-room when I passed in. A lady had fainted, the music had stopped; there was a shuffling of chairs and a pressing forward. The lady was not Charlotte, as I feared, but Mrs. Marden, who had suddenly been taken ill. I remember the relief with which I learned this, for to see Charlotte stricken would have been anguish, and her mother's condition gave a channel to her agitation. It was of course all a matter for the people of the house and for the ladies, and I could have no share in attending to my friends or in conducting them to their carriage. Mrs. Marden revived and insisted on going home, after which I uneasily withdrew.

I called the next morning to ask about her and was informed that she was better, but when I asked if Miss Marden would see me the message sent down was that it was impossible. There was nothing for me to do all day but to roam about with a beating heart. But toward evening I received a line in pencil, brought by hand—"Please come; mother wishes you." Five minutes afterward I was at the door again and ushered into the drawing-room. Mrs. Marden lay upon the sofa, and as soon as I looked at her I saw the shadow of death in her face. But the first thing she said was that she was better, ever so much better; her poor old heart had been behaving queerly again, but now it was quiet. She gave me her hand and I bent over her with my eyes in hers, and in this way I was able to read what she didn't speak—"I'm really very ill, but appear to take what I say exactly as I say it." Charlotte stood there beside her, looking not frightened now, but intensely grave, and not meeting my eyes. "She has told me—she has told me!" her mother went on.

"She has told you?" I stared from one of them to the other, wondering if Mrs. Marden meant that the girl had spoken to her of the circumstances on the balcony.

"That you spoke to her again—that you're admirably faithful."

I felt a thrill of joy at this; it showed me that that memory had been uppermost, and also that Charlotte had wished to say the thing that would soothe her mother most, not the thing that would alarm her. Yet I now knew, myself, as well as if Mrs. Marden had told me, that she knew and had known at the moment what her daughter had seen. "I spoke—I spoke, but she gave me no answer," I said.

"She will now, won't you, Chartie? I want it so, I want it!" the poor lady murmured, with ineffable wistfulness.

"You're very good to me," Charlotte said to me, seriously and sweetly, looking fixedly on the carpet. There was something different in her, different from all the past. She had recognised something, she felt a coercion. I could see that she was trembling.

"Ah, if you would let me show you *how* good I can be!" I exclaimed, holding out my hands to her. As I uttered the words I was touched with the knowledge that something had happened. A form had constituted itself on the other side of the bed, and the form leaned over Mrs. Marden. My whole being went forth into a mute prayer that Charlotte shouldn't see it and that I should be able to betray nothing. The impulse to glance toward Mrs. Marden was even stronger than the involuntary movement of taking in Sir Edmund Orme; but I could resist even that, and Mrs. Marden was perfectly still. Charlotte got up to give me her hand, and with the definite act she saw. She gave, with a shriek, one stare of dismay, and another sound, like a wail of one of the lost, fell at the same instant on my ear. But I had already sprung toward the girl to cover her, to veil her face. She had already thrown herself into my arms. I held her there a moment—bending over her, given up to her, feeling each of her throbs with my own and not knowing which was which; then, all of a sudden, coldly, I gathered that we were alone. She released herself. The figure beside the sofa had vanished; but Mrs. Marden lay in her place with closed eyes, with something in her stillness that gave us both another terror. Charlotte expressed it in the cry of "Mother,

mother!" with which she flung herself down. I fell on my knees beside her. Mrs. Marden had passed away.

Was the sound I heard when Chartie shrieked—the other and still more tragic sound I mean—the despairing cry of the poor lady's death-shock or the articulate sob (it was like a waft from a great tempest), of the exercised and pacified spirit? Possibly the latter, for that was, mercifully, the last of Sir Edmund Orme.

GEORGINA'S REASONS

I.

SHE WAS CERTAINLY a singular girl, and if he felt at the end that he didn't know her nor understand her, it is not surprising that he should have felt it at the beginning. But he felt at the beginning what he did not feel at the end, that her singularity took the form of a charm which—once circumstances had made them so intimate—it was impossible to resist or conjure away. He had a strange impression (it amounted at times to a positive distress, and shot through the sense of pleasure, morally speaking, with the acuteness of a sudden twinge of neuralgia) that it would be better for each of them that they should break off short and never see each other again. In later years he called this feeling a foreboding, and remembered two or three occasions when he had been on the point of expressing it to Georgina. Of course, in fact, he never expressed it; there were plenty of good reasons for that. Happy love is not disposed to assume disagreeable duties; and Raymond Benyon's love was happy, in spite of grave presentiments, in spite of the singularity of his mistress and the insufferable rudeness of her parents. She was a tall, fair girl, with a beautiful cold eye, and a smile of which the perfect sweetness, proceeding from the lips, was full of compensation; she had auburn hair, of a hue that could be qualified as nothing less than gorgeous, and she seemed to move through life with a stately grace, as she would have walked through an old-fashioned minuet. Gentlemen connected with the navy have the advantage of seeing many types of women; they are able to compare the ladies of New York with those of Valparaiso, and those of Halifax with those of the Cape of Good Hope. Raymond Benyon had had these opportunities, and, being fond of women, he had learned his lesson; he was in a position to appreciate

28

Georgina Gressie's fine points. She looked like a duchess—I don't mean that in foreign ports Benyon had associated with duchesses—and she took everything so seriously. That was flattering for the young man, who was only a lieutenant, detailed for duty at the Brooklyn navy-yard, without a penny in the world but his pay; with a set of plain, numerous, seafaring, God-fearing relations in New Hampshire, a considerable appearance of talent, a feverish, disguised ambition, and a slight impediment in his speech. He was a spare, tough young man; his dark hair was straight and fine, and his face, a trifle pale, smooth and carefully drawn. He stammered a little, blushing when he did so, at long intervals. I scarcely know how he appeared on shipboard, but on shore, in his civilian's garb, which was of the neatest, he had as little as possible an aroma of winds and waves. He was neither salt nor brown nor red nor particularly "hearty." He never twitched up his trousers, nor, so far as one could see, did he, with his modest, attentive manner, carry himself as a person accustomed to command. Of course, as a subaltern, he had more to do in the way of obeying. He looked as if he followed some sedentary calling, and was indeed supposed to be decidedly intellectual. He was a lamb with women, to whose charms he was, as I have hinted, susceptible; but with men he was different, and, I believe, as much of a wolf as was necessary. He had a manner of adoring the handsome, insolent queen of his affections (I will explain in a moment why I call her insolent); indeed, he looked up to her literally, as well as sentimentally, for she was the least bit the taller of the two.

He had met her the summer before on the piazza of an hotel at Fort Hamilton, to which, with a brother-officer, in a dusty buggy, he had driven over from Brooklyn to spend a tremendously hot Sunday—the kind of day when the navy-yard was loathsome; and the acquaintance had been renewed by his calling in Twelfth Street on New Year's day—a considerable time to wait for a pretext, but which proved the impression had not been transitory. The acquaintance ripened, thanks to a zealous cultivation (on his part) of occasions which Providence, it must be confessed, placed at his disposal none too liberally; so that now Georgina took up all his thoughts and a considerable part of his time. He was in love with her, beyond a doubt; but he could not flatter himself that she was smitten with him, though she seemed willing (what was so strange) to quarrel with her family about him. He didn't see how she could really care for him—she was marked out by nature for so much greater a fortune; and he used to say to her, "Ah, you don't—there's no use talking, you don't—really care for me at all!" To which she answered, "Really? You are very particular. It seems to me it's real enough if I let you touch one of my finger-tips!" That was one of her ways of being insolent. Another was simply her manner of looking at him, or at other people, when they spoke to her, with her hard, divine blue eye—looking quietly, amusedly, with the air of considering, wholly from her own point of view, what they might have said, and then turning her head or her back, while, without taking the trouble to answer them, she broke into a short, liquid, irrelevant laugh. This may seem to contradict what I said just now about her taking the young lieutenant in the navy seriously. What I mean is that she appeared to take him more seriously than she took anything else. She said to him once, "At any rate you have the merit of not being a shop-keeper;" and it was by this epithet she was pleased to designate most of the young men who at that time flourished in the best society of New York. Even if she had rather a free way of expressing general indifference, a young lady is supposed to be serious enough when she consents to marry you. For the rest, as regards a certain haughtiness that might be observed in Georgina Gressie, my story will probably throw sufficient light upon it. She remarked to Benyon once that it was none of his business why she liked him, but that, to please herself, she didn't mind telling him she thought the great Napoleon, before he was celebrated, before he had command of the army of Italy, must have looked something like him; and she sketched in a few words the sort of figure she imagined the incipient Bonaparte to have been— short, lean, pale, poor, intellectual, and with a tremendous future under his hat. Benyon asked himself whether he had a tremendous future, and what in the world Georgina expected of him in the coming years. He was flattered at the comparison, he was ambitious enough not to be frightened at it, and he guessed that she perceived a certain analogy between herself and the Empress Josephine. She would make a very good empress—that was true; Georgina was remarkably imperial. This may not at first seem to make it more clear why she should take into her favour an aspirant who, on the face of the matter, was not original, and whose Corsica was a flat New England seaport; but it afterwards became plain that he owed his brief happiness—it was very brief—to her father's opposition;

her father's and her mother's, and even her uncles' and her aunts'. In those days, in New York, the different members of a family took an interest in its alliances; and the house of Gressie looked askance at an engagement between the most beautiful of its daughters and a young man who was not in a paying business. Georgina declared that they were meddlesome and vulgar; she could sacrifice her own people, in that way, without a scruple; and Benyon's position improved from the moment that Mr. Gressie—ill-advised Mr. Gressie—ordered the girl to have nothing to do with him. Georgina was imperial in this—that she wouldn't put up with an order. When, in the house in Twelfth Street, it began to be talked about that she had better be sent to Europe with some eligible friend, Mrs. Portico for instance, who was always planning to go and who wanted as a companion some young mind, fresh from manuals and extracts, to serve as a fountain of history and geography—when this scheme for getting Georgina out of the way began to be aired, she immediately said to Raymond Benyon, "Oh yes, I'll marry you!" She said it in such an offhand way that, deeply as he desired her, he was almost tempted to answer, "But, my dear, have you really thought about it?"

II.

THIS little drama went on, in New York, in the ancient days, when Twelfth Street had but lately ceased to be suburban, when the squares had wooden palings, which were not often painted, when there were poplars in important thoroughfares and pigs in the lateral ways, when the theatres were miles distant from Madison Square, and the battered rotunda of Castle Garden echoed with expensive vocal music, when "the park" meant the grass-plats of the City Hall, and the Bloomingdale road was an eligible drive, when Hoboken, of a summer afternoon, was a genteel resort, and the handsomest house in town was on the corner of Fifth Avenue and Fifteenth Street. This will strike the modern reader, I fear, as rather a primitive epoch; but I am not sure that the strength of human passions is in proportion to the elongation of a city. Several of them, at any rate, the most robust and most familiar—love, ambition, jealousy, resentment, greed—subsisted in considerable force in the little circle at which we have glanced, where a view by no means favourable was taken of Raymond Benyon's attentions to

Miss Gressie. Unanimity was a family trait among these people (Georgina was an exception), especially in regard to the important concerns of life, such as marriages and closing scenes. The Gressies hung together; they were accustomed to do well for themselves and for each other. They did everything well: got themselves born well (they thought it excellent to be born a Gressie), lived well, married well, died well, and managed to be well spoken of afterwards. In deference to this last-mentioned habit, I must be careful what I say of them. They took an interest in each other's concerns, an interest that could never be regarded as of a meddlesome nature, inasmuch as they all thought alike about all their affairs, and interference took the happy form of congratulation and encouragement. These affairs were invariably lucky, and, as a general thing, no Gressie had anything to do but feel that another Gressie had been almost as shrewd and decided as he himself would have been. The great exception to that, as I have said, was this case of Georgina, who struck such a false note, a note that startled them all, when she told her father that she should like to unite herself to a young man engaged in the least paying business that any Gressie had ever heard of. Her two sisters had married into the most flourishing firms, and it was not to be thought of that—with twenty cousins growing up around her—she should put down the standard of success. Her mother had told her a fortnight before this that she must request Mr. Benyon to cease coming to the house; for hitherto his suit had been of the most public and resolute character. He had been conveyed up-town, from the Brooklyn ferry, in the "stage," on certain evenings, had asked for Miss Georgina at the door of the house in Twelfth Street, and had sat with her in the front parlour if her parents happened to occupy the back, or in the back if the family had disposed itself in the front. Georgina, in her way, was a dutiful girl, and she immediately repeated her mother's admonition to Benyon. He was not surprised, for, though he was aware that he had not, as yet, a great knowledge of society, he flattered himself he could tell when and where a polite young man was not wanted. There were houses in Brooklyn where such an animal was much appreciated, and there the signs were quite different.

They had been discouraging, except on Georgia's part, from the first of his calling in Twelfth Street. Mr. and Mrs. Gressie used to look at each other in silence when he came in, and indulge in strange perpendicular salutations, without any shaking of hands.

People did that at Portsmouth, N. H., when they were glad to see you; but in New York there was more luxuriance, and gesture had a different value. He had never, in Twelfth Street, been asked to "take anything," though the house had a delightful suggestion, a positive aroma, of sideboards, as if there were mahogany "cellarettes" under every table. The old people, moreover, had repeatedly expressed surprise at the quantity of leisure that officers in the navy seemed to enjoy. The only way in which they had not made themselves offensive was by always remaining in the other room; though at times even this detachment, to which he owed some delightful moments, presented itself to Benyon as a form of disapprobation. Of course, after Mrs. Gressie's message, his visits were practically at an end: he wouldn't give the girl up, but he wouldn't be beholden to her father for the opportunity to converse with her. Nothing was left for the tender couple—there was a curious mutual mistrust in their tenderness—but to meet in the squares, or in the topmost streets, or in the side-most avenues, on the spring afternoons. It was especially during this phase of their relations that Georgina struck Benyon as imperial. Her whole person seemed to exhale a tranquil, happy consciousness of having broken a law. She never told him how she arranged the matter at home, how she found it possible always to keep the appointments (to meet him out of the house) that she so boldly made, in what degree she dissimulated to her parents, and how much, in regard to their continued acquaintance, the old people suspected and accepted. If Mr. and Mrs. Gressie had forbidden him the house, it was not, apparently, because they wished her to walk with him in the Tenth Avenue or to sit at his side under the blossoming lilacs in Stuyvesant Square. He didn't believe that she told lies in Twelfth Street; he thought she was too imperial to lie; and he wondered what she said to her mother when, at the end of nearly a whole afternoon of vague peregrination with her lover, this rustling, bristling matron asked her where she had been. Georgina was capable of simply telling the truth; and yet if she simply told the truth it was a wonder that she had not been still more simply packed off to Europe. Benyon's ignorance of her pretexts is a proof that this rather oddly-mated couple never arrived at perfect intimacy, in spite of a fact which remains to be related. He thought of this afterwards, and thought how strange it was that he had not felt more at liberty to ask her what she did for him, and how she did it, and how much she suffered for him. She would probably not have admitted that she suffered at all, and she had no wish to pose for a martyr.

Benyon remembered this, as I say, in the after years, when he tried to explain to himself certain things which simply puzzled him; it came back to him with the vision, already faded, of shabby cross-streets, straggling toward rivers, with red sunsets, seen through a haze of dust, at the end; a vista through which the figures of a young man and a girl slowly receded and disappeared, strolling side by side, with the relaxed pace of desultory talk, but more closely linked as they passed into the distance, linked by its at last appearing safe to them—in the Tenth Avenue—that the young lady should take his arm. They were always approaching that inferior thoroughfare; but he could scarcely have told you, in those days, what else they were approaching. He had nothing in the world but his pay, and he felt that this was rather a "mean" income to offer Miss Gressie. Therefore he didn't put it forward; what he offered, instead, was the expression—crude often, and almost boyishly extravagant—of a delighted admiration of her beauty, the tenderest tones of his voice, the softest assurances of his eye, and the most insinuating pressure of her hand at those moments when she consented to place it in his arm. All this was an eloquence which, if necessary, might have been condensed into a single sentence; but those few words were scarcely needed when it was as plain that he expected, in general, she would marry him, as it was indefinite that he counted upon her for living on a few hundred a year. If she had been a different girl he might have asked her to wait, might have talked to her of the coming of better days, of his prospective promotion, of its being wiser, perhaps, that he should leave the navy and look about for a more lucrative career. With Georgina it was difficult to go into such questions; she had no taste whatever for detail. She was delightful as a woman to love, because when a young man is in love he discovers that; but she could not be called helpful, for she never suggested anything. That is, she never had done so till the day she really proposed—for that was the form it took—to become his wife without more delay. "Oh yes, I will marry you:" these words, which I quoted a little way back, were not so much the answer to something he had said at the moment as the light conclusion of a report she had just made (for the first time) of her actual situation in her father's house.

III.

"I AM afraid I shall have to see less of you," she had begun by saying. "They watch me so much."

"It is very little already," he answered. "What is once or twice a week?"

"That's easy for you to say. You are your own master, but you don't know what I go through."

"Do they make it very bad for you, dearest? Do they make scenes?" Benyon asked.

"No, of course not. Don't you know us enough to know how we behave? No scenes; that would be a relief. However, I never make them myself, and I never will—that's one comfort for you, for the future, if you want to know. Father and mother keep very quiet, looking at me as if I were one of the lost, with little hard, piercing eyes, like gimlets. To me they scarcely say anything, but they talk it all over with each other, and try and decide what is to be done. It's my belief that my father has written to the people in Washington—what do you call it?—the Department—to have you moved away from Brooklyn—to have you sent to sea."

"I guess that won't do much good. They want me in Brooklyn; they don't want me at sea."

"Well, they are capable of going to Europe for a year, on purpose to take me," Georgina said.

"How can they take you if you won't go? And if you should go, what good would it do if you were only to find me here when you came back, just the same as you left me?"

"Oh, well!" said Georgina, with her lovely smile, "of course they think that absence would cure me of——cure me of——" And she paused, with a kind of cynical modesty, not saying exactly of what.

"Cure you of what, darling? Say it, please say it," the young man murmured, drawing her hand surreptitiously into his arm.

"Of my absurd infatuation!"

"And would it, dearest?"

"Yes, very likely. But I don't mean to try. I shall not go to Europe—not when I don't want to. But it's better I should see less of you—even that I should appear—a little—to give you up"

"A little? What do you call a little?"

Georgina said nothing for a moment. "Well, that, for instance, you shouldn't hold my hand quite so tight!" And she disengaged this conscious member from the pressure of his arm.

"What good will that do?" Benyon asked.

"It will make them think it's all over—that we have agreed to part."

"And as we have done nothing of the kind, how will that help us?"

They had stopped at the crossing of a street; a heavy dray was lumbering slowly past them. Georgina, as she stood there, turned her face to her lover and rested her eyes for some moments on his own. At last, "Nothing will help us; I don't think we are very happy," she answered, while her strange, ironical, inconsequent smile played about her beautiful lips.

"I don't understand how you see things. I thought you were going to say you would marry me," Benyon rejoined, standing there still, though the dray had passed.

"Oh yes, I will marry you!" And she moved away across the street. That was the way she had said it, and it was very characteristic of her. When he saw that she really meant it, he wished they were somewhere else—he hardly knew where the proper place would be—so that he might take her in his arms. Nevertheless, before they separated that day he had said to her he hoped she remembered they would be very poor, reminding her how great a change she would find it. She answered that she shouldn't mind, and presently she said that if this was all that prevented them the sooner they were married the better. The next time he saw her she was quite of the same opinion; but he found, to his surprise, it was now her conviction that she had better not leave her father's house. The ceremony should take place secretly, of course; but they would wait awhile to let their union be known.

"What good will it do us, then?" Raymond Benyon asked.

Georgina coloured. "Well, if you don't know, I can't tell you!"

Then it seemed to him that he did know. Yet, at the same time, he could not see why, once the knot was tied, secrecy should be required. When he asked what especial event they were to wait for, and what should give them the signal to appear as man and wife, she answered that her parents would probably forgive her if they were to discover, not too abruptly, after six months, that she had taken the great step. Benyon supposed that she had ceased to care whether they forgave her or not; but he had already perceived that the nature of women is a queer mosaic. He had believed her capable of marrying him out of bravado, but the pleasure of defiance was absent if the marriage was kept to themselves. It now appeared that she was not especially anxious to defy; she was disposed rather to manage and temporise.

"Leave it to me; leave it to me. You are only a blundering man," Georgina said. "I shall know much better than you the right moment for saying, 'Well, you may as well make the best of it, because we have already done it!'"

That might very well be, but Benyon didn't quite understand, and he was awkwardly anxious (for a lover) till it came over him afresh that there was one thing at any rate in his favour, which was simply that the finest girl he had ever seen was ready to throw herself into his arms. When he said to her, "There is one thing I hate in this plan of yours—that, for ever so few weeks, so few days, your father should support my wife"—when he made this homely remark, with a little flush of sincerity in his face, she gave him a specimen of that unanswerable laugh of hers, and declared that it would serve Mr. Gressie right for being so barbarous and so horrid. It was Benyon's view that from the moment she disobeyed her father she ought to cease to avail herself of his protection; but I am bound to add that he was not particularly surprised at finding this a kind of honour in which her feminine nature was little versed. To make her his wife first—at the earliest moment—whenever she would, and trust to fortune and the new influence he should have, to give him, as soon thereafter as possible, complete possession of her: this finally presented itself to the young officer as the course most worthy of a lover and a gentleman. He would be only a pedant who would take nothing because he could not get everything at once. They wandered further than usual this afternoon, and the dusk was thick by the time he brought her back to her father's door. It was not his habit to come so near it, but to-day they had so much to talk about that he actually stood with her for ten minutes at the foot of the steps. He was keeping her hand in his, and she let it rest there while she said—by way of a remark that should sum up all their reasons and reconcile their differences—

"There's one great thing it will do, you know: it will make me safe."

"Safe from what?"

"From marrying any one else."

"Ah, my girl, if you were to do that——!" Benyon exclaimed; but he didn't mention the other branch of the contingency. Instead of this, he looked aloft at the blind face of the house (there were only dim lights in two or three windows, and no apparent eyes) and up and down the empty street, vague in the friendly twilight; after which he drew Georgina Gressie to his breast and gave her a long, passionate kiss. Yes, decidedly, he felt they had better be married. She had run quickly up the steps, and while she stood there, with her hand on the bell, she almost hissed at him, under her breath, "Go away, go away; Amanda's coming!" Amanda was the parlour-maid; and it was in those terms that the Twelfth Street Juliet dismissed her Brooklyn Romeo. As he wandered back into the Fifth Avenue, where the evening air was conscious of a vernal fragrance from the shrubs in the little precinct of the pretty Gothic church ornamenting that pleasant part of the street, he was too absorbed in the impression of the delightful contact from which the girl had violently released herself to reflect that the great reason she had mentioned a moment before was a reason for their marrying, of course, but not in the least a reason for their not making it public. But, as I said in the opening lines of this chapter, *if* he did not understand his mistress's motives at the end, he cannot be expected to have understood them at the beginning.

IV.

MRS. PORTICO, as we know, was always talking about going to Europe; but she had not yet—I mean a year after the incident I have just related—put her hand upon a youthful cicerone. Petticoats, of course, were required; it was necessary that her companion should be of the sex which sinks most naturally upon benches, in galleries and cathedrals, and pauses most frequently upon staircases that ascend to celebrated views. She was a widow with a good fortune and several sons, all of whom were in Wall Street, and none of them capable of the relaxed pace at which she expected to take her foreign tour. They were all in a state of tension; they went through life standing. She was a short, broad, high-coloured woman, with a loud voice and superabundant black hair, arranged in a way peculiar to herself, with so many combs and bands that it had the appearance of a national coiffure. There was an impression in New York, about 1845, that the style was Danish; some one had said something about having seen it in Schleswig-Holstein. Mrs. Portico had a bold, humorous, slightly flamboyant look; people who saw her for the first time received an impression that her late husband had married the daughter of a bar-keeper or the proprietress of a menagerie. Her high, hoarse, good-natured voice seemed to connect her in some way with public life; it was not pretty enough to suggest that she might have been an actress. These ideas quickly passed away, however, even if you were not sufficiently initiated to know—as all the Gressies, for instance, knew so well—that her origin, so far from being enveloped in mystery, was almost the sort of thing she might have boasted of. But, in spite of the high pitch of her appearance she didn't boast of anything; she was a genial, easy, comical, irreverent person, with a large charity, a democratic, fraternising turn of mind, and a contempt for many worldly standards, which she expressed not in the least in general axioms (for she had a mortal horror of philosophy), but in violent ejaculations on particular occasions. She had not a grain of moral timidity, and she fronted a delicate social problem as sturdily as she would have barred the way of a gentleman she might have met in her vestibule with the plate-chest. The only thing which prevented her being a bore in orthodox circles was that she was incapable of discussion. She never lost her temper, but she lost her vocabulary, and ended quickly by praying that heaven would give her an opportunity to act out what she believed. She was an old friend of Mr. and Mrs. Gressie, who esteemed her for the antiquity of her lineage and the frequency of her subscriptions, and to whom she rendered the service of making them feel liberal—like people too sure of their own position to be frightened. She was their indulgence, their dissipation, their point of contact with dangerous heresies; so long as they continued to see her they could not be accused of being narrow-minded—a matter as to which they were perhaps vaguely conscious of the necessity of taking their precautions. Mrs. Portico never asked herself whether she liked the Gressies; she had no disposition for morbid analysis, she accepted transmitted associations, and found, somehow, that her acquaintance with these people helped her to relieve herself. She was always making scenes in their drawing-room, scenes half indignant, half jocose, like all her manifestations, to which it must be confessed that they adapted themselves beautifully. They never "met" her, in the language of controversy; but always collected to watch her, with smiles and comfortable platitudes, as if they envied her superior richness of temperament. She took an interest in Georgina, who seemed to her different from the others, with suggestions about her of being likely not to marry so unrefreshingly as her sisters had done, and of a high, bold standard of duty. Her sisters had married from duty, but Mrs. Portico would rather have chopped off one of her large plump hands than behave herself so well as that. She had, in her daughterless condition, a certain ideal of a girl who should be beautiful and romantic, with wistful eyes, and a little persecuted, so that she, Mrs. Portico, might get her out of her troubles. She looked to Georgina, to a considerable degree, to give actuality to this vision; but she had really never understood Georgina at all. She ought to have been shrewd, but she lacked this refinement, and she never understood anything until after many disappointments and vexations. It was difficult to startle her, but she was much startled by a communication that this young lady made her one fine spring morning. With her florid appearance and her speculative mind, she was probably the most innocent woman in New York.

Georgina came very early, earlier even than visits were paid in New York thirty years ago; and instantly, without any preface, looking her straight in the face, told Mrs. Portico that she was in great trouble and must appeal to her for assistance. Georgina had in her aspect no symptom of distress; she was as fresh and beautiful as the April day itself; she held up her head and smiled, with a sort of familiar challenge, looking like a young woman who would naturally be on good terms with fortune. It was not in the least in the tone of a person making a confession or relating a misadventure that she presently said, "Well, you must know, to begin with—of course, it will surprise you—that I am married."

"Married, Georgina Gressie!" Mrs. Portico repeated, in her most resonant tones.

Georgina got up, walked with her majestic step across the room, and closed the door. Then she stood there, her back pressed against the mahogany panels, indicating only by the distance she had placed between herself and her hostess the consciousness of an irregular position. "I am not Georgina Gressie—I am Georgina Benyon; and it has become plain, within a short time, that the natural consequence will take place."

Mrs. Portico was altogether bewildered. "The natural conse-quence?" she exclaimed, staring.

"Of one's being married, of course; I suppose you know what that is. No one must know anything about it. I want you to take me to Europe."

Mrs. Portico now slowly rose from her place and approached her visitor, looking at her from head to foot as she did so, as if to mea-sure the truth of her remarkable announcement. She rested her hands on Georgina's shoulders a moment, gazing into her blooming face, and then she drew her closer and kissed her. In this way the girl was conducted back to the sofa, where, in a conversation of extreme intimacy, she opened Mrs. Portico's eyes wider than they had ever been opened before. She was Raymond Benyon's wife; they had been married a year, but no one knew anything about it. She had kept it from every one, and she meant to go on keeping it. The ceremony had taken place in a little Episcopal church at Haarlem, one Sunday afternoon, after the service. There was no one in that dusty suburb who knew them; the clergyman, vexed at being detained, and wanting to go home to tea, had made no trouble; he tied the knot before they could turn round. It was ri-diculous how easy it had been. Raymond had told him frankly that it must all be under the rose, as the young lady's family disapproved of what she was doing. But she was of legal age, and perfectly free; he could see that for himself. The parson had given a grunt as he looked at her over his spectacles; it was not very complimentary, it seemed to say that she was indeed no chicken. Of course she looked old for a girl; but she was not a girl now, was she? Raymond had certified his own identity as an officer in the United States navy (he had papers, besides his uniform, which he wore), and intro-duced the clergyman to a friend he had brought with him, who was also in the navy, a venerable paymaster. It was he who gave Georgina away, as it were; he was a dear old man, a regular grand-mother, and perfectly safe. He had been married three times him-self, and the first time in the same way. After the ceremony she went back to her father's; but she saw Mr. Benyon the next day. After that she saw him—for a little while—pretty often. He was always begging her to come to him altogether; she must do him that justice. But she wouldn't—she wouldn't now—perhaps she wouldn't ever. She had her reasons, which seemed to her very good but were very difficult to explain. She would tell Mrs. Portico in plenty of time what they were. But that was not the question now, whether they were good or bad; the question was for her to get away from the country for several months—far away from any one who had ever known her. She should like to go to some little place in Spain or Italy, where she should be out of the world until everything was over.

Mrs. Portico's heart gave a jump as this serene, handsome, domestic girl, sitting there with a hand in hers and pouring forth her extraordinary tale, spoke of everything being over. There was a glossy coldness in it, an unnatural lightness, which suggested— poor Mrs. Portico scarcely knew what. If Georgina was to become a mother it was to be supposed she would remain a mother. She said there was a beautiful place in Italy—Genoa—of which Raymond had often spoken, and where he had been more than once, he admired it so much; couldn't they go there and be quiet for a little while? She was asking a great favour, that she knew very well; but if Mrs. Portico wouldn't take her she would find some one who would. They had talked of such a journey so often; and, certainly, if Mrs. Portico had been willing before, she ought to be much more willing now. The girl declared that she *would* do something, go somewhere, keep, in one way or another, her situation unperceived. There was no use talking to her about telling; she would rather die than tell. No doubt it seemed strange, but she knew what she was about. No one had guessed anything yet—she had succeeded perfectly in doing what she wished—and her father and mother believed—as Mrs. Portico had believed, hadn't she?—that, any time the last year, Raymond Benyon was less to her than he had been before. Well, so he was; yes, he was. He had gone away—he was off, goodness knew where—in the Pacific; she was alone, and now she would remain alone. The family believed it was all over, with his going back to his ship, and other things, and they were right; for it was over, or it would be soon.

V.

MRS. PORTICO, by this time, had grown almost afraid of her young friend; she had so little fear, she had even, as it were, so little shame. If the good lady had been accustomed to analysing things a little more, she would have said she had so little conscience. She looked at Georgina with dilated eyes—her visitor was so much the calmer of the two—and exclaimed, and murmured, and sank back, and sprang forward, and wiped her forehead with her pocket-handkerchief. There were things she didn't understand; that they should all have been so deceived, that they should have thought Georgina was giving her lover up (they flattered themselves she was discouraged or had grown tired of him) when she was really only making it impossible she should belong to any one else. And with this, her inconsequence, her capriciousness, her absence of motive, the way she contradicted herself, her apparent belief that she could hush up such a situation for ever! There was nothing shameful in having married poor Mr. Benyon, even in a little church at Haarlem, and being given away by a paymaster; it was much more shameful to be in such a state without being prepared to make the proper explanations. And she must have seen very little of her husband; she must have given him up, so far as meeting him went, almost as soon as she had taken him. Had not Mrs. Gressie herself told Mrs. Portico, in the preceding October it must have been, that there now would be no need of sending Georgina away, inasmuch as the affair with the little navy-man—a project in every way so unsuitable—had quite blown over?

"After our marriage I saw him less—I saw him a great deal less," Georgina explained; but her explanation only appeared to make the mystery more dense.

"I don't see, in that case, what on earth you married him for!"

"We had to be more careful; I wished to appear to have given him up. Of course we were really more intimate; I saw him differently," Georgina said, smiling.

"I should think so! I can't for the life of me see why you weren't discovered."

"All I can say is we weren't. No doubt it's remarkable. We managed very well—that is, I managed; he didn't want to manage at all. And then father and mother are incredibly stupid!"

Mrs. Portico exhaled a comprehensive moan, feeling glad, on the whole, that she hadn't a daughter, while Georgina went on to furnish a few more details. Raymond Benyon, in the summer, had been ordered from Brooklyn to Charlestown, near Boston, where, as Mrs. Portico perhaps knew, there was another navy-yard, in which there was a temporary press of work, requiring more oversight. He had remained there several months, during which he had written to her urgently to come to him, and during which, as well, he had received notice that he was to rejoin his ship a little later. Before doing so he came back to Brooklyn for a few weeks, to wind up his work there, and then she had seen him—well, pretty often. That was the best time of all the year that had elapsed since their marriage. It was a wonder at home that nothing had then been guessed, because she had really been reckless, and Benyon had even tried to force on a disclosure. But they were dense, that was very certain. He had besought her again and again to put an end to their false position, but she didn't want it any more than she had wanted it before. They had had rather a bad parting; in fact, for a pair of lovers, it was a very queer parting indeed. He didn't know, now, the thing she had come to tell Mrs. Portico. She had not written to him. He was on a very long cruise. It might be two years before he returned to the United States. "I don't care how long he stays away," Georgina said, very simply.

"You haven't mentioned why you married him. Perhaps you don't remember!" Mrs. Portico broke out, with her masculine laugh.

"Oh yes; I loved him."

"And you have got over that?"

Georgina hesitated a moment. "Why, no, Mrs. Portico, of course I haven't. Raymond's a splendid fellow."

"Then why don't you live with him? You don't explain that."

"What would be the use when he's always away? How can one live with a man who spends half his life in the South Seas? If he wasn't in the navy it would be different; but to go through everything—I mean everything that making our marriage known would bring upon me: the scolding and the exposure and the ridicule, the scenes at home—to go through it all just for the idea, and yet to be alone here, just as I was before, without my husband after all, with none of the good of him"—and here Georgina looked at her hostess as if with the certitude that such an enumeration of inconveniences would touch her effectually—"really, Mrs. Portico, I am bound to say I don't think that would be worth while; I haven't the courage for it."

"I never thought you were a coward," said Mrs. Portico.

"Well, I am not, if you will give me time. I am very patient."

"I never thought that either."

"Marrying changes one," said Georgina, still smiling.

"It certainly seems to have had a very odd effect upon you. Why don't you make him leave the navy and arrange your life comfortably, like every one else?"

"I wouldn't for the world interfere with his prospects—with his promotion. That is sure to come for him, and to come immediately, he has such talents. He is devoted to his profession; it would ruin him to leave it."

"My dear young woman, you are a living wonder!" Mrs. Portico exclaimed, looking at her companion as if she had been in a glass case.

"So poor Raymond says," Georgina answered, smiling more than ever.

"Certainly, I should have been very sorry to marry a navy-man; but if I had married him I would stick to him, in the face of all the scoldings in the universe!"

"I don't know what your parents may have been; I know what mine are," Georgina replied, with some dignity. "When he's a captain we shall come out of hiding."

"And what shall you do meanwhile? What will you do with your children? Where will you hide them? What will you do with this one?"

Georgina rested her eyes on her lap for a minute; then, raising them, she met those of Mrs. Portico. "Somewhere in Europe," she said, in her sweet tone.

"Georgina Gressie, you're a monster!" the elder lady cried.

"I know what I am about, and you will help me," the girl went on.

"I will go and tell your father and mother the whole story— that's what I will do!"

"I am not in the least afraid of that—not in the least. You will help me; I assure you that you will."

"Do you mean I will support the child? "

Georgina broke into a laugh. "I do believe you would, if I were to ask you! But I won't go so far as that; I have something of my own. All I want you to do is to be with me."

"At Genoa; yes, you have got it all fixed! You say Mr. Benyon is so fond of the place. That's all very well; but how will he like his baby being deposited there?"

"He won't like it at all. You see I tell you the whole truth," said Georgina, gently.

"Much obliged; it's a pity you keep it all for me! It is in his power, then, to make you behave properly. *He* can publish your marriage, if you won't; and if he does you will have to acknowledge your child."

"Publish, Mrs. Portico? How little you know my Raymond! He will never break a promise; he will go through fire first."

"And what have you got him to promise?"

"Never to insist on a disclosure against my will; never to claim me openly as his wife till I think it is time; never to let any one know what has passed between us if I choose to keep it still a secret—to keep it for years—to keep it for ever. Never do anything in the matter himself, but to leave it to me. For this he has given me his solemn word of honour, and I know what that means!"

Mrs. Portico, on the sofa, fairly bounced.

"You do know what you are about! And Mr. Benyon strikes me as more demented even than yourself. I never heard of a man putting his head into such a noose. What good can it do him?"

"What good? The good it did him was that it gratified me. At the time he took it he would have made any promise under the sun. It was a condition I exacted just at the very last, before the marriage took place. There was nothing at that moment he would have refused me; there was nothing I couldn't have made him do. He was in love to that degree—but I don't want to boast," said Georgina, with quiet grandeur. "He wanted—he wanted—" she added; but then she paused.

"He doesn't seem to have wanted much!" Mrs. Portico cried, in a tone which made Georgina turn to the window, as if it might have reached the street. Her hostess noticed the movement and went on, "Oh, my dear, if I ever do tell your story I will tell it so that people will hear it!"

"You never will tell it. What I mean is that Raymond wanted the sanction—of the affair at the church—because he saw that I would never do without it. Therefore, for him, the sooner we had it the better, and, to hurry it on, he was ready to take any pledge."

"You have got it pat enough," said Mrs. Portico, in homely phrase. "I don't know what you mean by sanctions, or what you wanted of 'em."

Georgina got up, holding rather higher than before that beautiful head which, in spite of the embarrassments of this interview, had not yet perceptibly abated its elevation. "Would you have liked me to—to not marry?"

Mrs. Portico rose also, and, flushed with the agitation of unwonted knowledge—it was as if she had discovered a skeleton in her favourite cupboard—faced her young friend for a moment. Then her conflicting sentiments resolved themselves into an abrupt question, implying, for Mrs. Portico, much subtlety: "Georgina Gressie, were you really in love with him?"

The question suddenly dissipated the girl's strange, studied, wilful coldness; she broke out, with a quick flash of passion—a passion that, for the moment, was predominately anger, "Why else, in heaven's name, should I have done what I have done? Why else should I have married him? What under the sun had I to gain?"

A certain quiver in Georgina's voice, a light in her eye which seemed to Mrs. Portico more spontaneous, more human, as she uttered these words, caused them to affect her hostess rather less painfully than anything she had yet said. She took the girl's hand and emitted indefinite admonitory sounds. "Help me, my dear old friend, help me," Georgina continued, in a low, pleading tone; and in a moment Mrs. Portico saw that the tears were in her eyes.

"You are a precious mixture, my child!" she exclaimed. "Go straight home to your own mother and tell her everything; that is your best help."

"You are kinder than my mother. You mustn't judge her by yourself."

"What can she do to you? How can she hurt you? We are not living in pagan times," said Mrs. Portico, who was seldom so historical. "Besides, you have no reason to speak of your mother—to think of her even—so! She would have liked you to marry a man of some property; but she has always been a good mother to you."

At this rebuke Georgina suddenly kindled again; she was, indeed, as Mrs. Portico had said, a precious mixture. Conscious, evidently, that she could not satisfactorily justify her present stiffness, she wheeled round upon a grievance which absolved her from self-defence. "Why, then, did he make that promise, if he loved me? No man who really loved me would have made it, and no man that was a man as I understand being a man! He might have seen that I only did it to test him—to see if he wanted to take advantage of being left free himself. It is a proof that he doesn't love me—not as he ought to have done; and in such a case as that a woman isn't bound to make sacrifices!"

Mrs. Portico was not a person of a nimble intellect; her mind moved vigorously, but heavily; yet she sometimes made happy guesses. She saw that Georgina's emotions were partly real and partly fictitious, that, as regards this last matter especially, she was trying to "get up" a resentment, in order to excuse herself. The pretext was absurd, and the good lady was struck with its being heartless on the part of her young visitor to reproach poor Benyon with a concession on which she had insisted, and which could only be a proof of his devotion, inasmuch as he left her free while he bound himself. Altogether, Mrs. Portico was shocked and dismayed at such a want of simplicity in the behaviour of a young person whom she had hitherto believed to be as candid as she was stylish, and her appreciation of this discovery expressed itself in the uncompromising remark, "You strike me as a very bad girl, my dear; you strike me as a very bad girl!"

VI.

IT will doubtless seem to the reader very singular that, in spite of this reflection, which appeared to sum up her judgment of the matter, Mrs. Portico should in the course of a very few days have consented to everything that Georgina asked of her. I have thought it well to narrate at length the first conversation that took place between them, but I shall not trace further the successive phases of the girl's appeal, or the steps by which—in the face of a hundred robust and salutary convictions—the loud, kind, sharp, simple, sceptical, credulous woman took under her protection a damsel whose obstinacy she could not speak of without getting red with anger. It was the simple fact of Georgina's personal condition that moved her; this young lady's greatest eloquence was the seriousness of her predicament She might be bad, and she had a splendid, careless, insolent, fair-faced way of admitting it, which at moments, incoherently, inconsistently, irresistibly, transmuted the cynical confession into tears of weakness; but Mrs. Portico had known her from her rosiest years, and when Georgina declared that she couldn't go home, that she wished to be with her and not with her mother, that she couldn't expose herself—she absolutely couldn't—and that she must remain with her and her only till the day they should sail, the poor lady was forced to make that day a reality. She was over-mastered, she was cajoled, she was, to a certain extent, fascinated. She had to accept Georgina's rigidity (she had none of her own to oppose to it—she was only violent, she was not continuous), and once she did this it was plain, after all, that to take her young friend to Europe was to help her, and to leave her alone was not to help her. Georgina literally frightened Mrs. Portico into compliance. She was evidently capable of strange things if thrown upon her own devices. So, from one day to another, Mrs. Portico announced that she was really at last about to sail for foreign lands (her doctor having told her that if she didn't look out she would get too old to enjoy them), and that she had invited that robust Miss Gressie, who could stand so long on her feet, to accompany her. There was joy in the house of Gressie at this announcement, for, though the danger was over, it was a great general advantage to Georgina to go, and the Gressies were always elated at the prospect of an advantage. There was a danger that she might meet Mr. Benyon on the other side of the world; but it didn't seem likely that Mrs. Portico would lend herself to a plot of that kind. If she had taken it into her head to favour their love-affair she would have done it openly, and Georgina would have been married by this time. Her arrangements were made as quickly as her decision had been—or rather had appeared—slow; for this concerned those mercurial young men down town. Georgina was perpetually at her house; it was understood in Twelfth Street that she was talking over her future travels with her kind friend. Talk there was, of course, to a considerable degree; but after it was settled they should start nothing more was said about the motive of the journey. Nothing was said, that is, till the night before they sailed; then a few plain words passed between them. Georgina had already taken leave of her relations in Twelfth Street, and was to sleep at Mrs. Portico's in order to go down to the ship at an early hour. The two ladies were sitting together in the firelight, silent with the consciousness of corded luggage, when the elder one suddenly remarked to her companion that she seemed to be taking a great deal upon herself in assuming that Raymond Benyon wouldn't force her hand. He might choose to acknowledge his child, if she didn't; there were promises and promises, and many people would consider they had been let off when circumstances were so altered. She would have to reckon with Mr. Benyon more than she thought.

"I know what I am about," Georgina answered. "There is only one promise for him. I don't know what you mean by circumstances being altered."

"Everything seems to me to be altered," poor Mrs. Portico murmured, rather tragically.

"Well, he isn't, and he never will! I am sure of him, as sure as that I sit here. Do you think I would have looked at him if I hadn't known he was a man of his word?"

"You have chosen him well, my dear," said Mrs. Portico, who by this time was reduced to a kind of bewildered acquiescence.

"Of course I have chosen him well. In such a matter as this he will be perfectly splendid." Then suddenly, "Perfectly splendid, that's why I cared for him," she repeated, with a flash of incongruous passion.

This seemed to Mrs. Portico audacious to the point of being sublime; but she had given up trying to understand anything that the girl might say or do. She understood less and less after they had disembarked in England and begun to travel southward; and she understood least of all when, in the middle of the winter, the event came off with which in imagination she had tried to familiarise herself, but which, when it occurred, seemed to her beyond measure strange and dreadful. It took place at Genoa; for Georgina had made up her mind that there would be more privacy in a big town than in a little; and she wrote to America that both Mrs. Portico and she had fallen in love with the place and would spend two or three months there. At that time people in the United States knew much less than to-day about the comparative attractions of foreign cities; and it was not thought surprising that absent New Yorkers should wish to linger in a seaport where they might find apartments, according to Georgina's report, in a palace painted in fresco by Vandyke and Titian. Georgina, in her letters, omitted, it will be seen, no detail that could give colour to Mrs. Portico's long stay at Genoa. In such a palace—where the travellers hired twenty gilded rooms for the most insignificant sum—a remarkably fine boy came into the world. Nothing could have been more successful and comfortable than this transaction—Mrs. Portico was almost appalled at the facility and felicity of it. She was by this time in a pretty bad way; and—what had never happened to her before in her life—she suffered from chronic depression of spirits. She hated to have to lie, and now she was lying all the time. Everything she wrote home, everything that had been said or done in connection with their stay in Genoa, was a lie. The way they remained indoors to avoid meeting chance compatriots was a lie. Compatriots in Genoa, at that period, were very rare; but nothing could exceed the business-like completeness of Georgina's precautions. Her nerve, her self-possession, her apparent want of feeling, excited on Mrs. Portico's part a kind of gloomy suspense; a morbid anxiety to see how far her companion would go took possession of the excellent woman who, a few months before, hated to fix her mind on disagreeable things. Georgina went very far indeed; she did everything in her power to dissimulate the origin of her child. The record of his birth was made under a false name, and he was baptized at the nearest church by a Catholic priest. A magnificent contadina was brought to light by the doctor in a village in the hills, and this big, brown, barbarous creature, who, to do her justice, was full of handsome, familiar smiles and coarse tenderness, was constituted nurse to Raymond Benyon's son. She nursed him for a fortnight under the mother's eye, and she was then sent back to her village with the baby in her arms and sundry gold coin knotted into a corner of her pocket-handkerchief. Mr. Gressie had given his daughter a liberal letter of credit on a London banker, and she was able, for the present, to make abundant provision for the little one. She called Mrs. Portico's attention to the fact that she spent none of her money on futilities; she kept it all for her small pensioner in the Genoese hills. Mrs. Portico beheld these strange doings with a stupefaction that occasionally broke into passionate protest; then she relapsed into a brooding sense of having now been an accomplice so far that she must be an accomplice to the end.

VII.

THE two ladies went down to Rome—Georgina was in wonderful trim—to finish the season, and here Mrs. Portico became convinced that she intended to abandon her offspring. She had not driven into the country to see the nursling before leaving Genoa; she had said that she couldn't bear to see it in such a place and among such people, Mrs. Portico, it must be added, had felt the force of this plea, felt it as regards a plan of her own, given up after being hotly entertained for a few hours, of devoting a day, by herself, to a visit to the big contadina. It seemed to her that if she should see the child in the sordid hands to which Georgina had consigned it, she would become still more of a participant than she was already. This young woman's blooming hardness, after they got to Rome, acted upon her like a kind of Medusa-mask. She had seen a horrible thing, she had been mixed up with it, and her motherly heart had received a mortal chill. It became more clear to her every day that, though Georgina would continue to send the infant money in considerable quantities, she had dispossessed herself of it for ever. Together with this induction a fixed idea settled in her mind—the project of taking the baby herself, of making him her own, of arranging that matter with the father. The countenance she had given Georgina up to this point was an effective pledge that she would not expose her; but she could adopt the poor little mortal without exposing her, she could say that he was a lovely baby—he was lovely, fortunately—whom she had picked up in a wretched village in Italy, a village that had been devastated by brigands. She could pretend—she could pretend; oh, yes, of course, she could pretend! Everything was imposture now, and she could go on to lie as she had begun. The falsity of the whole business sickened her; it made her so yellow that she scarcely knew herself in her glass. None the less, to rescue the child, even if she had to become falser still, would be in some measure an atonement for the treachery to which she had already surrendered herself. She began to hate Georgina, who had dragged her into such an abyss, and if it had not been for two considerations she would have insisted on their separating. One was the deference she owed to Mr. and Mrs. Gressie, who had reposed such a trust in her; the other was that she must keep hold of the mother till she had got possession of the infant Meanwhile, in this forced communion, her detestation of her companion increased; Georgina came to appear to her a creature of clay and iron. She was exceedingly afraid of her, and it seemed to her now a wonder of wonders that she should ever have trusted her enough to come so far. Georgina showed no consciousness of the change in Mrs. Portico, though there was, indeed, at present, not even a pretence of confidence between the two. Miss Gressie—that was another lie to which Mrs. Portico had to lend herself—was bent on enjoying Europe, and was especially delighted with Rome. She certainly had the courage of her undertaking, and she confessed to Mrs. Portico that she had left Raymond Benyon, and meant to continue to leave him, in ignorance of what had taken place at

Genoa. There was a certain confidence, it must be said, in that. He was now in Chinese waters, and she probably should not see him for years. Mrs. Portico took counsel with herself, and the result of her cogitation was that she wrote to Mr. Benyon that a charming little boy had been born to him, and that Georgina had put him to nurse with Italian peasants; but that, if he would kindly consent to it, she, Mrs. Portico, would bring him up much better than that. She knew not how to address her letter, and Georgina, even if she should know, which was doubtful, would never tell her; so she sent the missive to the care of the Secretary of the Navy, at Washington, with an earnest request that it might immediately be forwarded. Such was Mrs. Portico's last effort in this strange business of Georgina's. I relate rather a complicated fact in a very few words when I say that the poor lady's anxieties, indignations, repentances, preyed upon her until they fairly broke her down. Various persons whom she knew in Rome notified her that the air of the Seven Hills was plainly unfavourable to her; and she had made up her mind to return to her native land when she found that, in her de-pressed condition, malarial fever had laid its hand upon her. She was unable to move, and the matter was settled for her in the course of an illness which, happily, was not prolonged. I have said that she was not obstinate, and the resistance she made on the present occa-sion was not worthy even of her spasmodic energy. Brain-fever made its appearance, and she died at the end of three weeks, during which Georgina's attentions to her patient and protectress had been unremitting. There were other Americans in Rome who, after this sad event, extended to the bereaved young lady every comfort and hospitality. She had no lack of opportunities for returning under a proper escort to New York. She selected, you may be sure, the best, and re-entered her father's house, where she took to plain dressing; for she sent all her pocket-money, with the utmost se-crecy, to the little boy in the Genoese hills.

VIII.

"WHY should he come if he doesn't like you? He is under no ob-ligation, and he has his ship to look after. Why should he sit for an hour at a time, and why should he be so pleasant?"

"Do you think he is very pleasant?" Kate Theory asked, turning away her face from her sister. It was important that Mildred should not see how little the expression of that charming countenance corresponded with the inquiry.

This precaution was useless, however, for in a moment Mildred said, from the delicately draped couch on which she lay at the open window, "Kate Theory, don't be affected."

"Perhaps it's for you he comes. I don't see why he shouldn't; you are far more attractive than I, and you have a great deal more to say. How can he help seeing that you are the cleverest of the clever? You can talk to him of everything: of the dates of the different eruptions, of the statues and bronzes in the museum, which you have never seen, *poverina*, but which you know more about than he does, than any one does. What was it you began on last time? Oh yes, you poured forth floods about Magna Græcia. And then—and then—"

But with this Kate Theory paused; she felt it wouldn't do to speak the words that had risen to her lips. That her sister was as beautiful as a saint, and as delicate and refined as an angel—she had been on the point of saying something of that sort. But Mildred's beauty and delicacy were the fairness of mortal disease, and to praise her for her refinement was just to remind her that she had the tenuity of a consumptive. So, after she had checked herself, the younger girl—she was younger only by a year or two—simply kissed her tenderly and settled the knot of the lace handkerchief that was tied over her head. Mildred knew what she had been going to say, knew why she had stopped. Mildred knew everything, without ever leaving her room, or leaving, at least, that little *salon* of their own, at the pension, which she had made so pretty by simply lying there, at the window that had the view of the bay and of Vesuvius, and telling Kate how to arrange and how to rearrange everything. Since it began to be plain that Mildred must spend her small remnant of years altogether in warm climates, the lot of the two sisters had been cast in the ungarnished hostelries of southern Europe. Their little sitting-room was sure to be very ugly, and Mildred was never happy till it was remodelled. Her sister fell to work, as a matter of course, the first day, and changed the place of all the tables, sofas, chairs, till every combination had been tried and the invalid thought at last that there was a little effect.

Kate Theory had a taste of her own, and her ideas were not always the same as her sister's; but she did whatever Mildred liked, and if the poor girl had told her to put the door-mat on the dining-table, or the clock under the sofa, she would have obeyed without a murmur. Her own ideas, her personal tastes, had been folded up and put away, like garments out of season, in drawers and trunks, with camphor and lavender. They were not, as a general thing, for southern wear, however indispensable to comfort in the climate of New England, where poor Mildred had lost her health. Kate Theory, ever since this event, had lived for her companion, and it was almost an inconvenience for her to think that she was attractive to Captain Benyon. It was as if she had shut up her house and was not in a position to entertain. So long as Mildred should live, her own life was suspended; if there should be any time afterwards, perhaps she would take it up again; but for the present, in answer to any knock at her door, she could only call down from one of her dusty windows that she was not at home. Was it really in these terms she should have to dismiss Captain Benyon? If Mildred said it was for her he came she must perhaps take upon herself such a duty; for, as we have seen, Mildred knew everything, and she must therefore be right. She knew about the statues in the museum, about the excavations at Pompeii, about the antique splendour of Magna Græcia. She always had some instructive volume on the table beside her sofa, and she had strength enough to hold the book for half-an-hour at a time. That was about the only strength she had now. The Neapolitan winter had been remarkably soft, but after the first month or two she had been obliged to give up her little walks in the garden. It lay beneath her window like a single enormous bouquet; as early as May, that year, the flowers were so dense. None of them, however, had a colour so intense as the splendid blue of the bay, which filled up all the rest of the view. It would have looked painted if you had not been able to see the little movement of the waves. Mildred Theory watched them by the hour, and the breathing crest of the volcano, on the other side of Naples, and the great sea-vision of Capri, on the horizon, changing its tint while her eyes rested there, and wondered what would become of her sister after she was gone. Now that Percival was married—he was their only brother, and from one day to the other was to come down to Naples to show them his new wife, as yet a complete stranger, or revealed only in the few letters she had written them during her wedding-tour—now that Percival was to be quite taken up, poor Kate's situation would be much more grave. Mildred felt that she should be able to judge better after she should have seen

her sister-in-law how much of a home Kate might expect to find
with the pair; but even if Agnes should prove—well, more satisfactory than her letters, it was a wretched prospect for Kate—this living as a mere appendage to happier people. Maiden-aunts were
very well, but being a maiden-aunt was only a last resource, and
Kate's first resources had not even been tried.

Meanwhile the latter young lady wondered as well, wondered
in what book Mildred had read that Captain Benyon was in love
with her. She admired him, she thought, but he didn't seem a man
that would fall in love with one like that. She could see that he was
on his guard: he wouldn't throw himself away. He thought too
much of himself, or at any rate he took too good care of himself,
in the manner of a man to whom something had happened which
had given him a lesson. Of course what had happened was that his
heart was buried somewhere, in some woman's grave; he had
loved some beautiful girl—much more beautiful, Kate was sure,
than she, who thought herself meagre and dusky—and the maiden
had died, and his capacity to love had died with her. He loved her
memory; that was the only thing he would care for now. He was
quiet, gentle, clever, humorous, and very kind in his manner; but
if any one save Mildred had said to her that if he came three times
a week to Posilippo, it was for anything but to pass his time (he
had told them he didn't know another lady in Naples), she would
have felt that this was simply the kind of thing—usually so idiotic—
that people always thought it necessary to say. It was very easy
for him to come; he had the big ship's boat, with nothing else
to do; and what could be more delightful than to be rowed
across the bay, under a bright awning, by four brown sailors with
Louisiana in blue letters on their immaculate white shirts and in gilt
letters on their fluttering hat-ribbons? The boat came to the steps
of the garden of the pension, where the orange-trees hung over
and made vague yellow balls shine back out of the water. Kate
Theory knew all about that, for Captain Benyon had persuaded
her to take a turn in the boat, and if they had only had another lady
to go with them he could have conveyed her to the ship and
shown her all over it. It looked beautiful, just a little way off, with
the American flag hanging loose in the Italian air. They would
have another lady when Agnes should arrive; then Percival would
remain with Mildred while they took this excursion. Mildred had
stayed alone the day she went in the boat; she had insisted on it,

and, of course it was really Mildred who had persuaded her; though now that Kate came to think of it, Captain Benyon had, in his quiet, waiting way—he turned out to be waiting long after you thought he had let a thing pass—said a good deal about the pleasure it would give him. Of course, everything would give pleasure to a man who was so bored. He was keeping the *Louisiana* at Naples, week after week, simply because these were the commodore's orders. There was no work to be done there, and his time was on his hands; but of course the commodore, who had gone to Constantinople with the two other ships, had to be obeyed to the letter, however mysterious his motives. It made no difference that he was a fantastic, grumbling, arbitrary old commodore; only a good while afterwards it occurred to Kate Theory that, for a reserved, correct man, Captain Benyon had given her a considerable proof of confidence in speaking to her in these terms of his superior officer. If he looked at all hot when he arrived at the pension she offered him a glass of cold "orangeade." Mildred thought this an unpleasant drink—she called it messy; but Kate adored it and Captain Benyon always accepted it.

IX.

THE day I speak of, to change the subject, she called her sister's attention to the extraordinary sharpness of a zigzaging cloud-shadow on the tinted slope of Vesuvius; but Mildred remarked in answer only that she wished her sister would marry the Captain. It was in this familiar way that constant meditation led Miss Theory to speak of him; it shows how constantly she thought of him, for, in general, no one was more ceremonious than she, and the failure of her health had not caused her to relax any form that it was possible to keep up. There was a kind of slim erectness even in the way she lay on her sofa; and she always received the doctor as if he were calling for the first time.

"I had better wait till he asks me," Kate Theory said. "Dear Milly, if I were to do some of the things you wish me to do, I should shock you very much."

"I wish he would marry you, then. You know there is very little time, if I wish to see it."

"You will never see it, Mildred. I don't see why you should take so for granted that I would accept him."

"You will never meet a man who has so few disagreeable qualities. He is probably not very well off. I don't know what is the pay of a captain in the navy"

"It's a relief to find there is something you don't know," Kate Theory broke in.

"But when I am gone," her sister went on, calmly, "when I am gone there will be plenty for both of you."

The younger girl, at this, was silent for a moment; then she exclaimed, "Mildred, you may be out of health, but I don't see why you should be dreadful!"

"You know that since we have been leading this life we have seen no one we liked better," said Milly. When she spoke of the life they were leading—there was always a soft resignation of regret and contempt in the allusion—she meant the southern winters, the foreign climates, the vain experiments, the lonely waitings, the wasted hours, the interminable rains, the bad food, the pottering, humbugging doctors, the damp pensions, the chance encounters, the fitful apparitions of fellow-travellers.

"Why shouldn't you speak for yourself alone? I am glad you like him, Mildred."

"If you don't like him, why do you give him orangeade?"

At this inquiry Kate began to laugh, and her sister continued—

"Of course you are glad I like him, my dear. If I didn't like him, and you did, it wouldn't be satisfactory at all. I can imagine nothing more miserable; I shouldn't die in any sort of comfort."

Kate Theory usually checked this sort of allusion—she was always too late—with a kiss; but on this occasion she added that it was a long time since Mildred had tormented her so much as she had done to-day. "You will make me hate him," she added.

"Well, that proves you don't already," Milly rejoined; and it happened that almost at this moment they saw, in the golden afternoon, Captain Benyon's boat approaching the steps at the end of the garden. He came that day, and he came two days later, and he came yet once again after an interval equally brief, before Percival Theory arrived with Mrs. Theory from Rome.

He seemed anxious to crowd into these few days, as he would have said, a good deal of intercourse with the two remarkably nice girls—or nice women, he hardly knew which to call them—whom in the course of a long, idle, rather tedious detention at Naples, he had discovered in the lovely suburb of Posilippo. It was the

American consul who had put him into relation with them. The
sisters had had to sign in the consul's presence some law-papers,
transmitted to them by the man of business who looked after their
little property in America, and the kindly functionary, taking advantage of the pretext (Captain Benyon happened to come into the
consulate as he was starting, indulgently, to wait upon the ladies) to
bring together "two parties" who, as he said, ought to appreciate
each other, proposed to his fellow-officer in the service of the
United States that he should go with him as witness of the little
ceremony. He might, of course, take his clerk, but the Captain
would do much better; and he represented to Benyon that the Miss
Theorys (singular name, wasn't it?) suffered, he was sure, from a
lack of society; also that one of them was very sick, that they were
real pleasant and extraordinarily refined, and that the sight of a
compatriot literally draped, as it were, in the national banner would
cheer them up more than most anything, and give them a sense of
protection. They had talked to the consul about Benyon's ship,
which they could see from their windows, in the distance, at its
anchorage. They were the only American ladies then at Naples—
the only residents, at least—and the Captain wouldn't be doing the
polite thing unless he went to pay them his respects. Benyon felt
afresh how little it was in his line to call upon strange women; he
was not in the habit of hunting up female acquaintance, or of looking out for the particular emotions which the sex only can inspire.
He had his reasons for this abstention, and he seldom relaxed it; but
the consul appealed to him on rather strong grounds. And he suffered himself to be persuaded. He was far from regretting, during
the first weeks at least, an act which was distinctly inconsistent with
his great rule—that of never exposing himself to the danger of be-
coming entangled with an unmarried woman. He had been obliged
to make this rule, and had adhered to it with some success. He was
fond of women, but he was forced to restrict himself to superficial
sentiments. There was no use tumbling into situations from which
the only possible issue was a retreat. The step he had taken with
regard to poor Miss Theory and her delightful little sister was an
exception on which at first he could only congratulate himself.
That had been a happy idea of the ruminating old consul; it made
Captain Benyon forgive him his hat, his boots, his shirt-front—a
costume which might be considered representative, and the
effect of which was to make the observer turn with rapture to a

half-naked lazzarone. On either side the acquaintance had helped the time to pass, and the hours he spent at the little pension at Posilippo left a sweet, and by no means innutritive, taste behind.

As the weeks went by his exception had grown to look a good deal like a rule; but he was able to remind himself that the path of retreat was always open to him. Moreover, if he should fall in love with the younger girl there would be no great harm, for Kate Theory was in love with her sister, and it would matter very little to her whether he advanced or retreated. She was very attractive, or rather she was very attracting. Small, pale, attentive without rigidity, full of pretty curves and quick movements, she looked as if the habit of watching and serving had taken complete possession of her, and was literally a little sister of charity. Her thick black hair was pushed behind her ears, as if to help her to listen, and her clear brown eyes had the smile of a person too full of tact to carry a sad face to a sick-bed. She spoke in an encouraging voice, and had soothing and unselfish habits. She was very pretty, producing a cheerful effect of contrasted black and white, and dressed herself daintily, so that Mildred might have something agreeable to look at. Benyon very soon perceived that there was a fund of good service in her. Her sister had it all now; but poor Miss Theory was fading fast, and then what would become of this precious little force? The answer to such a question that seemed most to the point was that it was none of his business. He was not sick—at least not physically—and he was not looking out for a nurse. Such a companion might be a luxury, but was not, as yet, a necessity. The welcome of the two ladies, at first, had been simple, and he scarcely knew what to call it but sweet; a bright, gentle, jocular friendliness remained the tone of their intercourse. They evidently liked him to come; they liked to see his big transatlantic ship hover about those gleaming coasts of exile. The fact of Miss Mildred being always stretched on her couch—in his successive visits to foreign waters Benyon had not unlearned (as why should he?) the pleasant American habit of using the lady's personal name—made their intimacy seem greater, their differences less; it was as if his hostesses had taken him into their confidence and he had been—as the consul would have said—of the same party. Knocking about the salt parts of the globe, with a few feet square on a rolling frigate for his only home, the pretty flower-decked sitting-room of the quiet American sisters became, more than anything he had hitherto known, his interior. He had dreamed once of having an interior, but the dream had vanished in lurid smoke, and no such vision had come to him again. He had a feeling that the end of this was drawing nigh; he was sure that the advent of the strange brother, whose wife was certain to be disagreeable, would make a difference. That is why, as I have said, he came as often as possible the last week, after he had learned the day on which Percival Theory would arrive. The limits of the exception had been reached.

He had been new to the young ladies at Posilippo, and there was no reason why they should say to each other that he was a very different man from the ingenuous youth who, ten years before, used to wander with Georgina Gressie down vistas of plank-fences brushed over with advertisements of quack medicines. It was natural he should be, and we, who know him, would have found that he had traversed the whole scale of alteration. There was nothing ingenuous in him now; he had the look of experience, of having been seasoned and hardened by the years. His face, his complexion, were the same; still smooth-shaven and slim, he always passed, at first, for a decidedly youthful mariner. But his expression was old, and his talk was older still—the talk of a man who had seen much of the world (as indeed he had to-day) and judged most things for himself, with a humorous scepticism which, whatever concessions it might make, superficially, for the sake of not offending, for instance, two remarkably nice American women who had kept most of their illusions, left you with the conviction that the next minute it would go quickly back to its own stand-point. There was a curious contradiction in him; he struck you as serious, and yet he could not be said to take things seriously. This was what made Kate Theory feel so sure that he had lost the object of his affections; and she said to herself that it must have been under circumstances of peculiar sadness, for that was, after all, a frequent accident, and was not usually thought, in itself, a sufficient stroke to make a man a cynic. This reflection, it may be added, was, on the young lady's part, just the least bit acrimonious. Captain Benyon was not a cynic in any sense in which he might have shocked an innocent mind; he kept his cynicism to himself, and was a very clever, courteous, attentive gentleman. If he was melancholy, you knew it chiefly by his jokes, for they were usually at his own expense; and if he was indifferent, it was all the more to his credit that he should have exerted himself to entertain his countrywomen.

X.

THE last time he called before the arrival of the expected brother he found Miss Theory alone, and sitting up, for a wonder, at her window. Kate had driven into Naples to give orders at the hotel for the reception of the travellers, who required accommodation more spacious than the villa at Posilippo (where the two sisters had the best rooms) could offer them; and the sick girl had taken advantage of her absence, and of the pretext afforded by a day of delicious warmth, to transfer herself for the first time in six months to an arm-chair. She was practising, as she said, for the long carriage-journey to the north, where, in a quiet corner they knew of, on the Lago Maggiore, her summer was to be spent. Raymond Benyon remarked to her that she had evidently turned the corner and was going to get well, and this gave her a chance to say various things that were in her mind. She had various things on her mind, poor Mildred Theory, so caged and restless, and yet so resigned and patient as she was; with a clear, quick spirit, in the most perfect health, ever reaching forward, to the end of its tense little chain, from her wasted and suffering body; and, in the course of the perfect summer afternoon, as she sat there, exhilarated by the success of her effort to get up and by her comfortable opportunity, she took her friendly visitor into the confidence of most of her anxieties. She told him, very promptly and positively, that she was not going to get well at all, that she had probably not more than a twelvemonth yet to live, and that he would oblige her very much by not forcing her to waste any more breath in contradicting him on that head. Of course she couldn't talk much; therefore she wished to say to him only things that he would not hear from any one else. Such for instance was her present secret—Katie's and hers—the secret of their fearing so much that they shouldn't like Percival's wife, who was not from Boston but from New York. Naturally, that by itself would be nothing, but from what they had heard of her set—this subject had been explored by their correspondents—they were rather nervous, nervous to the point of not being in the least reassured by the fact that the young lady would bring Percival a fortune. The fortune was a matter of course, for that was just what they had heard about Agnes's circle—that the stamp of money was on all their thoughts and doings. They were very rich and very new and very splashing, and evidently had very little in common with the two Miss Theorys, who, moreover, if the truth must be told (and this was a

great secret), did not care much for the letters their sister-in-law
had hitherto addressed them. She had been at a French boarding-
school in New York, and yet (and this was the greatest secret of all)
she wrote to them that she had performed a part of the journey
through France in a "diligance"! Of course, they would see the
next day; Miss Mildred was sure she should know in a moment
whether Agnes would like them. She could never have told him all
this if her sister had been there, and Captain Benyon must promise
never to tell Kate how she had chattered. Kate thought always that
they must hide everything, and that even if Agnes should be a
dreadful disappointment they must never let any one guess it. And
yet Kate was just the one who would suffer, in the coming years,
after she herself had gone. Their brother had been everything to
them, but now it would all be different. Of course it was not to be
expected that he should have remained a bachelor for their sake:
she only wished he had waited till she was dead and Kate was married. One of these events, it was true, was much less sure than the
other; Kate might never marry, much as she wished she would. She
was quite morbidly unselfish, and didn't think she had a right to
have anything of her own—not even a husband.

Miss Mildred talked a good while about Kate, and it never occurred to her that she might bore Captain Benyon. She didn't, in
point of fact; he had none of the trouble of wondering why this
poor, sick, worried lady was trying to push her sister down his
throat. Their peculiar situation made everything natural, and the
tone she took with him now seemed only what their pleasant relations for the last three months led up to. Moreover, he had an
excellent reason for not being bored: the fact, namely, that, after all,
with regard to her sister, Miss Mildred appeared to him to keep
back more than she uttered. She didn't tell him the great thing—
she had nothing to say as to what that charming girl thought of
Raymond Benyon. The effect of their interview, indeed, was to
make him shrink from knowing, and he felt that the right thing for
him would be to get back into his boat, which was waiting at the
garden-steps, before Kate Theory should return from Naples. It
came over him, as he sat there, that he was far too interested in
knowing what this young lady thought of him. She might think
what she pleased; it could make no difference to him. The best
opinion in the world—if it looked out at him from her tender
eyes—would not make him a whit more free or more happy.

Women of that sort were not for him, women whom one could not see familiarly without falling in love with them, and whom it was no use to fall in love with unless one was ready to marry them. The light of the summer-afternoon, and of Miss Mildred's pure spirit, seemed suddenly to flood the whole subject. He saw that he was in danger, and he had long since made up his mind that from this particular peril it was not only necessary but honourable to flee. He took leave of his hostess before her sister reappeared, and had the courage even to say to her that he should not come back often after that; they would be so much occupied by their brother and his wife! As he moved across the glassy bay, to the rhythm of the oars, he wished either that the sisters would leave Naples or that his confounded commodore would send for him.

When Kate returned from her errand, ten minutes later, Milly told her of the Captain's visit, and added that she had never seen anything so sudden as the way he left her. "He wouldn't wait for you, my dear, and he said he thought it more than likely that he should never see us again. It is as if he thought you were going to die too!"

"Is his ship called away?" Kate Theory asked.

"He didn't tell me so; he said we should be so busy with Percival and Agnes."

"He has got tired of us; that is all. There is nothing wonderful in that; I knew he would."

Mildred said nothing for a moment; she was watching her sister, who was very attentively arranging some flowers. "Yes, of course, we are very dull, and he is like everybody else."

"I thought you thought he was so wonderful," said Kate—"and so fond of us."

"So he is; I am surer of that than ever. That's why he went away so abruptly."

Kate looked at her sister now. "I don't understand."

"Neither do I, *cara*. But you will, one of these days."

"How, if he never comes back?"

"Oh, he will—after a while—when I am gone. Then he will explain; that, at least, is clear to me."

"My poor precious, as if I cared!" Kate Theory exclaimed, smiling as she distributed her flowers. She carried them to the window, to place them near her sister, and here she paused a moment, her eye caught by an object, far out in the bay, with which she was not unfamiliar. Mildred noticed its momentary look, and followed its direction.

"It's the Captain's gig going back to the ship," Milly said. "It's so still one can almost hear the oars."

Kate Theory turned away, with a sudden, strange violence, a movement and exclamation which, the very next minute, as she became conscious of what she had said—and, still more, of what she felt—smote her own heart (as it flushed her face) with surprise and with the force of a revelation. "I wish it would sink him to the bottom of the sea!"

Her sister stared, then caught her by the dress, as she passed from her, drawing her back with a weak hand. "Oh, my darling dear!" And she drew Kate down and down toward her, so that the girl had nothing for it but to sink on her knees and bury her face in Mildred's lap. If that ingenious invalid did not know everything now, she knew a great deal.

XI.

MRS. PERCIVAL proved very pretty; it is more gracious to begin with this declaration, instead of saying, in the first place, that she proved very vapid. It took a long day to arrive at the end of her silliness, and the two ladies at Posilippo, even after a week had passed, suspected that they had only skirted its edges. Kate Theory had not spent half an hour in her company before she gave a little private sigh of relief; she felt that a situation which had promised to be embarrassing was now quite clear, was even of a primitive simplicity. She would spend with her sister-in-law, in the coming time, one week in the year; that was all that would be mortally possible. It was a blessing that one could see exactly what she was, for in that way the question settled itself. It would have been much more tiresome if Agnes had been a little less obvious; then one would have had to hesitate and consider and weigh one thing against another. She was pretty and silly, as distinctly as an orange is yellow and round; and Kate Theory would as soon have thought of looking to her to give interest to the future as she would have thought of looking to an orange to impart solidity to the prospect of dinner. Mrs. Percival travelled in the hope of meeting her American acquaintance, or of making acquaintance with such Americans as she did meet, and for the purpose of buying mementos

for her relations. She was perpetually adding to her store of articles
in tortoise-shell, in mother-of-pearl, in olive-wood, in ivory, in
filigree, in tartan lacquer, in mosaic; and she had a collection of
Roman scarfs and Venetian beads which she looked over exhaus-
tively every night before she went to bed. Her conversation bore
mainly upon the manner in which she intended to dispose of these
accumulations. She was constantly changing about, among each
other, the persons to whom they were respectively to be offered.
At Rome one of the first things she said to her husband after entering the Coliseum had been, "I guess I will give the ivory work-box
to Bessie and the Roman pearls to Aunt Harriet!" She was always
hanging over the travellers' book at the hotel; she had it brought
up to her, with a cup of chocolate, as soon as she arrived. She
searched its pages for the magical name of New York, and she indulged in infinite conjecture as to who the people were—the name
was sometimes only a partial cue—who had inscribed it there.
What she most missed in Europe, and what she most enjoyed, was
the New Yorkers; when she met them she talked about the people
in their native city who had "moved" and the streets they had
moved to. "Oh yes, the Drapers are going up town, to Twenty-
fourth Street, and the Vanderdeckens are going to be in Twenty-
third Street, right back of them. My uncle, Mr. Henry Platt, thinks
of building round there." Mrs. Percival Theory was capable of repeating statements like these thirty times over—of lingering on
them for hours. She talked largely of herself, of her uncles and
aunts, of her clothes—past, present and future. These articles, in
especial, filled her horizon; she considered them with a compla-
cency which might have led you to suppose that she had invented the custom of draping the human form. Her main point
of contact with Naples was the purchase of coral; and all the
while she was there the word "set"—she used it as if every one
would understand—fell with its little flat, common sound upon
the ears of her sisters-in-law, who had no sets of anything. She
cared little for pictures and mountains; Alps and Apennines were
not productive of New Yorkers, and it was difficult to take an
interest in Madonnas who flourished at periods when apparently
there were no fashions, or at any rate no trimmings.

I speak here not only of the impression she made upon her husband's anxious sisters, but of the judgment passed on her (he went
so far as that, though it was not obvious how it mattered to him)

by Raymond Benyon. And this brings me at a jump (I confess it's a very small one) to the fact that he did, after all, go back to Posilippo. He stayed away for nine days, and at the end of this time Percival Theory called upon him to thank him for the civility he had shown his kinswomen. He went to this gentleman's hotel, to return his visit, and there he found Miss Kate, in her brother's sitting-room. She had come in by appointment from the villa, and was going with the others to look at the royal palace, which she had not yet had an opportunity to inspect. It was proposed (not by Kate), and presently arranged, that Captain Benyon should go with them; and he accordingly walked over marble floors for half an hour, exchanging conscious commonplaces with the woman he loved. For this truth had rounded itself during those nine days of absence; he discovered that there was nothing particularly sweet in his life when once Kate Theory had been excluded from it. He had stayed away to keep himself from falling in love with her; but this expedient was in itself illuminating, for he perceived that, according to the vulgar adage, he was locking the stable-door after the horse had been stolen. As he paced the deck of his ship and looked toward Posilippo his tenderness crystallised; the thick, smoky flame of a sentiment that knew itself forbidden, and was angry at the knowledge, now danced upon the fuel of his good resolutions. The latter, it must be said, resisted, declined to be consumed. He determined that he would see Kate Theory again, for a time just sufficient to bid her good bye and to add a little explanation. He thought of his explanation very lovingly, but it may not strike the reader as a happy inspiration. To part from her dryly, abruptly, without an allusion to what he might have said if everything had been different—that would be wisdom, of course, that would be virtue, that would be the line of a practical man, of a man who kept himself well in hand. But it would be virtue terribly unrewarded—it would be virtue too austere even for a person who flattered himself that he had taught himself stoicism. The minor luxury tempted him irresistibly, since the larger—that of happy love—was denied him; the luxury of letting the girl know that it would not be an accident—oh, not at all—that they should never meet again. She might easily think it was, and thinking it was would doubtless do her no harm. But this wouldn't give him his pleasure—the platonic satisfaction of expressing to her at the same time his belief that they might have made each other happy and the necessity of his renunciation. That, probably, wouldn't hurt her either, for she had given him no proof whatever that she cared for him. The nearest approach to it was the way she walked beside him now, sweet and silent, without the least reference to his not having come back to the villa. The place was cool and dusky, the blinds were drawn to keep out the light and noise, and the little party wandered through the high saloons, where precious marbles and the gleam of gilding and satin made reflections in the rich dimness. Here and there the cicerone, in slippers, with Neapolitan familiarity, threw open a shutter to show off a picture or a tapestry. He strolled in front with Percival Theory and his wife, while this lady, drooping silently from her husband's arm as they passed, felt the stuff of the curtains and the sofas. When he caught her in these experiments the cicerone, in expressive deprecation, clasped his hands and lifted his eyebrows; whereupon Mrs. Theory exclaimed to her husband, "Oh, bother his old king!" It was not striking to Captain Benyon why Percival Theory had married the niece of Mr. Henry Platt. He was less interesting than his sisters—a smooth, cool, correct young man, who frequently took out a pencil and did a little arithmetic on the back of a letter. He sometimes, in spite of his correctness, chewed a toothpick, and he missed the American papers, which he used to ask for in the most unlikely places. He was a Bostonian converted to New York; a very special type.

"Is it settled when you leave Naples?" Benyon asked of Kate Theory.

"I think so; on the twenty-fourth. My brother has been very kind; he has lent us his carriage, which is a large one, so that Mildred can lie down. He and Agnes will take another; but of course we shall travel together."

"I wish to heaven I were going with you!" Captain Benyon said. He had given her the opportunity to respond, but she did not take it; she merely remarked, with a vague laugh, that of course he couldn't take his ship over the Apennines. "Yes, there is always my ship," he went on. "I am afraid that in future it will carry me far away from you."

They were alone in one of the royal apartments; their companions had passed, in advance of them, into the adjoining room. Benyon and his fellow-visitor had paused beneath one of the immense chandeliers of glass, which in the clear, coloured gloom, through which one felt the strong outer light of Italy beating in, suspended its twinkling drops from the decorated vault. They looked round them confusedly, made shy for the moment by Benyon's having struck a note more serious than any that had hitherto sounded between them, looked at the sparse furniture, draped in white overalls, at the scagliola floor, in which the great cluster of crystal pendants seemed to shine again.

"You are master of your ship—can't you sail it as you like?" Kate Theory asked, with a smile.

"I am not master of anything. There is not a man in the world less free. I am a slave. I am a victim."

She looked at him with kind eyes; something in his voice suddenly made her put away all thought of the defensive airs that a girl, in certain situations, is expected to assume. She perceived that he wanted to make her understand something, and now her only wish was to help him to say it. "You are not happy," she murmured simply, her voice dying away in a kind of wonderment at this reality.

The gentle touch of her words—it was as if her hand had stroked his cheek—seemed to him the sweetest thing he had ever known. "No, I am not happy, because I am not free. If I were—if I were, I would give up my ship, I would give up everything, to follow you. I can't explain; that is part of the hardness of it. I only want you to know it, that if certain things were different, if everything was different, I might tell you that I believe I should have a right to speak to you. Perhaps some day it will change; but probably then it will be too late. Meanwhile, I have no right of any kind. I don't want to trouble you, and I don't ask of you—anything! It is only to have spoken just once. I don't make you understand, of course. I am afraid I seem to you rather a brute, perhaps even a humbug. Don't think of it now; don't try to understand. But some day, in the future, remember what I have said to you, and how we stood here, in this strange old place, alone! Perhaps it will give you a little pleasure."

Kate Theory began by listening to him with visible eagerness; but in a moment she turned away her eyes. "I am very sorry for you," she said, gravely.

"Then you do understand enough?"

"I shall think of what you have said—in the future."

Benyon's lips formed the beginning of a word of tenderness, which he instantly suppressed; and in a different tone, with a bitter smile and a sad shake of the head, raising his arms a moment and letting them fall, he rejoined, "It won't hurt any one, your remembering this!"

"I don't know whom you mean." And the girl, abruptly, began to walk to the end of the room. He made no attempt to tell her whom he meant, and they proceeded together in silence till they overtook their companions.

XII.

THERE were several pictures in the neighbouring room, and Percival Theory and his wife had stopped to look at one of them, of which the cicerone announced the title and the authorship as Benyon came up. It was a modern portrait of a Bourbon princess, a woman young, fair, handsome, covered with jewels. Mrs. Percival appeared to be more struck with it than with anything the palace had yet offered to her sight, while her sister-in-law walked to the window, which the custodian had opened, to look out into the garden. Benyon noticed this; he was conscious that he had given the girl something to reflect upon, and his ears burned a little as he stood beside Mrs. Percival and looked up, mechanically, at the royal lady. He already repented a little of what he had said; for, after all, what was the use? And he hoped the others wouldn't observe that he had been making love.

"Gracious, Percival! Do you see who she looks like?" Mrs. Theory said to her husband.

"She looks like a lady who has a big bill at Tiffany's," this gentleman answered.

"She looks like my sister-in-law; the eyes, the mouth, the way the hair's done—the whole thing."

"Which do you mean? You have got about a dozen."

"Why, Georgina, of course—Georgina Roy. She's awfully like."

"Do you call her your sister-in-law?" Percival Theory asked. "You must want very much to claim her."

"Well, she's handsome enough. You have got to invent some new name, then. Captain Benyon, what do you call your brother-in-law's second wife?" Mrs. Percival continued, turning to her neighbour, who still stood staring at the portrait. At first he had looked without seeing; then sight, and hearing as well, became quick. They were suddenly peopled with thrilling recognitions.

The Bourbon princess—the eyes, the mouth, the way the hair was done, these things took on an identity, and the gaze of the painted face seemed to fasten itself to his own. But who in the world was Georgina Roy, and what was this talk about sisters-in-law? He turned to the little lady at his side a countenance unexpectedly puzzled by the problem she had lightly presented to him.

"Your brother-in-law's second wife? That's rather complicated."

"Well, of course, he needn't have married again," said Mrs. Percival, with a small sigh.

"Whom did he marry?" asked Benyon, staring. Percival Theory had turned away. "Oh, if you are going into her relationships," he murmured, and joined his sister at the brilliant window, through which, from the distance, the many-voiced uproar of Naples came in.

"He married first my sister Cora, and she died five years ago. Then he married *her*;" and Mrs. Percival nodded at the princess.

Benyon's eyes went back to the portrait; he could see what she meant—it stared out at him. "Her? Georgina?"

"Georgina Gressie! Gracious, do you know her?"

It was very distinct—that answer of Mrs. Percival's, and the question that followed it as well. But he had the resource of the picture; he could look at it, seem to take it very seriously, though it danced up and down before him. He felt that he was turning red, then he felt that he was turning pale. "The brazen impudence!" That was the way he could speak to himself now of the woman he had once loved, and whom he afterwards hated, till this had died out too. Then the wonder of it was lost in the quickly growing sense that it would make a difference for him—a great difference. Exactly what, he didn't see yet; only a difference that swelled and swelled as he thought of it, and caught up, in its expansion, the girl who stood behind him so quietly, looking into the Italian garden.

The custodian drew Mrs. Percival away to show her another princess, before Benyon answered her last inquiry. This gave him time to recover from his first impulse, which had been to answer it with a negative; he saw in a moment that an admission of his acquaintance with Mrs. Roy (Mrs. Roy!—it was prodigious!) was necessarily helping him to learn more. Besides, it needn't be compromising. Very likely Mrs. Percival would hear one day that he had once wanted to marry her. So, when he joined his companions a minute later he remarked that he had known Miss Gressie years before, and had even admired her considerably, but had lost sight of her entirely in later days. She had been a great beauty, and it was a wonder that she had not married earlier. Five years ago, was it? No, it was only two. He had been going to say that in so long a time it would have been singular he should not have heard of it. He had been away from New York for ages; but one always heard of marriages and deaths. This was a proof, though two years was rather long. He led Mrs. Percival insidiously into a further room, in advance of the others, to whom the cicerone returned. She was delighted to talk about her "connections," and she supplied him with every detail. He could trust himself now; his self-possession was complete, or, so far as it was wanting, the fault was that of a sudden gaiety which he could not, on the spot, have accounted for. Of course it was not very flattering to them—Mrs. Percival's own people—that poor Cora's husband should have consoled himself; but men always did it (talk of widows!) and he had chosen a girl who was—well, very fine-looking, and the sort of successor to Cora that they needn't be ashamed of. She had been awfully admired, and no one had understood why she had waited so long to marry. She had had some affair as a girl—an engagement to an officer in the army—and the man had jilted her, or they had quarrelled, or something or other. She was almost an old maid—well, she was thirty, or very nearly—but she had done something good now. She was handsomer than ever, and tremendously striking. William Roy had one of the biggest incomes in the city, and he was quite affectionate. He had been intensely fond of Cora—he often spoke of her still, at least to her own relations; and her portrait, the last time Mrs. Percival was in his house (it was at a party, after his marriage to Miss Gressie), was still in the front parlour. Perhaps by this time he had had it moved to the back; but she was sure he would keep it somewhere, anyway. Poor Cora had had no children; but Georgina was making that all right; she had a beautiful boy. Mrs. Percival had what she would have called quite a pleasant chat with Captain Benyon about Mrs. Roy. Perhaps *he* was the officer—she never thought of that! He was sure he had never jilted her? And he had never quarrelled with a lady? Well, he must be different from most men.

He certainly had the air of being so before he parted that afternoon with Kate Theory. This young lady, at least, was free to think him wanting in that consistency which is supposed to be a distinctively masculine virtue. An hour before he had taken an eternal farewell of her; and now he was alluding to future meetings, to future visits, proposing that, with her sister-in-law, she should appoint an early day for coming to see the *Louisiana*. She had supposed she understood him, but it would appear now that she had not understood him at all. His manner had changed too. More and more off his guard, Raymond Benyon was not aware how much more hopeful an expression it gave him, his irresistible sense that somehow or other this extraordinary proceeding of his wife's would set him free. Kate Theory felt rather weary and mystified, all the more for knowing that henceforth Captain Benyon's variations would be the most important thing in life for her.

XIII.

THAT officer, on his ship in the bay, lingered very late on the deck that night—lingered there, indeed, under the warm southern sky, in which the stars glittered with a hot, red light, until the early dawn began to show. He smoked cigar after cigar; he walked up and down by the hour; he was agitated by a thousand reflections; he repeated to himself that it made a difference—an immense difference; but the pink light had deepened in the east before he had discovered in what the change consisted. By that time he saw it clearly—it consisted in Georgina's being in his power now, in place of his being in hers. He laughed as he sat alone in the darkness at the thought of what she had done. It had occurred to him more than once that she would do it; he believed her capable of anything; but the accomplished fact had a freshness of comicality. He thought of William Roy, of his big income, of his being "quite affectionate," of his blooming son and heir, of his having found such a worthy successor to poor Mrs. Cora. He wondered whether Georgina had mentioned to him that she had a husband living, but was strongly of the belief that she had not. Why should she, after all? She had neglected to mention it to so many others. He had thought he knew her, in so many years, that he had nothing more to learn about her, but this ripe stroke revived his sense of her audacity. Of course it was what she had been waiting for, and if she had not done it sooner it was because she had hoped he would be lost at sea in one of his long cruises and relieve her of the necessity of a crime. How she must hate him to-day for not having been lost, for being alive, for continuing to put her in the wrong! Much as she hated him, however, his own loathing was at least a match for hers. She had done him the foulest of wrongs—she had ravaged his life. That he should ever detest in this degree a woman whom he had once loved as he loved her he would not have thought possible in his innocent younger years. But neither would he have thought it possible then that a woman should be such a cold-blooded devil as she had been. His love had perished in his rage, his blinding, impotent rage, at finding that he had been duped and measuring his impotence. When he learned, years before, from Mrs. Portico, what she had done with her baby, of whose entrance into life she herself had given him no intimation, he felt that he was face to face with a full revelation of her nature. Before that it had puzzled him, it had mocked him; his relations with her were bewildering, stupe-fying. But when, after obtaining, with difficulty and delay, a leave of absence from Government, and betaking himself to Italy to look for the child and assume possession of it, he had encountered abso-lute failure and defeat, then the case presented itself to him more simply. He perceived that he had mated himself with a creature who just happened to be a monster, a human exception altogether. That was what he couldn't pardon—her conduct about the child; never, never, never! To him she might have done what she chose—dropped him, pushed him out into eternal cold, with his hands fast tied—and he would have accepted it, excused her almost, admitted that it had been his business to mind better what he was about. But she had tortured him through the poor little irrecover-able son whom he had never seen, through the heart and the human vitals that she had not herself, and that he had to have, poor wretch, for both of them.

All his effort, for years, had been to forget those horrible months, and he had cut himself off from them so that they seemed at times to belong to the life of another person. But to-night he lived them over again; he retraced the different gradations of darkness through which he had passed, from the moment, so soon after his extraor-dinary marriage, when it came over him that she already repented and meant, if possible, to elude all her obligations. This was the moment when he saw why she had reserved herself—in the strange vow she extracted from him—an open door for retreat; the mo-ment, too, when her having had such an inspiration (in the midst of her momentary good faith, if good faith it had ever been) struck him as a proof of her essential depravity. What he had tried to forget came back to him: the child that was not his child produced for him when he fell upon that squalid nest of peasants in the Genoese country, and then the confessions, retractations, contradictions, lies, terrors, threats, and general bottomless, baffling mendacity and idiocy of every one in the place. The child was gone; that had been the only definite thing. The woman who had taken it to nurse had a dozen different stories, her husband had as many, and every one in the village had a hundred more. Georgina had been sending money—she had managed, apparently, to send a good deal—and the whole country seemed to have been living on it and making merry. At one moment, the baby had died and received a most expensive burial; at another, he had been entrusted (for more healthy air, Santissima Madonna!) to the woman's cousin, in another village. According to a version which for a day or two Benyon had inclined to think the least false, he had been taken by the cousin (for his beauty's sake) to Genoa, when she went for the first time in her life to the town to see her daughter in service there, and had been confided for a few hours to a third woman, who was to keep him while the cousin walked about the streets, but who, having no child of her own, took such a fancy to him that she refused to give him up, and a few days later left the place (she was a Pisana) never to be heard of more. The cousin had forgotten her name—it had happened six months before. Benyon spent a year looking up and down Italy for his child, and inspecting hundreds of swaddled infants, inscrutable candidates for recognition. Of course he could only get further and further from real knowledge, and his search was arrested by the conviction that it was making him mad. He set his teeth and made up his mind, or tried to, that the baby had died in the hands of its nurse. This was, after all, much the likeliest supposition, and the woman had maintained it, in the hope of being rewarded for her candour, quite as often as she had asseverated that it was still somewhere, alive, in the hope of being remunerated for her good news. It may be imagined with what sentiments toward his wife Benyon had emerged from this episode. To-night his memory went further back—back to the beginning and to the days when he had had to ask himself, with all the crudity of his first surprise, what in the name of perversity she had wished to do with him. The answer to this speculation was so old, it had dropped so out of the line of recurrence, that it was now almost new again. Moreover, it was only approximate, for, as I have already said, he could comprehend such baseness as little at the end as at the beginning. She had found herself on a slope which her nature forced her to descend to the bottom. She did him the honour of wishing to enjoy his society, and she did herself the honour of thinking that their intimacy, however brief, must have a certain consecration. She felt that with him, after his promise (he would have made any promise to lead her on), she was secure, secure as she had proved to be, secure as she must think herself. That security had helped her to ask herself, after the first flush of passion was over, and her native, her twice-inherited worldliness had had time to open its eyes again, why she should keep faith with a man whose deficiencies (as a husband before the world—another affair) had been so scientifically exposed to her by her parents. So she had simply determined *not* to keep faith; and her determination, at least, she did keep.

By the time Benyon turned in he had satisfied himself, as I say, that Georgina was now in his power; and this seemed to him such an improvement in his situation that he allowed himself, for the next ten days, a license which made Kate Theory almost as happy as it made her sister, though she pretended to understand it far less. Mildred sank to her rest, or rose to fuller comprehensions, within the year, in the Isle of Wight; and Captain Benyon, who had never written so many letters as since they left Naples, sailed westward about the same time as the sweet survivor. For the *Louisiana* at last was ordered home.

XIV.

CERTAINLY, I will see you if you come, and you may appoint any day or hour you like. I should have seen you with pleasure any time these last years. Why should we not be friends, as we used to be? Perhaps we shall be yet. I say "perhaps" only, on purpose, because your note is rather vague about your state of mind. Don't come with any idea about making me nervous or uncomfortable. I am not nervous by nature, thank heaven, and I won't, I positively won't (do you hear, dear Captain Benyon?) be uncomfortable. I have been so (it served me right) for years and years; but I am very happy now. To remain so is the very definite intention of yours ever

GEORGINA ROY.

This was the answer Benyon received to a short letter that he despatched to Mrs. Roy after his return to America. It was not till he had been there some weeks that he wrote to her. He had been occupied in various ways: he had had to look after his ship; he had had to report at Washington; he had spent a fortnight with his mother at Portsmouth, N. H.; and he had paid a visit to Kate Theory in Boston. She herself was paying visits; she was staying with various relatives and friends. She had more colour—it was very delicately rosy—than she had had of old, in spite of her black dress; and the effect of her looking at him seemed to him to make her eyes grow still prettier. Though sisterless now, she was not without duties, and Benyon could easily see that life would press hard on her unless some one should interfere. Every one regarded her as just the person to do certain things. Every one thought she could do everything, because she had nothing else to do. She used to read to the blind, and, more onerously, to the deaf. She looked after other people's children while the parents attended anti-slavery conventions.

She was coming to New York, later, to spend a week at her brother's, but beyond this she had no idea what she should do. Benyon felt it to be awkward that he should not be able just now to tell her; and this had much to do with his coming to the point, for he accused himself of having rather hung fire. Coming to the point, for Benyon, meant writing a note to Mrs. Roy (as he must call her), in which he asked whether she would see him if he should present himself. The missive was short; it contained, in addition to what I have hinted, little more than the remark that he had something of importance to say to her. Her reply, which we have just read, was prompt. Benyon designated an hour, and rang the doorbell of her big modern house, whose polished windows seemed to shine defiance at him.

As he stood on the steps, looking up and down the straight vista of the Fifth Avenue, he perceived that he was trembling a little, that he was nervous, if she were not. He was ashamed of his agitation, and he pulled himself vigorously together. Afterwards he saw that what had made him nervous was not any doubt of the goodness of his cause, but his revived sense (as he drew near her) of his wife's hardness, her capacity for insolence. He might only break himself against that, and the prospect made him feel helpless. She kept him waiting for a long time after he had been introduced; and as he walked up and down her drawing-room, an immense, florid, expensive apartment, covered with blue satin, gilding, mirrors and bad frescoes, it came over him as a certainty that her delay was calculated. She wished to annoy him, to weary him; she was as ungenerous as she was unscrupulous. It never occurred to him that, in spite of the bold words of her note, she, too, might be in a tremor, and if any one in their secret had suggested that she was afraid to meet him, he would have laughed at this idea. This was of bad omen for the success of his errand; for it showed that he recognised the ground of her presumption—his having the superstition of old promises. By the time she appeared he was flushed, very angry. She closed the door behind her, and stood there looking at him, with the width of the room between them.

The first emotion her presence excited was a quick sense of the strange fact that, after all these years of loneliness, such a magnificent person should be his wife. For she was magnificent, in the maturity of her beauty, her head erect, her complexion splendid, her auburn tresses undimmed, a certain plenitude in her very glance. He saw in a moment that she wished to seem to him beautiful, she had endeavoured to dress herself to the best effect. Perhaps, after all, it was only for this she had delayed; she wished to give herself every possible touch. For some moments they said nothing; they had not stood face to face for nearly ten years, and they met now as adversaries. No two persons could possibly be more interested in taking each other's measure. It scarcely belonged to Georgina, however, to have too much the air of timidity, and after a moment, satisfied, apparently, that she was not to receive a broadside, she advanced, slowly, rubbing her jewelled hands and smiling. He wondered why she should smile, what thought was in her mind. His impressions followed each other with extraordinary quickness of pulse, and now he saw, in addition to what he had already perceived, that she was waiting to take her cue: she had determined on no definite line. There was nothing definite about her but her courage; the rest would depend upon him. As for her courage, it seemed to glow in the beauty which grew greater as she came nearer, with her eyes on his and her fixed smile; to be expressed in the very perfume that accompanied her steps. By this time he had got a still further impression, and it was the strangest of all. She was ready for anything, she was capable of anything, she wished to surprise him with her beauty, to remind him that it belonged, after all, at the bottom of

everything, to him. She was ready to bribe him, if bribing should
be necessary. She had carried on an intrigue before she was twenty;
it would be more, rather than less, easy for her now that she was
thirty. All this and more was in her cold, living eyes, as, in the prolonged silence, they engaged themselves with his; but I must not
dwell upon it, for reasons extraneous to the remarkable fact. She
was a truly amazing creature.

"Raymond!" she said, in a low voice—a voice which might
represent either a vague greeting or an appeal.

He took no heed of the exclamation, but asked her why she had
deliberately kept him waiting, as if she had not made a fool enough
of him already. She couldn't suppose it was for his pleasure he had
come into the house.

She hesitated a moment, still with her smile. "I must tell you I
have a son, the dearest little boy. His nurse happened to be engaged
for the moment, and I had to watch him. I am more devoted to
him than you might suppose."

He fell back from her a few steps." I wonder if you are insane,"
he murmured.

"To allude to my child? Why do you ask me such questions
then? I tell you the simple truth. I take every care of this one. I am
older and wiser. The other one was a complete mistake; he had no
right to exist."

"Why didn't you kill him then with your own hands, instead of
that torture?"

"Why didn't I kill myself? That question would be more to the
point. You are looking wonderfully well," she broke off, in another
tone; "hadn't we better sit down?"

"I didn't come here for the advantage of conversation," Benyon
answered. And he was going on, but she interrupted him.

"You came to say something dreadful, very likely; though I
hoped you would see it was better not. But just tell me this, before
you begin. Are you successful, are you happy? It has been so provoking, not knowing more about you."

There was something in the manner in which this was said that
caused him to break into a loud laugh; whereupon she added—

"Your laugh is just what it used to be. How it comes back to me!
You *have* improved in appearance," she continued.

She had seated herself, though he remained standing; and she
leaned back in a low, deep chair, looking up at him, with her arms

folded. He stood near her and over her, as it were, dropping his baffled eyes on her, with his hand resting on the corner of the chimney-piece. "Has it never occurred to you that I may deem myself absolved from the promise I made you before I married you?"

"Very often, of course. But I have instantly dismissed the idea. How can you be 'absolved'? One promises, or one doesn't. I attach no meaning to that, and neither do you." And she glanced down at the front of her dress.

Benyon listened, but he went on as if he had not heard her. "What I came to say to you is this : that I should like your consent to my bringing a suit for divorce against you."

"A suit for divorce? I never thought of that."

"So that I may marry another woman. I can easily obtain a divorce on the ground of your desertion. It will simplify our situation."

She stared a moment, then her smile solidified, as it were, and she looked grave; but he could see that her gravity, with her lifted eyebrows, was partly assumed. "Ah, you want to marry another woman!" she exclaimed, slowly, thoughtfully. He said nothing, and she went on, "Why don't you do as I have done?"

"Because I don't want my children to be——"

Before he could say the words she sprang up, checking him with a cry. "Don't say it; it isn't necessary! Of course I know what you mean; but they won't be if no one knows it."

"I should object to knowing it myself; it's enough for me to know it of yours."

"Of course I have been prepared for your saying that."

"I should hope so!" Benyon exclaimed. "You may be a bigamist, if it suits you, but to me the idea is not attractive. I wish to marry——" and, hesitating a moment, with his slight stammer, he repeated, "I wish to marry——"

"Marry, then, and have done with it!" cried Mrs. Roy.

He could already see that he should be able to extract no consent from her; he felt rather sick. "It's extraordinary to me that you shouldn't be more afraid of being found out," he said, after a moment's reflection. "There are two or three possible accidents."

"How do you know how much afraid I am? I have thought of every accident, in dreadful nights. How do you know what my life is, or what it has been all these horrid years? But every one is dead."

"You look wasted and worn, certainly."

"Ah, don't compliment me!" Georgina exclaimed. "If I had never known you—if I had not been through all this—I believe I should have been handsome. When did you hear of my marriage? Where were you at the time?"

"At Naples, more than six months ago, by a mere chance."

"How strange that it should have taken you so long! Is the lady a Neapolitan? They don't mind what they do over there."

"I have no information to give you beyond what I have just said," Benyon rejoined. "My life doesn't in the least regard you."

"Ah, but it does from the moment I refuse to let you divorce me."

"You refuse?" Benyon said, softly.

"Don't look at me that way! You haven't advanced so rapidly as I used to think you would; you haven't distinguished yourself so much," she went on, irrelevantly.

"I shall be promoted commodore one of these days," Benyon answered. "You don't know much about it, for my advancement has already been extraordinary rapid." He blushed as soon as the words were out of his mouth. She gave a light laugh on seeing it; but he took up his hat and added, "Think over a day or two what I have proposed to you. It's a perfectly possible proceeding. Think of the temper in which I ask it."

"The temper?" she stared. "Pray, what have you to do with temper?" And as he made no reply, smoothing his hat with his glove, she went on, "Years ago, as much as you please! you had a good right, I don't deny, and you raved, in your letters, to your heart's content. That's why I wouldn't see you; I didn't wish to take it full in the face. But that's all over now; time is a healer; you have cooled off, and by your own admission you have consoled yourself. Why do you talk to me about temper? What in the world have I done to you but let you alone?"

"What do you call this business?" Benyon asked, with his eye flashing all over the room.

"Ah, excuse me, that doesn't touch you; it's my affair. I leave you your liberty, and I can live as I like. If I choose to live in this way, it may be queer (I admit it is, tremendously), but you have nothing to say to it. If I am willing to take the risk, you may be. If I am willing to play such an infernal trick upon a confiding gentleman (I will put it as strongly as you possibly could), I don't see what you have to say to it except that you are exceedingly glad such a woman as that isn't known to be your wife!" She had been cool and deliberate up to this time, but with these words her latent agitation broke out. "Do you think I have been happy? Do you think I have enjoyed existence? Do you see me freezing up into a stark old maid?"

"I wonder you stood out so long," said Benyon.

"I wonder I did! They were bad years."

"I have no doubt they were!"

"You could do as you pleased," Georgina went on. "You roamed about the world, you formed charming relations. I am delighted to hear it from your own lips. Think of my going back to my father's house—that family vault—and living there, year after year, as Miss Gressie! If you remember my father and mother—they are round in Twelfth Street, just the same—you must admit that I paid for my folly!"

"I have never understood you; I don't understand you now," said Benyon.

She looked at him a moment "I adored you."

"I could damn you with a word!" he exclaimed.

XV.

THE moment he had spoken she grasped his arm and held up her other hand, as if she were listening to a sound outside the room. She had evidently had an inspiration, and she carried it into instant effect. She swept away to the door, flung it open, and passed into the hall, whence her voice came back to Benyon as she addressed a person who apparently was her husband. She had heard him enter the house at his habitual hour, after his long morning at business; the closing of the door of the vestibule had struck her ear. The parlour was on a level with the hall, and she greeted him without impediment. She asked him to come in and be introduced to Captain Benyon, and he responded with due solemnity. She returned in advance of him, her eyes fixed upon Benyon and lighted with defiance, her whole face saying to him vividly, "Here is your opportunity; I give it to you with my own hands. Break your promise and betray me if you dare! You say you can damn me with a word; speak the word and let us see!"

Benyon's heart beat faster, as he felt that it was indeed a chance; but half his emotion came from the spectacle, magnificent in its

way, of her unparalleled impudence. A sense of all that he had escaped in not having had to live with her rolled over him like a
wave, while he looked strangely at Mr. Roy, to whom this privi-
lege had been vouchsafed. He saw in a moment his successor had a
constitution that would carry it. Mr. Roy suggested squareness and
solidity; he was a broad-based, comfortable, polished man, with a
surface in which the rank tendrils of irritation would not easily
obtain a foothold. He had a broad, blank face, a capacious mouth,
and a small, light eye, to which, as he entered, he was engaged in
adjusting a double gold-rimmed glass. He approached Benyon with
a prudent, civil, punctual air, as if he habitually met a good many
gentlemen in the course of business, and though, naturally, this was
not that sort of occasion, he was not a man to waste time in pre-
liminaries. Benyon had immediately the impression of having seen
him, or his equivalent, a thousand times before. He was middle-
aged, fresh-coloured, whiskered, prosperous, indefinite. Georgina
introduced them to each other—she spoke of Benyon as an old
friend, whom she had known long before she had known Mr. Roy,
who had been very kind to her years ago, when she was a girl.

"He is in the navy. He has just come back from a long cruise."

Mr. Roy shook hands—Benyon gave him his before he knew
it—said he was very happy, smiled, looked at Benyon from head to
foot, then at Georgina, then round the room, then back at Benyon
again—at Benyon, who stood there, without sound or movement,
with a dilated eye and a pulse quickened to a degree of which Mr.
Roy could have little idea. Georgina made some remark about their
sitting down, but William Roy replied that he hadn't time for that,
if Captain Benyon would excuse him. He should have to go
straight into the library and write a note to send back to his office,
where, as he just remembered, he had neglected to give, in leaving
the place, an important direction.

"You can wait a moment, surely," Georgina said. "Captain
Benyon wants so much to see you."

"Oh yes, my dear; I can wait a minute, and I can come back."

Benyon saw, accordingly, that he was waiting, and that Georgina
was waiting too. Each was waiting for him to say something,
though they were waiting for different things. Mr. Roy put his
hands behind him, balanced himself on his toes, hoped that Captain
Benyon had enjoyed his cruise—though he shouldn't care much
for the navy himself—and evidently wondered at the vacuity of his

wife's visitor. Benyon knew he was speaking, for he indulged in two or three more observations, after which he stopped. But his meaning was not present to our hero. This personage was conscious of only one thing, of his own momentary power, of everything that hung on his lips; all the rest swam before him; there was vagueness in his ears and eyes. Mr. Roy stopped, as I say, and there was a pause, which seemed to Benyon of tremendous length. He knew, while it lasted, that Georgina was as conscious as himself that he felt his opportunity, that he held it there in his hand, weighing it noiselessly in the palm, and that she braved and scorned, or rather that she enjoyed, the danger. He asked himself whether he should be able to speak if he were to try, and then he knew that he should not, that the words would stick in his throat, that he should make sounds which would dishonour his cause. There was no real choice nor decision, then, on Benyon's part; his silence was after all the same old silence, the fruit of other hours and places, the stillness to which Georgina listened while he felt her eager eyes fairly eat into his face, so that his cheeks burned with the touch of them. The moments stood before him in their turn; each one was distinct. "Ah, well," said Mr. Roy, "perhaps I interrupt; I will just dash off my note." Benyon knew that he was rather bewildered, that he was making a protest, that he was leaving the room; knew presently that Georgina again stood before him alone.

"You are exactly the man I thought you!" she announced, as joyously as if she had won a bet.

"You are the most horrible woman I can imagine. Good God, if I had to live with you!" That is what he said to her in answer.

Even at this she never flinched; she continued to smile in triumph. "He adores me—but what's that to you? Of course you have all the future," she went on; "but I know you as if I had made you!"

Benyon considered a moment. "If he adores you, you are all right. If our divorce is pronounced you will be free, and then he can marry you properly, which he would like ever so much better."

"It's too touching to hear you reason about it. Fancy me telling such a hideous story—about myself—me—me!" And she touched her breasts with her white fingers.

Benyon gave her a look that was charged with all the sickness of his helpless rage. "You—you!" he repeated, as he turned away from her and passed through the door which Mr. Roy had left open.

She followed him into the hall, she was close behind him; he moved before her as she pressed. "There was one more reason," she said. "I wouldn't be forbidden. It was my hideous pride. That's what prevents me now."

"I don't care what it is," Benyon answered, wearily, with his hand on the knob of the door.

She laid hers on his shoulder; he stood there an instant, feeling it, wishing that her loathsome touch gave him the right to strike her to the earth, to strike her so that she should never rise again.

"How clever you are, and intelligent always, as you used to be; to feel so perfectly and know so well—without more scenes—that it's hopeless—my ever consenting! If I have, with you, the shame of having made you promise, let me at least have the profit!"

His back had been turned to her, but at this he glanced round. "To hear you talk of shame—!"

"You don't know what I have gone through; but, of course, I don't ask any pity from you. Only I should like to say something kind to you before we part. I admire you so much. Who will ever tell her, if you don't? How will she ever know, then? She will be as safe as I am. You know what that is," said Georgina, smiling.

He had opened the door wide while she spoke, apparently not heeding her, thinking only of getting away from her for ever. In reality he heard every word she said, and felt to his marrow the lowered, suggestive tone in which she made him that last recommendation. Outside, on the steps—she stood there in the doorway—he gave her his last look. "I only hope you will die. I shall pray for that!" And he descended into the street and took his way.

It was after this that his real temptation came. Not the temptation to return betrayal for betrayal; that passed away even in a few days, for he simply knew that he couldn't break his promise, that it imposed itself on him as stubbornly as the colour of his eyes or the stammer of his lips; it had gone forth into the world to live for itself, and was far beyond his reach or his authority. But the temptation to go through the form of a marriage with Kate Theory, to let her suppose that he was as free as herself and that their children, if they should have any, would, before the law, have a right to exist—this attractive idea held him fast for many weeks, and caused him to pass some haggard nights and days. It was perfectly possible she might never learn his secret, and that, as no one could either suspect it or have an interest in bringing it to light, they both might live and die in security and honour. This vision fascinated him; it was, I say, a real temptation. He thought of other solutions—of telling her that he was married (without telling her to whom), and inducing her to overlook such an accident and content herself with a ceremony in which the world would see no flaw. But after all the contortions of his spirit it remained as clear to him as before that dishonour was in everything but renunciation. So, at last, he renounced. He took two steps which attested this act to himself. He addressed an urgent request to the Secretary of the Navy that he might, with as little delay as possible, be despatched on another long voyage; and he returned to Boston to tell Kate Theory that they must wait. He could explain so little that, say what he would, he was aware that he could not make his conduct seem natural, and he saw that the girl only trusted him, that she never understood. She trusted without understanding, and she agreed to wait. When the writer of these pages last heard of the pair they were waiting still.

1884.

LORD BEAUPRÉ

I.

SOME REFERENCE HAD been made to Northerley, which was within an easy drive, and Firminger described how he had dined there the night before and had found a lot of people. Mrs. Ashbury, one of the two visitors, inquired who these people might be, and he mentioned half a dozen names, among which was that of young Raddle, which had been a good deal on people's lips, and even in the newspapers, on the occasion, still recent, of his stepping into the fortune, exceptionally vast even as the product of a patent glue, left him by a father whose ugly name on all the vacant spaces of the world had exasperated generations of men.

"Oh, is he there?" asked Mrs. Ashbury, in a tone which might have been taken as a vocal rendering of the act of pricking up one's ears. She didn't hand on the information to her daughter, who was talking—if a beauty of so few phrases could have been said to talk—with Mary Gosselin, but in the course of a few moments she put down her teacup with a failure of suavity, and, getting up, gave the girl a poke with her parasol. "Come, Maud, we must be stirring."

"You pay us a very short visit," said Mrs. Gosselin, intensely demure over the fine web of her knitting. Mrs. Ashbury looked hard for an instant into her bland eyes, then she gave poor Maud another poke. She alluded to a reason and expressed regrets; but she got her daughter into motion, and Guy Firminger passed through the garden with the two ladies, to put them into their carriage. Mrs. Ashbury protested particularly against any further escort. While he was absent the other parent and child, sitting together on their pretty lawn in the yellow light of the August afternoon, talked of the frightful way Maud Ashbury had "gone off," and of something else as to which there was more to say when their third visitor came back.

"Don't think me grossly inquisitive if I ask you where they told the coachman to drive," said Mary Gosselin, as the young man dropped near her into a low wicker chair, stretching his long legs as if he had been one of the family.

Firminger stared. "Upon my word, I didn't particularly notice; but I think the old lady said 'Home.'"

"There, mamma dear!" the girl exclaimed triumphantly.

But Mrs. Gosselin only knitted on, persisting in profundity. She replied that "Home" was a feint, that Mrs. Ashbury would already have given another order, and that it was her wish to hurry off to Northerley that had made her keep them from going with her to the carriage, in which they would have seen her take a suspected direction. Mary explained to Guy Firminger that her mother had perceived poor Mrs. Ashbury to be frantic to reach the house at which she had heard that Mr. Raddle was staying. The young man stared again, and wanted to know what she desired to do with Mr. Raddle. Mary replied that her mother would tell him what Mrs. Ashbury desired to do with poor Maud.

"What all Christian mothers desire," said Mrs. Gosselin. "Only she doesn't know how."

"To marry the dear child to Mr. Raddle," Mary added, smiling.

Firminger's vagueness expanded with the subject. "Do you mean you want to marry *your* dear child to that little cad?" he asked, of the elder lady.

"I speak of the general duty—not of the particular case," said Mrs. Gosselin.

"Mamma *does* know how," Mary went on.

"Then, why ain't you married?"

"Because we're not acting, like the Ashburys, with injudicious precipitation. Is that correct?" the girl demanded, laughing, of her mother.

"Laugh at me, my dear, as much as you like—it's very lucky you've got me," Mrs. Gosselin declared.

"She means I can't manage for myself," said Mary, to the visitor.

"What nonsense you talk!" Mrs. Gosselin murmured, counting stitches.

"I can't, mamma, I can't; I admit it," Mary continued.

"But injudicious precipitation and—what's the other thing?— creeping prudence, seem to come out in very much the same place," the young man objected.

"Do you mean since I too wither on the tree?"

"It only comes back to saying how hard it is nowadays to marry one's daughters," said the lucid Mrs. Gosselin, saving Firminger, however, the trouble of an ingenious answer. "I don't contend that, at the best, it's easy."

But Guy Firminger would not have struck you as capable of much conversational effort as he lounged there in the summer softness, with ironic familiarities, like one of the old friends who rarely deviate into sincerity. He was a robust but loose-limbed young man, with a well-shaped head and a face smooth, fair, and kind. He was in knickerbockers, and his clothes, which had seen service, were composed of articles that didn't match. His laced boots were dusty—he had evidently walked a certain distance; an indication confirmed by the lingering, sociable way in which, in his basket-seat, he tilted himself towards Mary Gosselin. It pointed to a pleasant reason for a long walk. This young lady, of five-and-twenty, had black hair and blue eyes; a combination often associated with the effect of beauty. The beauty in this case, however, was dim and latent, not vulgarly obvious, and if her height and slenderness gave that impression of length of line which, as we know, is the fashion, Mary Gosselin had, on the other hand, too much expression to be generally admired. Every one thought her intellectual; a few of the most simple-minded even thought her plain. What Guy Firminger thought—or rather what he took for granted, for he was not built up on depths of reflection—will probably appear from this narrative.

"Yes, indeed; things have come to a pass that's awful for *us,*" the girl announced.

"For *us,* you mean," said Firminger. "We're hunted like the ostrich; we're trapped and stalked and run to earth. We go in fear—I assure you we do."

"Are *you* hunted, Guy?" Mrs. Gosselin. asked, with an inflection of her own.

"Yes, Mrs. Gosselin, even *moi qui vous parle,* the ordinary male of commerce, inconceivable as it may appear. I know something about it."

"And of whom do you go in fear?" Mary Gosselin took up an uncut book and a paper-knife which she had laid down on the advent of the other visitors.

"My dear child, of Diana and her nymphs, of the spinster at large. She's always out with her rifle. And it isn't only that; you

know there's always a second gun, a walking arsenal, at her heels. I
forget, for the moment, who Diana's mother was, and the geneal-
ogy of the nymphs; but not only do the old ladies know the
younger ones are out—they distinctly go *with* them."

"Who was Diana's mother, my dear?" Mrs. Gosselin inquired of
her daughter.

"She was a beautiful old lady with pink ribbons in her cap and a
genius for knitting," the girl replied, cutting her book.

"Oh, I'm not speaking of you two dears; you're not like any one
else; you're an immense comfort," said Guy Firminger. "But
they've reduced it to a science, and I assure you that if one were
any one in particular, if one were not protected by one's obscurity,
one's life would be a burden. Upon my honor, one wouldn't escape. I've seen it, I've watched them. Look at poor Beaupré—look
at little Raddle over there. I object to him, but I bleed for him."

"Lord Beaupré won't marry again," said Mrs. Gosselin, with an
air of conviction.

"So much the worse for him!"

"Come—that's a concession to our charms!" Mary laughed.

But the ruthless young man explained away his concession. "I
mean that to be married's the only protection—or else to be engaged."

"To be permanently engaged—wouldn't that do?" Mary Gosselin
asked.

"Beautifully—I would try it if I were a *parti*."

"And how's the little boy?" Mrs. Gosselin presently inquired.

"What little boy?"

"Your little cousin—Lord Beaupré's child; isn't it a boy?"

"Oh, poor little beggar, he isn't up to much. He was awfully cut
up by scarlet fever."

"You're not the rose indeed, but you're tolerably near it," the
elder lady presently continued.

"What do you call near it? Not even in the same garden—not in
any garden at all, alas!"

"There are three lives—but after all!"

"Dear lady, don't be homicidal!"

"What do you call the 'rose?'" Mary asked of her mother.

"The title," said Mrs. Gosselin, promptly but softly.

Something in her tone made Firminger laugh aloud. "You don't
mention the property."

"Oh, I mean the whole thing."

"Is the property very large?" said Mary Gosselin.

"Fifty thousand a year," her mother responded; at which the young man laughed out again.

"Take care, mamma, or we shall be thought to be out with our guns!" the girl interposed; a recommendation that drew from Guy Firminger the just remark that there would be time enough for that when his prospects should be worth speaking of. He leaned over to pick up his hat and stick, as if it were his time to go; but he didn't go for another quarter of an hour, and during these minutes his prospects received some frank consideration. He was Lord Beaupré's first cousin, and the three intervening lives were his lordship's own, that of his little sickly son, and that of his uncle the Major, who was also Guy's uncle, and with whom the young man was at present staying. It was from homely Trist, the Major's house, that he had walked over to Mrs. Gosselin's. Frank Firminger, who had married in youth a woman with something of her own, and eventually left the army, had nothing but girls, but he was only of middle age, and might possibly still have a son. At any rate, his life was a very good one. Beaupré might marry again, and, marry or not, he was barely thirty-three, and might live to a great age. The child, moreover, poor little devil, would doubtless, with the growing consciousness of an incentive (there was none like feeling you were in people's way), develop a capacity for duration; so that altogether Guy professed himself, with the best will in the world, unable to take a rosy view of the disappearance of obstacles. He treated the subject with a jocularity that, in view of the remoteness of his chance, was not wholly tasteless, and the discussion, between old friends and in the light of this extravagance, was less crude than perhaps it sounds. The young man quite declined to see any latent brilliancy in his future. They had all been lashing him up, his poor dear mother, his uncle Frank, and Beaupré as well, to make that future political; but even if he should get in (he was nursing—oh, so languidly!—a possible opening), it would only be into the shallow edge of the stream. He would stand there like a tall idiot, with the water up to his ankles. He didn't know how to swim—in that element; he didn't know how to do anything.

"I think you're very perverse, my dear," said Mrs. Gosselin. "I'm sure you have great dispositions."

"For what—except for sitting here and talking with you and Mary? I revel in this sort of thing, but I scarcely like anything else."

"You'd do very well, if you weren't so lazy," Mary said. "I believe you're the very laziest person in the world."

"So do I—the very laziest in the world," the young man contentedly replied. "But how can I regret it, when it keeps me so quiet, when (I might even say) it makes me so amiable?"

"You'll have, one of these days, to get over your quietness, and perhaps even a little over your amiability," Mrs. Gosselin sagaciously stated.

"I devoutly hope not."

"You'll have to perform the duties of your position."

"Do you mean keep my stump of a broom in order and my crossing irreproachable?"

"You may say what you like; you will be a *parti*." Mrs. Gosselin continued.

"Well, then, if the worst comes to the worst, I shall do what I said just now: I shall get some good plausible girl to see me through."

"The proper way to 'get' her will be to marry her. After you're married you won't be a *parti*."

"Dear mamma, he'll think you're already levelling your rifle!" Mary Gosselin laughingly wailed.

Guy Firminger looked at her a moment. "I say, Mary, wouldn't *you* do?"

"For the good plausible girl? Should I be plausible enough?"

"Surely—what could be more natural? Everything would seem to contribute to the suitability of our alliance. I should be known to have known you for years—from childhood's sunny hour; I should be known to have bullied you, and even to have been bullied *by* you, in the period of pinafores. My relations from a tender age with your brother, which led to our school-room romps in holidays, and to the happy footing on which your mother has always been so good as to receive me here, would add to all the presumptions of intimacy. People would accept such a conclusion as inevitable."

"Among all your reasons you don't mention the young lady's attractions," said Mary Gosselin.

Firminger stared a moment, his clear eye lighted by his happy thought. "I don't mention the young man's. They would be so obvious, on one side and the other, as to be taken for granted."

"And is it your idea that one should pretend to be engaged to you all one's life?"

"Oh no; simply till I should have had time to look round. I'm determined not to be hustled and bewildered into matrimony—to be dragged to the shambles before I know where I am. With such an arrangement as the one I speak of I should be able to take my time, to keep my head, to make my choice."

"And how would the young lady make hers?"

"How do you mean, hers?"

"The selfishness of men is something exquisite. Suppose the young lady—if it's conceivable that you should find one idiotic enough to be a party to such a transaction—suppose the poor girl herself should happen to wish to be *really* engaged?"

Guy Firminger thought a moment, with his slow but not stupid smile. "Do you mean to *me?*"

"To you—or to some one else."

"Oh, if she'd give me notice, I'd let her off."

"Let her off till you could find a substitute?"

"Yes; but I confess it would be a great inconvenience. People wouldn't take the second one so seriously."

"She would have to make a sacrifice; she would have to wait till you should know where you were," Mrs. Gosselin suggested.

"Yes, but where would *her* advantage come in?" Mary persisted.

"Only in the pleasure of charity; the moral satisfaction of doing a fellow a good turn," said Firminger.

"You must think people are keen to oblige you!"

"Ah, but surely I could count on *you*, couldn't I?" the young man asked.

Mary had finished cutting her book; she got up and flung it down on the tea-table. "What a preposterous conversation!" she exclaimed with force, tossing the words from her as she tossed her book; and, looking round her vaguely a moment, without meeting Guy Firminger's eyes, she walked away to the house.

Firminger sat watching her; then he said serenely to her mother: "Why has our Mary left us?"

"She has gone to get something, I suppose."

"What has she gone to get?"

"A little stick, to beat you, perhaps."

"You don't mean I've been objectionable?"

"Dear, no—I'm joking. One thing is very certain," pursued Mrs. Gosselin; "that you ought to work—to try to get on exactly as if nothing could ever happen. Oughtn't you?" She threw off the question mechanically as her visitor continued silent.

"I'm sure she doesn't like it!" he exclaimed, without heeding her appeal.

"Doesn't like what?"

"My free play of mind. It's perhaps too much in the key of our old romps."

"You're very clever; she always likes *that*," said Mrs. Gosselin. "You ought to go in for something serious, for something honorable," she continued, "just as much as if you had nothing at all to look to."

"Words of wisdom, dear Mrs. Gosselin," Firminger replied, rising slowly from his relaxed attitude. "But what *have* I to look to?"

She raised her mild, deep eyes to him as he stood before her— she might have been a fairy godmother. "Everything!"

"But you know I can't poison them!"

"That won't be necessary."

He looked at her an instant; then, with a laugh, "One might think *you* would undertake it!"

"I almost would—for *you*. Good-bye."

"Take care—if they *should* be carried off!" But Mrs. Gosselin only repeated her good-bye, and the young man departed before Mary had come back.

II.

NEARLY two years after Guy Firminger had spent that friendly hour in Mrs. Gosselin's little garden in Hampshire this far-seeing woman was enabled (by the return of her son, who in New York, in an English bank, occupied a position in which they all rejoiced, to such great things might it possibly lead) to resume possession, for the season, of the little London house which her husband had left her to live in, but which her native thrift, in determining her to let it for a term, had converted into a source of income. Hugh Gosselin, who was thirty years old, and at twenty-three, before his father's death, had been dispatched to America to exert himself, was understood to be doing very well—so well that his devotion to the interests of his employers had been rewarded, for the first time, with a real holiday. He was to remain in England from May to August, undertaking, as he said, to make it all right if during this time his mother should occupy (to contribute to his entertainment) the habitation in Chester Street. He was a small, preoccupied young man, with a sharpness as acquired as a new hat; he struck his mother and sister as intensely American. For the first few days after his arrival they were startled by his intonations, though they admitted that they had an escape when he reminded them that he might have brought with him an accent embodied in a wife.

"When you do take one," said Mrs. Gosselin, who regarded such an accident over there as inevitable, "you must charge her high for it."

It was not with this question, however, that the little family in Chester Street was mainly engaged, but with the last incident in the extraordinary succession of events which, like a chapter of romance, had in the course of a few months converted their vague and impecunious friend into a personage envied and honored. It was as if a blight had been cast on all Guy Firminger's hindrances. On the day Hugh Gosselin sailed from New York the delicate little boy at Bosco had succumbed to an attack of diphtheria. His father had died of typhoid the previous winter at Naples; his uncle, a few weeks later, had had a fatal accident in the hunting-field. So strangely, so rapidly had the situation cleared up, had his fate and theirs worked for him. Guy had opened his eyes one morning to an earldom which carried with it a fortune not alone nominally but really great. Mrs. Gosselin and Mary had not written to him, but they knew he was at Bosco; he had remained there after the funeral of the late little lord. Mrs. Gosselin, who heard everything, had heard somehow that he was behaving with the greatest consideration, giving the guardians, the trustees, whatever they were called, plenty of time to do everything. Everything was comparatively simple; in the absence of collaterals there were so few other people concerned. The principal relatives were poor Frank Firminger's widow and her girls, who had seen themselves so near to new honors and comforts. Probably the girls would expect their cousin Guy to marry one of them, and think it the least he could decently do; a view the young man himself (if he were very magnanimous) might possibly embrace. The question would be whether he would be very magnanimous. These young ladies exhausted in their three persons the numerous varieties of plainness. On the other hand,

Guy Firminger—or Lord Beaupré, as one would have to begin to call him now—was unmistakably kind. Mrs. Gosselin appealed to her son as to whether their noble friend were not unmistakably kind.

"Of course I've known him always, and that time he came out to America—when was it? four years ago—I saw him every day. I like him awfully, and all that; but since you push me, you know," said Hugh Gosselin, "I'm bound to say that the first thing to mention in any description of him would be—if you wanted to be quite correct—that he's unmistakably selfish."

"I see—I see," Mrs. Gosselin unblushingly replied. "Of course I know what you mean," she added, in a moment. "But is he any more so than any one else? Every one's unmistakably selfish."

"Every one but you and Mary," said the young man.

"And *you,* dear!" his mother smiled. "But a person may be kind, you know—mayn't he?—at the same time that he *is* selfish. There are different sorts."

"Different sorts of kindness?" Hugh Gosselin asked, with a laugh; and the inquiry undertaken by his mother occupied them for the moment, demanding a subtlety of treatment from which they were not conscious of shrinking, of which rather they had an idea that they were perhaps exceptionally capable. They came back to the temperate view that Guy would never put himself out, would probably never do anything great, but might show himself all the same a delightful member of society. Yes, he was probably selfish, like other people; but unlike most of them he was, somehow, amiably, attachingly, sociably, almost lovably selfish. Without doing anything great he would yet be a great success—a big, pleasant, gossiping, lounging, and, in its way, doubtless very splendid, presence. He would have no ambition, and it was ambition that made selfishness ugly. Hugh and his mother were sure of this last point until Mary, before whom the discussion, when it reached this stage, happened to be carried on, checked them by asking whether that, on the contrary, were not just what was supposed to make it fine.

"Oh, he only wants to be comfortable," said her brother; "but he *does* want it!"

"There'll be a tremendous rush for him," Mrs. Gosselin prophesied to her son.

"Oh, he'll never marry. It will be too much trouble."

"It's done here without any trouble—for the men. One sees how long you've been out of the country."

"There was a girl in New York whom he might have married—he really liked her. But he wouldn't turn round for her."

"Perhaps she wouldn't turn round for *him*," said Mary.

"I dare say she'll turn round *now*," Mrs. Gosselin rejoined; on which Hugh mentioned that there was nothing to be feared from her, all her revolutions had been accomplished. He added that nothing would make any difference—so intimate was his conviction that Beaupré would preserve his independence.

"Then I think he's not so selfish as you say," Mary declared; "or, at any rate, one will never know whether he is. Isn't married life the great chance to show it?"

"Your father never showed it," said Mrs. Gosselin; and as her children were silent in presence of this tribute to the departed, she added, smiling, "Perhaps you think that *I* did!" They embraced her, to indicate what they thought, and the conversation ended when she had remarked that Lord Beaupré was a man who would be perfectly easy to manage *after* marriage, with Hugh's exclaiming that this was doubtless exactly why he wished to keep out of it.

Such was evidently his wish, as they were able to judge in Chester Street when he came up to town. He appeared there oftener than was to have been expected, not taking himself, in his new character, at all too seriously to find stray half-hours for old friends. It was plain that he was going to do just as he liked, that he was not a bit excited or uplifted by his change of fortune. Mary Gosselin observed that he had no imagination—she even reproached him with the deficiency to his face; an incident which showed indeed how little seriously *she* took him. He had no idea of playing a part, and yet he would have been clever enough. He wasn't even systematic about being simple; his simplicity was a series of accidents and indifferences. Never was a man more conscientiously superficial. There were matters on which he valued Mrs. Gosselin's judgment and asked her advice—without, as usually appeared later, ever taking it; such questions, mainly, as the claims of a predecessor's servants, and those, in respect to social intercourse, of the clergyman's family. He didn't like his parson—what was a fellow to do when he didn't like his parson? What he did like was to talk with Hugh about American investments, and it was amusing to Hugh, though he tried not to show his amusement, to find himself looking at Guy Firminger in the light of capital. To Mary he addressed from the first the oddest snatches of confidential discourse, rendered in fact, however, by the levity of his tone, considerably less confidental than in intention. He had something to tell her that he joked about, yet without admitting that it was any less important for being laughable. It was neither more nor less than that Charlotte Firminger, the eldest of his late uncle's four girls, had designated to him in the clearest manner the person she considered he ought to marry. She appealed to his sense of justice, she spoke and wrote, or at any rate she looked and moved, she sighed and sang, in the name of common honesty. He had had four letters from her that week, and to his knowledge there were a series of people in London, people she could bully, whom she had got to promise to take her in for the season. She was going to be on the spot, she was going to follow him up. He took his stand on common honesty, but he had a mortal horror of Charlotte. At the same time, when a girl had a jaw like that and had marked you—really *marked* you, mind, you felt your safety oozing away. He had given them during the past three months, all those terrible girls, every sort of present that Bond Street could supply; but these demonstrations had only been held to constitute another pledge. Therefore what was a fellow to do? Besides, there were other portents; the air was thick with them, as the sky over battle-fields was darkened by the flight of vultures. They were flocking, the birds of prey, from every quarter, and every girl in England, by Jove! was going to be thrown at his head. What had he done to deserve such a fate? He wanted to stop in England and see all sorts of things through; but how could he stand there and face such a charge? Yet what good would it do to bolt? Wherever he should go there would be fifty of them there first. On his honor he could say that he didn't deserve it; he had never, to his own sense, been a flirt, such a flirt at least as to have given any one a handle. He appealed candidly to Mary Gosselin to know whether his past conduct justified such penalties. "*Have* I been a flirt—have I given any one a handle?" he inquired, with pathetic intensity.

She met his appeal by declaring that he had been awful, committing himself right and left; and this manner of treating his affliction contributed to the sarcastic publicity (as regarded the little house in Chester Street) which presently became its natural element. Lord Beaupré's comical and yet thoroughly grounded view of his danger was soon a frequent theme among the Gosselins, who however had their own reasons for not communicating the alarm. They had no motive for concealing their interest in their old friend, but their allusions to him among their other friends may be said on the whole to have been studied. His state of mind recalled of course to Mary and her mother the queer talk about his prospects that they had had in the country that afternoon on which Mrs. Gosselin had been so strangely prophetic (she confessed that she had had a flash of divination: the future had been mysteriously revealed to her), and poor Guy, too, had seen himself quite as he was to be. He had seen his nervousness, under inevitable pressure, deepen to a panic, and he now, in intimate hours, made no attempt to disguise that a panic had become his portion. It was a fixed idea with him that he should fall a victim to woven toils, be caught in a trap constructed with superior science. The science evolved in an enterprising age by this branch of industry, the manufacture of the trap matrimonial, he had terrible anecdotes to illustrate; and what had he on his lips but a scientific term when he declared, as he perpetually did, that it was his fate to be hypnotised?

Mary Gosselin reminded him, they each in turn reminded him, that his safeguard was to fall in love; were he once to put himself under that protection, all of the mothers and maids in Mayfair would not prevail against him. He replied that this was just the impossibility; it took leisure and calmness and opportunity and a free mind to fall in love, and never was a man less open to such experiences. He was literally fighting his way. He reminded the girl of his old fancy for pretending already to have disposed of his hand if he could put that hand on a young person who would like him well enough to be willing to participate in the fraud. She would have to place herself in rather a false position, of course—have to take a certain amount of trouble; but there would, after all, be a good deal of fun in it (there was always fun in duping the world) between the pair themselves, the two happy comedians.

"Why should they both be happy?" Mary Gosselin asked. "I understand why you should; but, frankly, I don't quite grasp the reason of *her* pleasure."

Lord Beaupré, with his sunny human eyes, thought a moment. "Why, for the lark, as they say, and that sort of thing. I should be awfully nice to her."

"She would require indeed to be in want of recreation!"

"Ah, but I should want a good sort—a quiet, reasonable one, you know!" he somewhat eagerly interposed.

"You're too delightful!" Mary Gosselin exclaimed, continuing to laugh. He thanked her for this appreciation, and she returned to her point—that she didn't really see the advantage his accomplice could hope to enjoy as her compensation for extreme disturbance.

Guy Firminger stared. "But what extreme disturbance?"

"Why, it would take a lot of time; it might become intolerable."

"You mean I ought to pay her—to hire her for the season?"

Mary Gosselin considered him a moment. "Wouldn't marriage come cheaper at once?" she asked, with a quieter smile.

"You *are* chaffing me!" he sighed, forgivingly. "Of course she would have to be good-natured enough to pity me,"

"Pity's akin to love. If she were good-natured enough to want to help you, she'd be good-natured enough to want to marry you. That would be *her* idea of help."

"Would it be *yours*?" Lord Beaupre asked, rather eagerly.

"You're too absurd! You must sail your own boat!" the girl answered, turning away.

That evening at dinner she stated to her companions that she had never seen a fatuity so dense, so serene, so preposterous as his lordship's.

"Fatuity, my dear! what do you mean?" her mother inquired.

"Oh, mamma, you know perfectly." Mary Gosselin spoke with a certain impatience.

"If you mean he's conceited, I'm bound to say I don't agree with you," her brother observed. "He's too indifferent to every one's opinion for that."

"He's not vain, he's not proud, he's not pompous," said Mrs. Gosselin.

Mary was silent a moment. "He takes more things for granted than any one I ever saw."

"What sort of things?"

"Well, one's interest in his affairs."

"With old friends surely a gentleman may."

"Of course," said Hugh Gosselin; "old friends have in turn the right to take for granted a corresponding interest on *his* part."

"Well, who could be nicer to us than he is, or come to see us oftener?" his mother asked.

"He comes exactly for the purpose I speak of—to talk about himself," said Mary.

"There are thousands of girls who would be delighted with his talk," Mrs. Gosselin returned.

"We agreed long ago that he's intensely selfish," the girl went on; "and if I speak of it to-day, it's not because that in itself is anything of a novelty. What I'm freshly struck with is simply that he more shamelessly shows it."

"He shows it, exactly," said Hugh; "he shows all there is. There it is, on the surface; there are not depths of it underneath."

"He's not hard," Mrs. Gosselin contended; "he's not impervious."

"Do you mean he's soft?" Mary asked.

"I mean he's yielding." And Mrs. Gosselin, with considerable expression, looked across at her daughter. She added, before they rose from dinner, that poor Beaupré had plenty of difficulties, and that she thought, for her part, they ought in common loyalty to do what they could to assist him.

For a week nothing more passed between the two ladies on the subject of their noble friend, and in the course of this week they had the amusement of receiving in Chester Street a member of Hugh's American circle, Mr. Bolton-Brown, a young man from New York. He was a person engaged in large affairs, for whom Hugh Gosselin professed the highest regard, from whom in New York he had received much hospitality, and for whose advent he had from the first prepared his companions. Mrs. Gosselin begged the amiable stranger to stay with them, and if she failed to overcome his hesitation, it was because his hotel was near at hand and he should be able to see them often. It became evident that he would do so, and, to the two ladies, as the days went by, equally evident that no objection to such a relation was likely to arise. Mr. Bolton-Brown was delightfully fresh; the most usual expressions acquired on his lips a well-nigh comical novelty, the most superficial sentiments, in the look with which he accompanied them, a really touching sincerity. He was unmarried and good-looking, clever and natural, and if he was not very rich, was at least very freehanded. He literally strewed the path of the ladies in Chester Street with flowers, he choked them with French confectionery. Hugh, however, who was often rather mysterious on monetary questions, placed in a light sufficiently clear the fact that his friend had in Wall Street (they knew all about Wall Street) improved each shining hour. They introduced him to Lord Beaupré, who thought him "tremendous fun," as Hugh said, and who immediately declared that the four must spend a Sunday at Bosco a week or two later. The date of this visit was fixed—Mrs. Gosselin had uttered a comprehensive acceptance; but after Guy Firminger had taken leave of them (this had been his first appearance since the odd conversation with Mary), our young lady confided to her mother that she should not be able to join the little party. She expressed the conviction that it would be all that was essential if Mrs. Gosselin should go with the two others. On being pressed to communicate the reason of this aloofness, Mary was able to give no better one than that she never had cared for Bosco.

"What makes you hate him so?" her mother presently broke out, in a tone which brought the red to the girl's cheek. Mary denied that she entertained for Lord Beaupré any sentiment so intense; to which Mrs. Gosselin rejoined, with some sternness and, no doubt, considerable wisdom: "Look out what you do, then, or you'll be thought by every one to be in love with him!"

III.

I KNOW not whether it was this danger—that of appearing to be moved to extremes—that weighed with Mary Gosselin; at any rate when the day arrived she had decided to be perfectly colorless and take her share of Lord Beaupré's hospitality. On perceiving that the house, when with her companions she reached it, was full of visitors, she consoled herself with the sense that such a share would be of the smallest. She even wondered whether its smallness might not be caused in some degree by the sufficiently startling presence, in this stronghold of the single life, of Maud Ashbury and her mother. It was true that during the Saturday evening she never saw their host address an observation to them; but she was struck, as she had been struck before, with the girl's cold and magnificent beauty. It was very well to say she had "gone off;" she was still handsomer than any one else. She had failed in everything she had tried; the campaign undertaken with so much energy against young Raddle had been conspicuously disastrous. Young Raddle had married his grandmother, or a person who might have filled such an office, and Maud was a year older, a year more disappointed, and a year more ridiculous. Nevertheless one could scarcely believe that a creature with such advantages would always fail, though, indeed, the poor girl was stupid enough to be a warning. Perhaps it would be at Bosco, or with the master of Bosco, that fate had appointed her to succeed. Except Mary herself, she was the only young unmarried woman on the scene, and Mary glowed with the generous sense of not being a competitor. She felt as much out of the question as the blooming wives, the heavy matrons, who formed the rest of the female contingent. Before the evening closed, however, her host, who, she saw, was delightful in his own house, mentioned to her that he had a couple of guests who had not been invited.

"Not invited?"

"They drove up to my door as they might have done to an inn. They asked for rooms, and complained of those that were given them. Don't pretend not to know who they are."

"Do you mean the Ashburys? How amusing !".

"Don't laugh; it freezes my blood."

"Do you really mean you're afraid of them?"

"I tremble like a leaf. Some monstrous ineluctable fate seems to look at me out of their eyes."

"That's because you secretly admire Maud. How can you help it? She's extremely good-looking, and if you get rid of her mother, she'll become a very nice girl."

"It's an odious thing, no doubt, to say about a young person under one's own roof, but I don't think I ever saw any one who happened to be less to my taste," said Guy Firminger. "I don't know why I don't turn them out even now."

Mary persisted in sarcasm. "Perhaps you can make her have a worse time by letting her stay."

"*Please* don't laugh," her interlocutor repeated. "Such a fact as I have mentioned to you seems to me to speak volumes—to show you what my life is."

"Oh, your life, your life!" Mary Gosselin murmured, with her mocking note.

"Don't you agree that at such a rate it may easily become impossible?"

"Many people would change with you. I don't see what there is for you to do but to bear your cross!"

"That's easy talk!" Lord Beaupré sighed.

"Especially from me, do you mean? How do you know I don't bear mine?"

"Yours?" he asked, vaguely.

"How do you know that *I'm* not persecuted, that *my* footsteps are not dogged, that *my* life isn't a burden?"

They were walking in the old gardens, the proprietor of which, at this, stopped short. "Do you mean by fellows who want to marry you?"

His tone produced on his companion's part an irrepressible peal of hilarity; but she walked on as she exclaimed:. "You speak as if there couldn't *be* such madmen!"

"Of course such a charming girl must be made up to," Guy Firminger conceded as he overtook her.

"I don't speak of it; I keep quiet about it."

"You realize then, at any rate, that it's all horrid when you don't care for them."

"I suffer in silence, because I know there are worse tribulations. It seems to me you ought to remember that," Mary continued. "Your cross is small compared with your crown. You've everything in the world that most people most desire, and I'm bound to say I think your life is made very comfortable for you. If you're oppressed by the quantity of interest and affection you inspire, you ought simply to make up your mind to bear up and be cheerful under it."

Lord Beaupré received this admonition with perfect good-humor; he professed himself able to do it full justice. He remarked that he would gladly give up some of his material advantages to be a little less badgered, and that he had been quite content with his former insignificance. No doubt, however, such annoyances were the essential drawbacks of ponderous promotions; one had to pay for everything. Mary was quite right to rebuke him; her own attitude, as a young woman much admired, was a lesson to his irritability. She cut this appreciation short, speaking of something else; but a few minutes later he broke out irrelevantly: "Why, if you are hunted as well as I, that dodge I proposed to you would be just the thing for us *both!*" He had evidently been reasoning it out.

Mary Gosselin was silent at first, she only paused gradually in their walk at a point where four long alleys met. In the centre of the circle, on a massive pedestal, rose in Italian bronze a florid, complicated image, so that the place made a charming Old World picture. The grounds of Bosco were stately without stiffness and full of marble terraces and misty avenues. The fountains in particular were royal. The girl had told her mother in London that she disliked this fine residence, but she now looked round her with a vague, pleased, sigh, holding up her glass (she had been condemned to wear one, with a long handle, since she was fifteen), to consider the weather-stained garden group. "What a perfect place of its kind!" she musingly exclaimed.

"Wouldn't it really be just the thing?" Lord Beaupré went on, with the eagerness of his idea.

"Wouldn't what be just the thing?"

"Why, the defensive alliance we've already talked of. You wanted to know the good it would do *you*. Now you see the good it would do you!"

"I don't like practical jokes," said Mary. "The remedy's worse than the disease," she added; and she began to follow one of the paths that took the direction of the house.

Poor Lord Beaupré was absurdly in love with his invention, he had all an inventor's importunity. He kept up his attempt to place his "dodge" in a favorable light, in spite of a further objection from his companion, who assured him that it was one of those contrivances which break down in practice in just the proportion in which they make a figure in theory. At last she said: "I was not sincere just now when I told you I'm worried. I'm *not* worried!"

"They *don't* buzz about you?" Guy Firminger asked.

She hesitated an instant. "They buzz about me; but at bottom it's flattering, and I don't mind it. Now please drop the subject."

He dropped the subject, though not without congratulating her on the fact that, unlike his infirm self, she could keep her head and her temper. His infirmity found a trap laid for it before they had proceeded twenty yards, as was proved by his sudden exclamation of horror. "Good heavens—if there isn't Lottie!"

Mary perceived, in effect, in the distance a female figure coming towards them over a stretch of lawn, and she simultaneously saw, as a gentleman passed from behind a clump of shrubbery, that it was not unattended. She recognized Charlotte Firminger, and she also distinguished the gentleman. She was moved to larger mirth at the dismay expressed by poor Firminger, but she was able to articulate: "Walking with Mr. Brown!"

Lord Beaupré stopped again before they were joined by the pair. "Does *he* buzz about you?"

"Mercy, what questions you ask!" his companion exclaimed.

"Does he—*please?*" the young man repeated, with odd intensity.

Mary looked at him an instant, she was puzzled by the deep annoyance that had flushed through the essential good-humor of his face. Then she saw that this annoyance had exclusive reference to poor Charlotte; so that it left her free to reply, with another laugh: "Well, yes—he does. But you know I like it!"

"I don't, then!" Before she could have asked him, even had she wished to, in what manner such a circumstance concerned him, he added, with his droll agitation: "I never invited *her,* either! Don't let her get at me!"

"What can I do?" Mary demanded, as the others advanced.

"Please take her away, keep her yourself! I'll take the American, I'll keep *him,*" he murmured, inconsequently, as a bribe.

"But I don't object to him."

"Do you like him so much?"

"Very much indeed," the girl replied.

The reply was perhaps lost upon her interlocutor, whose eye now fixed itself gloomily on the dauntless Charlotte. As Miss Firminger came nearer he exclaimed, almost loud enough for her to hear, "I think I shall *murder* her some day!"

Mary Gosselin's first impression had been that, in his panic, under the empire of that fixed idea to which he confessed himself subject, he attributed to his kinswoman machinations and aggressions of which she was incapable; an impression that might have been confirmed by this young lady's decorous placidity, her passionless eyes, her expressionless cheeks, and colorless tones. She was ugly, yet she was orthodox; she was not what writers of books called intense. But after Mary, to oblige their host, had tried, successfully enough, to be crafty, had drawn her on to stroll a little in advance of the two gentlemen, she became promptly aware, by the mystical influence of propinquity, that Miss Firminger was indeed full of views, of a purpose single, simple and strong, which gave her the effect of a person carrying with a stiff, steady hand, with eyes fixed and lips compressed, a cup charged to the brim. She had driven over to lunch, driven from somewhere in the neighborhood; she had picked up some weak woman as an escort. Mary, though she knew the neighborhood, failed to recognize her base of operations; and as Charlotte was not specific, ended by suspecting that, far from being entertained by friends, she had put up at an inn and hired a fly. This suspicion startled her; it gave her for the first time something of the measure of the passions engaged, and she wondered to what the insecurity complained of by Guy might lead. Charlotte, on arriving, had gone through a part of the house in quest of its master (the servants being unable to tell her where he was), and she had finally come upon Mr. Bolton-Brown, who was looking at old books in the library. He had placed himself at her service, as if he had been trained immediately to recognize in such a case his duty, and informing her that he believed Lord Beaupré to be in the grounds, had come out with her to help to find him. Lottie Firminger questioned her companion about this accommodating person; she intimated that he was rather odd but rather nice. Mary mentioned to her that Lord Beaupré thought highly of him; she believed they were going somewhere together. At this Miss Firminger turned round to look for them, but they had already disappeared, and the girl became ominously dumb.

Mary wondered afterwards what profit she could hope to derive from such proceedings; they struck her own sense, naturally, as disreputable and desperate. She was equally unable to discover the compensation they offered, in another variety, to poor Maud Ashbury, whom Lord Beaupré, the greater part of the day, neglected as conscientiously as he neglected his cousin. She asked herself if he should be blamed, and replied that the others should be blamed first. He got rid of Charlotte somehow after tea; she had to fall back to her mysterious lines. Mary knew this method would have been detestable to him—he hated to force his friendly nature; she was sorry for him and wished to lose sight of him. She wished not to be mixed up even indirectly with his tribulations, and the fevered faces of the Ashburys were particularly dreadful to her. She spent as much of the long summer afternoon as possible out of the house, which indeed on such an occasion, emptied itself of most of its inmates. Mary Gosselin asked her brother to join her in a devious ramble; she might have had other society, but she was in a mood to prefer his. These two were "great chums," and they had been separated so long that they had arrears of talk to make up. They had been at Bosco more than once, and though Hugh Gosselin said that the land of the free (which he had assured his sister was even more enslaved than dear old England) made one forget there were such spots on earth, they both remembered, a couple of miles away, a little ancient church to which the walk across the fields would be the right thing. They talked of other things as they went, and among them they talked of Mr. Bolton-Brown, in regard to whom Hugh, as scantily addicted to enthusiasm as to bursts of song (he was determined not to be taken in), became, in commendation, almost lyrical. Mary asked what he had done with his paragon, and he replied that he believed him to have gone out stealthily to sketch: they might come across him. He was extraordinarily clever at water-colors, but haunted with the fear that the public practice of such an art on Sunday was viewed with disfavor in England. Mary exclaimed that this was the respectable fact, and when her brother ridiculed the idea, she told him she had already noticed he had lost all sense of things at home, so that Mr. Bolton-Brown was apparently a better Englishman than he. "He is indeed—he's awfully artificial!" Hugh returned; but it must be added that in spite of this rigor their American friend, when they reached the goal of their walk, was to be perceived in an irregular attitude in the very churchyard. He was perched on an old flat tomb, with a box of colors beside him and a sketch half completed. Hugh asserted that this exercise was the only thing that Mr. Bolton-Brown really cared for, but the young man protested against the imputation in the face of an achievement so modest. He showed his sketch to Mary, however, and it consoled her for not having kept up her own experiments; she never could make her trees so leafy. He had found a lovely bit on the other side of the hill, a bit he should like to come back to, and he offered to show it to his friends. They were on the point of starting with him to look at it when Hugh Gosselin, taking out his watch, remembered the hour at which he had promised to be at the house again to give his mother, who wanted a little mild exercise, his arm. His sister, at this, said she would go back with him; but Bolton-Brown interposed an earnest inquiry. Mightn't she let Hugh keep his appointment and let _him_ take her over the hill and bring her home?

"Happy thought—_do_ that!" said Hugh, with a crudity that showed the girl how completely he had lost his English sense. He perceived, however, in an instant, that she was embarrassed, whereupon he went on: "My dear child, I've walked with girls so often in America that we really ought to let poor Brown walk with one in England." I know not if it was the effect of this plea or that of some further eloquence of their friend; at any rate, Mary Gosselin in the course of another minute had accepted the accident of Hugh's secession, had seen him depart with an injunction to her to render it clear to poor Brown that he had made quite a monstrous request. As she went over the hill with her companion she reflected that since she had granted the request, it was not in her interest to pretend she had gone out of her way. She wondered moreover whether her brother had wished to throw them together: it suddenly occurred to her that the whole incident might have been prearranged. The idea made her a little angry with Hugh; it led her however to entertain no resentment against the other party (if party Mr. Brown had been) to the transaction. He told her all the delight that certain sweet old corners of rural England excited in his mind, and she liked him for hovering near some of her own secrets.

Hugh Gosselin meanwhile, at Bosco, strolling on the terrace with his mother, who preferred walks that were as slow as conspiracies, and had had much to say to him about his extraordinary indiscretion, repeated over and over (it ended by irritating her), that as he himself had been out for hours with American girls, it was only fair to let their friend have a turn with an English one.

"Pay as much as you like, but don't pay with your sister!" Mrs. Gosselin replied; while Hugh submitted that it was just his sister who was required to make the payment *his*. She turned his logic to easy scorn, and she waited on the terrace till she had seen the two explorers reappear. When the ladies went to dress for dinner she expressed to her daughter her extreme disapproval of such conduct, and Mary did nothing more to justify herself than to exclaim at first "Poor dear man!" and then to say, "I was afraid you wouldn't like it." There were reservations in her silence that made Mrs. Gosselin uneasy, and she was glad that at dinner Mr. Bolton-Brown had to take in Mrs. Ashbury: it served him so right. This arrangement had, in Mrs. Gosselin's eyes, the added merit of serving Mrs. Ashbury right. She was more uneasy than ever when after dinner, in the drawing-room, she saw Mary sit for a period on the same small sofa with the culpable American. This young couple leaned back together familiarly, and their conversation had the air of being desultory without being in the least difficult. At last she quitted her place and went over to them, remarking to Mr. Bolton-Brown that she wanted him to come and talk a bit to *her*. She conducted him to another part of the room, which was vast and animated by scattered groups, and held him there very persuasively, quite maternally, till the approach of the hour at which the ladies would exchange looks and murmur good-nights. She made him talk about America, though he wanted to talk about England, and she judged that she gave him an impression of the kindest attention, though she was really thinking, in alternation, of three important things. One of these was a circumstance of which she had become conscious only just after sitting down with him— the prolonged absence of Lord Beaupré from the drawing-room; the second was the absence, equally marked (to her imagination), of Maud Ashbury, the third was a matter different altogether. "England gives one such a sense of immemorial continuity, something that drops like a plummet-line into the past," said the young American, ingeniously exerting himself, while Mrs. Gosselin, rigidly contemporaneous, strayed into deserts of conjecture. Had the fact that their host was out of the room any connection with the fact that the most beautiful, even though the most suicidal, of his satellites had quitted it? Yet if poor Guy was taking a turn by starlight on the terrace with the misguided girl, what had he done with his resentment at her invasion and by what inspiration of despair had Maud achieved such a triumph? The good lady studied Mrs. Ashbury's face across the room; she decided that triumph, accompanied perhaps with a shade of nervousness, looked out of her insincere eyes. An intelligent consciousness of ridicule was at any rate less present in them than ever. While Mrs. Gosselin had her infallible finger on the pulse of the occasion one of the doors opened to readmit Lord Beaupré, who struck her as pale, and who immediately approached Mrs. Ashbury with a remark evidently intended for herself alone. It led this lady to rise with a movement of dismay and, after a question or two, leave the room. Lord Beaupré left it again in her company. Mr. Bolton-Brown had also noticed the incident; his conversation languished, and he asked Mrs. Gosselin if she supposed anything had happened. She turned it over a moment, and then she said: "Yes, something will have happened to Miss Ashbury."

"What do you suppose? Is she ill?"

"I don't know; we shall see. They're capable of anything."

"Capable of anything?"

"I've guessed it—she wants to have a grievance."

"A grievance?" Mr. Bolton-Brown was mystified.

"Of course you don't understand; how should you? Moreover, it doesn't signify. But I'm so vexed with them (he's a very old friend of ours) that really, though I dare say I'm indiscreet, I can't speak civilly of them."

"Miss Ashbury's a wonderful type," said the young American.

This remark appeared to irritate his companion. "I see perfectly what has happened; she has made a scene."

"A scene?" Mr. Bolton-Brown was terribly out of it.

"She has tried to be injured—to provoke him, I mean, to some act of impatience, to some failure of temper, of courtesy. She has asked him if he wishes her to leave the house at midnight, and he may have answered—But no, he wouldn't!" Mrs. Gosselin suppressed the wild supposition.

"How you read it! She looks so quiet."

"Her mother has coached her, and—(I won't pretend to say *exactly* what has happened)—they've done, somehow, what they wanted; they've got him to do something to them that he'll have to make up for."

"What an evolution of ingenuity!" the young man laughed.

"It often answers."

"Will it in this case?"

Mrs. Gosselin was silent a moment. "It *may*."

"Really, you think?"

"I mean it might, if it weren't for something else."

"I'm too judicious to ask what that is."

"I'll tell you when we're back in town," said Mrs. Gosselin, getting up.

Lord Beaupré was restored to them, and the ladies prepared to withdraw. Before she went to bed Mrs. Gosselin asked him if there had been anything the matter with Maud; to which he replied, with abysmal blankness (she had never seen him wear just that face) that he was afraid Miss Ashbury was ill. She proved, in fact, in the morning too unwell to return to London: a piece of news communicated to Mrs. Gosselin at breakfast.

"She'll have to stay; I can't turn her out of the house," said Guy Firminger.

"Very well; let her stay her fill!"

"I wish you would stay, too," the young man went on.

"Do you mean to nurse her?"

"No, her mother must do that. I mean to keep me company."

"*You?* You're not going up?"

"I think I had better wait over to-day, or long enough to see what's the matter."

"Don't you *know* what's the matter?"

He was silent a moment. "I may have been nasty last night."

"You have compunctions? You're too good-natured."

"I dare say I hit rather wild. It will look better for me to stop over twenty-four hours."

Mrs. Gosselin fixed her eyes on a distant object. "Let no one ever say you're selfish!"

"*Does* any one ever say it?"

"You're too generous, you're too soft, you're too foolish. But if it will give you any pleasure, Mary and I will wait till tomorrow."

"And Hugh, too, won't he, and Bolton-Brown?"

"Hugh will do as he pleases. But don't keep the American."

"Why not? He's all right."

"That's why I want him to go," said Mrs. Gosselin, who could treat a matter with candor, just as she could treat it with humor, at the right moment.

The party at Bosco broke up, and there was a general retreat to town. Hugh Gosselin pleaded pressing business, he accompanied the young American to London. His mother and sister came back on the morrow, and Bolton-Brown went in to see them, as he often did, at tea-time. He found Mrs. Gosselin alone in the drawing-room, and she took such a convenient occasion to mention to him, what she had withheld on the eve of their departure from Bosco, the reason why poor Maud Ashbury's frantic assault on the master of that property would be vain. He was greatly surprised, the more so that Hugh hadn't told him. Mrs. Gosselin replied that Hugh didn't know: she had not seen him all day, and it had only just come out. Hugh's friend, at any rate, was deeply interested, and his interest took for several minutes the form of throbbing silence. At last Mrs. Gosselin heard a sound below, on which she said, quickly: "That's Hugh—I'll tell him now!" She left the room with the request that their visitor would wait for Mary, who would be down in a moment. During the instants that he spent alone the visitor lurched, as if he had been on a deck in a blow, to the window, and stood there with his hands in his pockets, staring vacantly into Chester Street; then, turning away, he gave himself, with an odd ejaculation, an impatient shake which had the effect of enabling

him to meet Mary Gosselin composedly enough when she came in.
It took her mother apparently some time to communicate the news
to Hugh, so that Bolton-Brown had a considerable margin for nervousness and hesitation before he could say to the girl, abruptly, but
with an attempt at a voice properly gay: "You must let me very
heartily congratulate you!"

Mary stared. "On what?"

"On your engagement."

"My engagement?"

"To Lord Beaupré"

Mary Gosselin looked strange; she colored. "Who told you I'm
engaged?"

"Your mother—just now."

"Oh!" the girl exclaimed, turning away. She went and rang the
bell for fresh tea, rang it with noticeable force. But she said "Thank
you very much!" before the servant came.

IV.

BOLTON-BROWN did something that evening towards disseminating
the news: he told it to the first people he met socially after leaving
Chester Street; and this although he had to do himself a certain
violence in speaking. He would have preferred to hold his peace;
therefore if he resisted his inclination it was for an urgent purpose.
This purpose was to prove to himself that he didn't mind. A perfect
indifference could be for him the only result of any understanding
Mary Gosselin might arrive at with any one, and he wanted to be
more and more conscious of his indifference. He was aware indeed that it required demonstration, and this was why he was almost feverishly active. He could mentally concede at least that he
had been surprised, for he had suspected nothing at Bosco. When
a fellow was attentive in America everyone knew it, and judged by
this standard Lord Beaupré made no show: how otherwise should
he have achieved that sweet accompanied ramble? Everything at
any rate was lucid now, except perhaps a certain ambiguity in
Hugh Gosselin, who on coming into the drawing-room with his
mother had looked flushed and grave, and had stayed only long
enough to kiss Mary and go out again. There had been nothing
effusive in the scene; but then there was nothing effusive in any
English scene. This helped to explain why Miss Gosselin had been

so blank during the minutes she spent with him before her mother came back.

He himself wanted to cultivate tranquillity, and he felt that he did so the next day in not going again to Chester Street. He went instead to the British Museum, where he sat quite like an elderly gentleman, with his hands crossed on the top of his stick and his eyes fixed on an Assyrian bull. When he came away, however, it was with the resolution to move briskly; so that he walked westward the whole length of Oxford Street and arrived at the Marble Arch. He stared for some minutes at this monument, as in the national collection he had stared at even less intelligible ones; then brushing away the apprehension that he should meet two persons riding together, he passed into the park. He didn't care a straw whom he met. He got upon the grass and made his way to the southern expanse, and when he reached the Row he dropped into a chair, rather tired, to watch the capering procession of riders. He watched it with a lustreless eye, for what he seemed mainly to extract from it was a vivification. of his disappointment. He had had a hope that he should not be forced to leave London without inducing Mary Gosselin to ride with him; but that prospect failed, for what he had accomplished in the British Museum was the determination to go to Paris. He tried to think of the attractions supposed to be evoked by that name, and while he was so engaged he recognized that a gentleman on horseback, close to the barrier of the Row, was making a sign to him. The gentleman was Lord Beaupré, who had pulled up his horse, and whose sign the young American lost no time in obeying. He went forward to speak to his late host, but during the instant of the transit he was able both to observe that Mary Gosselin was not in sight and to ask himself why she was not. She rode with her brother; why then didn't she ride with her future husband? It was singular at such a moment to see her future husband disporting himself alone. This personage conversed a few moments with Bolton-Brown, said it was too hot to ride, but that he ought to be mounted (*he* would give him a mount, if he liked), and was on the point of turning away when his interlocutor succumbed to the temptation to put his modesty to the test.

"Good-bye, but let me congratulate you first," said Bolton-Brown.

"Congratulate me? On what?" His look, his tone were very much what Mary Gosselin's had been.

"Why, on your engagement. Haven't you heard of it?"

Lord Beaupré stared a moment while his horse shifted uneasily. Then he laughed and said: "Which of them do you mean?"

"There's only one I know anything about. To Miss Gosselin," Brown added, after a puzzled pause.

"Oh yes, I see—thanks so much!" With this, letting his horse go, Lord Beaupré broke off, while Bolton-Brown stood looking after him and saying to himself that perhaps he *didn't* know! The chapter of English oddities was long.

But on the morrow the announcement was in *The Morning Post,* and that surely made it authentic. It was doubtless only superficially singular that Guy Firminger should have found himself unable to achieve a call in Chester Street until this journal had been for several hours in circulation. He appeared there just before luncheon, and the first person who received him was Mrs. Gosselin. He had always liked her, finding her infallible on the question of behavior; but he was on this occasion more than ever struck with her ripe astuteness, her independent wisdom.

"I knew what you wanted, I knew what you needed, I knew the subject on which you had pressed her," the good lady said; "and after Sunday I found myself really haunted with your dangers. There was danger in the air at Bosco, in your own defended house; it seemed to me too monstrous. I said to myself, 'We *can* help him, poor dear, and we *must*. It's the least one can do for so old and so good a friend.' I decided what to do: I simply put this other story about. In London that always answers. I knew that Mary pitied you really as much as I do, and that what she saw at Bosco had been a revelation—had at any rate brought your situation home to her. Yet, of course, she would be shy about saying out, for herself, 'Here I am—I'll do what you want.' The thing was for me to say it *for* her; so I said it first to that chattering American. He repeated it to several others, and there you are! I just forced her hand a little, but it's all right. All she has to do is not to contradict it. It won't be any trouble, and you'll be comfortable. That will be our reward!" smiled Mrs. Gosselin.

"Yes, all she has to do is not to contradict it," Lord Beaupré replied, musing a moment. "It *won't* be any trouble," he added, "and I *hope* I shall be comfortable." He thanked Mrs. Gosselin formally and liberally, and expressed all his impatience to assure Mary herself of his deep obligation to her; upon which his hostess promised to send her daughter to him on the instant: she would go and call her, so that they might be alone. Before Mrs. Gosselin left him, however, she touched on one or two points that had their little importance. Guy Firminger had asked for Hugh, but Hugh had gone to the City, and his mother mentioned candidly that he didn't take part in the game. She even disclosed his reason: he thought there was a want of dignity in it. Lord Beaupré stared at this, and after a moment exclaimed: "Dignity? Dignity be hanged! One must save one's life!"

"Yes, but the point poor Hugh makes is that one must save it by the use of one's *own* wits, or one's *own* arms and legs. But do you know what I said to him?" Mrs. Gosselin continued.

"Something very clever, I dare say."

"That if *we* were drowning, you'd be the very first to jump in. And we may fall overboard yet!" Fidgeting there, with his hands in his pockets, Lord Beaupré gave a laugh at this, but assured her that there was nothing in the world for which they mightn't count upon him. None the less she just permitted herself another warning, a warning, it is true, that was in his own interest, a reminder of a peril that he ought beforehand to look in the face. Wasn't there always the chance—just the bare chance—that a girl in Mary's position would, in the event, decline to let him off, decline to release him even on the day he should wish to marry? She wasn't speaking of Mary, but there were, of course, girls who would play him that trick. Guy Firminger considered this contingency; then he declared that it wasn't a question of "girls," it was simply a question of dear old Mary! If *she* should wish to hold him, so much the better; he would do anything in the world that she wanted. "Don't let us dwell on such vulgarities; but I had it on my conscience!" Mrs. Gosselin wound up.

She left him, but at the end of three minutes Mary came in, and the first thing she said was: "Before you speak a word, please understand this, that it's wholly mamma's doing. I hadn't dreamed of it, but she suddenly began to tell people."

"It was charming of her, and it's charming of you!" the visitor cried.

"It's not charming of any one, I think," said Mary Gosselin, looking at the carpet. "It's simply idiotic."

"Don't be nasty about it. It will be tremendous fun."

"I've only consented because mamma says we owe it to you," the girl went on.

"Never mind your reason—the end justifies the means. I can never thank you enough, nor tell you what a weight it lifts off my shoulders. Do you know I feel the difference already?—a peace that passeth understanding!" Mary replied that this was childish; how could such a feeble fiction last? At the very best it could live but an hour, and then he would be no better off than before. It would bristle moreover with difficulties and absurdities; it would be so much more trouble than it was worth. She reminded him that so ridiculous a service had never been asked of any girl, and at this he seemed a little struck; he said: "Ah, well, if it's positively disagreeable to you, we'll instantly drop the idea. But I—I thought you really liked me enough—!" She turned away impatiently, and he went on to argue imperturbably that she had always treated him in the kindest way in the world. He added that the worst was over, the start, they were off: the thing would be in all the evening papers. Wasn't it much simpler to accept it? That was all they would have to do; and all *she* would have to do would be not to gainsay it, and to smile and thank people when she was congratulated. She would have to *act* a little, but that would just be part of the fun. Oh, he hadn't the shadow of a scruple about taking the world in; the world deserved it richly, and she couldn't deny that this was what she had felt for him, that she had really been moved to compassion. He grew eloquent and charged her with having recognized in his predicament a genuine motive for charity. Their little plot would last what it could—it would be a part of their amusement to *make* it last. Even if it should be but a thing of a day, there would have been always so much gained. But they would be ingenious, they would find ways, they would have no end of sport.

"*You* must be ingenious; I can't," said Mary. "If people scarcely ever see us together, they'll guess we're trying to humbug them."

"But they *will* see us together. We *are* together. We've been together—I mean we've seen a lot of each other—all our lives."

"Ah, not *that* way!"

"Oh, trust me to work it right!" cried the young man, whose imagination had now evidently begun to glow in the air of their pious fraud.

"You'll find it a dreadful bore," said Mary Gosselin.

"Then I'll drop it, don't you see? And *you'll* drop it, of course, the moment *you've* had enough," Lord Beaupré punctually added. "But as soon as you begin to realize what a lot of good you do me you won't *want* to drop it. That is, if you're what I take you for!" laughed his lordship.

If a third person had been present at this conversation—and there was nothing in it surely that might not have been spoken before a trusty listener—that person would perhaps have thought, from the immediate expression of Mary Gosselin's face, that she was on the point of exclaiming "You take me for too big a fool!" No such ungracious words in fact, however, passed her lips; she only said after an instant: "What reason do you propose to give, on the day you need one, for our rupture?"

Her interlocutor stared. "To you, do you mean?"

"*I* sha'n't ask you for one. I mean to other people."

"Oh, I'll tell them you're sick of me. I'll put everything on you, and you'll put everything on me."

"You *have* worked it out!" Mary exclaimed.

"Oh, I shall be intensely considerate."

"Do you call that being considerate—publicly accusing me?"

Guy Firminger stared again. "Why, isn't that the reason *you'll* give?"

She looked at him an instant. "I won't tell you the reason I shall give."

"Oh, I shall learn it from others."

"I hope you'll like it when you do!" said Mary, with sudden gayety; and she added frankly though kindly the hope that he might soon light upon some young person who would really meet his requirements. He replied that he shouldn't be in a hurry—that was now just the comfort; and she, as if thinking over to the end the list of arguments against his clumsy contrivance, broke out: "And of course you mustn't dream of giving me anything—any tokens or presents."

"Then it won't look natural."

"That's exactly what I say. You can't make it deceive anybody."

"I *must* give you something—something that people can see. There must be some evidence! You can simply put my offerings away after a little and give them back." But about this Mary was visibly serious; she declared that she wouldn't touch anything that came from his hand, and she spoke in such a tone that he colored a little and hastened to say: "Oh, all right, I shall be thoroughly careful!" This appeared to complete their understanding; so that after it was settled that for the deluded world they *were* engaged, there was obviously nothing for him to do but to go. He therefore shook hands with her very gratefully and departed.

V.

He was able promptly to assure his accomplice that their little plot was working to a charm; it already made such a difference for the better. Only a week had elapsed, but he felt quite another man; his life was no longer spent in springing to arms, and he had ceased to sleep in his boots. The ghost of his great fear was laid; he could follow out his inclinations and attend to his neglected affairs. The news had been a bomb in the enemy's camp, and there were plenty of blank faces to testify to the confusion it had wrought. Every one was "sold" and every one made haste to clap him on the back. Lottie Firminger only had written in terms of which no notice could be taken, though of course he expected every time he came in to find her waiting in his hall. Her mother was coming up to town and he should have the family at his ears; but, taking them as a single body he could manage them, and that was a detail. The Ashburys had remained at Bosco till that establishment was favored with the tidings that so nearly concerned it (they were communicated to Maud's mother by the housekeeper), and then the beautiful sufferer had found in her defeat strength to seek another asylum. The two ladies had departed for a destination unknown; he didn't think they had turned up in London. Guy Firminger averred that there were precious portable objects which he was sure he should miss on returning to his country home.

He came every day to Chester Street, and was evidently much less bored than Mary had prefigured by this regular tribute to verisimilitude. It was amusement enough to see the progress of their comedy and to invent new touches for some of its scenes. The girl herself was amused; it was an opportunity like another for cleverness such as hers and had much in common with private theatricals, especially with the rehearsals, the most amusing part. Moreover, she was good-natured enough to be really pleased at the service it was impossible for her not to acknowledge that she had rendered. Each of the parties to this queer contract had anecdotes and suggestions for the other, and each reminded the other duly that they must at every step keep their story straight. Except for the exercise of this care Mary Gosselin found her duties less onorous than she had feared, and her part in general much more passive than active. It consisted, indeed, largely of murmuring thanks and smiling and looking happy and handsome; as well as perhaps also in saying in answer to many questions, that nothing as yet was fixed, and of trying to remain humble when people expressed without ceremony that such a match was a wonder for such a girl. Her mother on the other hand was devotedly active. She treated the situation with private humor but with public zeal and, making it both real and ideal, told so many fibs about it that there were none left for Mary. The girl had failed to understand Mrs. Gosselin's interest in this elaborate pleasantry; the good lady had seen in it from the first more than she herself had been able to see. Mary performed her task mechanically, sceptically, but Mrs. Gosselin attacked hers with conviction and had really the air at moments of thinking that their fable had crystallized into fact. Mary allowed her as little of this attitude as possible and was ironical about her duplicity; warnings which the elder lady received with gaiety until one day when repetition had made them act on her nerves. Then she begged her daughter, with sudden asperity, not to talk to her as if she were a fool. She had already had words with Hugh about some aspects of the affair—so much as this was evident in Chester Street; a smothered discussion which at the moment had determined the poor boy to go to Paris with Bolton-Brown. The young men came back together after Mary had been "engaged" three weeks, but she remained in ignorance of what passed between Hugh and his mother the night of his return. She had gone to the opera with Lady Whiteroy, after one of her invariable comments on Mrs. Gosselin's invariable remark that of course Guy Firminger would spend his evening in their box. The remedy for his trouble, Lord Beaupré's prospective bride had said, was surely worse than the disease; she was in perfect good faith when she wondered that his lordship's sacrifices, his laborious cultivation of appearances should "pay."

Hugh Gosselin dined with his mother and at dinner talked of Paris and of what he had seen and done there; he kept the conversation superficial and after he had heard how his sister, at the moment, was occupied, asked no question that might have seemed to denote an interest in the success of the experiment for which in going abroad he had declined responsibility. His mother could not help observing that he never mentioned Guy Firminger by either of his names, and it struck her as a part of the same detachment that later, upstairs (she sat with him while he smoked), he should suddenly say, as he finished a cigar:

"I return to New York next week."

"Before your time? What for?" Mrs. Gosselin was horrified.

"Oh, mamma, you know what for!"

"Because you still resent poor Mary's good-nature?"

"I don't understand it, and I don't like things I don't understand; therefore I'd rather not be here to see it. Besides, I really can't tell a pack of lies."

Mrs. Gosselin exclaimed and protested; she had arguments to prove that there was no call at present for the least deflection from the truth; all that any one had to reply to any question (and there could be none that was embarrassing save the ostensible determination of the date of the marriage) was that nothing was settled as yet—a form of words in which for the life of her she couldn't see any perjury. "Why, then, go in for anything in such bad taste, to culminate only in something so absurd?" Hugh demanded. "If the essential part of the matter can't be spoken of as fixed, nothing is fixed, the deception becomes transparent, and they give the whole idea away. It's child's play."

"That's why it's so innocent. All I can tell you is that practically their attitude answers; he's delighted with its success. Those dreadful women have given him up; they've already found some other victim."

"And how is it all to end, please?"

Mrs. Gosselin was silent a moment. "Perhaps it won't end."

"Do you mean that the engagement will become real?"

Again the good lady said nothing until she broke out: "My dear boy, can't you trust your poor old mummy?"

"Is *that* your speculation? Is that Mary's? I never heard of anything so odious!" Hugh Gosselin cried. But she defended his sister with eagerness, with a gloss of coaxing, maternal indignation, declaring that Mary's disinterestedness was complete—she had the perfect proof of it. Hugh was conscious as he lighted another cigar that the conversation was more fundamental than any that he had ever had with his mother, who however hung fire but for an instant when he asked her what this "perfect proof" might be. He didn't doubt of his sister, he admitted that; but the perfect proof would make the whole thing more luminous. It took finally the form of a confession from Mrs. Gosselin that the girl evidently liked—well, greatly liked—Mr. Bolton-Brown. Yes, the good lady had seen for herself at Bosco that the smooth young American was making up to her and that, time and opportunity aiding, something might very well happen which could not be regarded as satisfactory. She had been very frank with Mary, had besought her not to commit herself to a suitor who in the very nature of the case couldn't meet the most legitimate of their views. Mary, who pretended not to know what their "views" were, had denied that she was in danger; but Mrs. Gosselin had assured her that she had all the air of it and had said, triumphantly: "Agree to what Lord Beaupré asks of you, and I'll *believe* you." Mary had wished to be believed—so she had agreed. That was all the witchcraft any one had used.

Mrs. Gosselin out-talked her son, but there were two or three plain questions that he came back to; and the first of these bore upon the ground of her aversion to poor Bolton-Brown. He told her again, as he had told her before, that his friend was that rare bird, a maker of money who was also a man of culture. He was a gentleman to his finger-tips, accomplished, capable, kind, with a charming mother and two lovely sisters (she should see them!), the sort of fellow in short whom it was stupid not to appreciate.

"I believe it all; and if I had three daughters he should be very welcome to one of them."

"You might easily have had three daughters who wouldn't attract him at all! You've had the good fortune to have one who does, and I think you do wrong to interfere with it."

"My eggs are in one basket then, and that's a reason the more for preferring Lord Beaupré," said Mrs. Gosselin.

"Then it *is* your calculation—?" stammered Hugh in dismay; on which she colored and requested that he would be a little less rough with his mother. She would rather part with him immediately, sad as that would be, than that he should attempt to undo what she had done. When Hugh replied that it was not to Mary but to Beaupré himself that he judged it important he should speak, she informed him that a rash remonstrance might do his sister a cruel wrong. Dear Guy was *most* attentive.

"If you mean that he really cares for her there's the less excuse for his taking such a liberty with her. He's either in love with her or he isn't. If he is, let him make her a serious offer; if he isn't, let him leave her alone."

Mrs. Gosselin looked at her son with a kind of patient joy. "He's in love with her, but he doesn't know it."

"He ought to know it, and if he's so idiotic I don't see that we ought to consider him."

"Don't worry—he *shall* know it!" Mrs. Gosselin cried; and, continuing to struggle with Hugh, she insisted on the delicacy of the situation. She made a certain impression on him, though on confused grounds; she spoke at one moment as if he was to forbear because the matter was a make-believe that happened to contain a convenience for a distressed friend, and at another as if one ought to strain a point because there were great possibilities at stake. She was most lucid when she pictured the social position and other advantages of a peer of the realm. What had those of an American stockbroker, however amiable and with whatever shrill belongings in the background, to compare with them? She was inconsistent, but she was diplomatic, and the result of the discussion was that Hugh Gosselin became conscious of a dread of "injuring" his sister. He became conscious at the same time of a still greater apprehension, that of seeing her arrive at the agreeable in a tortuous, a second-rate manner. He might keep the peace to please his mother, but he couldn't enjoy it, and he actually took his departure, travelling in company with Bolton-Brown, who of course before going waited on the ladies in Chester Street to thank them for the kindness they had shown him. It couldn't be kept from Guy Firminger that Hugh was not happy, though when they met, which was only once or twice before he quitted London, Mary Gosselin's brother flattered himself that he was too proud to show it. He had always liked old loafing Guy, and it was disagreeable to him not to like him now; but he was aware that he must either quarrel with him definitely or not at all, and that he had passed his word to his mother. Therefore his attitude was strictly negative; he took with the parties to it no notice whatever of the "engagement," and he couldn't help it if to other people he had the air of not being initiated. They doubtless thought him strangely fastidious. Perhaps he was; the tone of London struck him in some respects as very horrid; he had grown in a manner away from it. Mary was impenetrable; tender, gay, charming, but with no patience, as she said, for his premature flight. Except when Lord Beaupré was present you would not have dreamed that he existed for her. In his company— he had to be present more or less of course—she was simply like any other English girl who disliked effusiveness. They had each the same manner, that of persons of rather a shy tradition who were on their guard against public "spooning." They practised their fraud with good taste, a good taste mystifying to Bolton-Brown, who thought their precautions excessive. When he took leave of Mary Gosselin her eyes consented for a moment to look deep down into his. He had been from the first of the opinion that they were beautiful, and he was more mystified than ever.

If Guy Firminger had failed to ask Hugh Gosselin whether he had a fault to find with what they were doing, this was, in spite of old friendship, simply because he was too happy now to care much whom he didn't please, to care at any rate for criticism. He had ceased to be critical himself, and his high prosperity could take his blamelessness for granted. His happiness would have been offensive if people generally hadn't liked him, for it consisted of a kind of monstrous candid comfort. To take all sorts of things for granted was still his great, his delightful characteristic; but it didn't prevent his showing imagination and tact and taste in particular circumstances. He made, in their little comedy, all the right jokes and none of the wrong ones: the girl had an acute sense that there were some jokes that would have been detestable. She gathered that it was universally supposed she was having an unprecedented season, and something of the glory of an enviable future seemed indeed to hang about her. People no doubt thought it odd that she didn't go about more with her future husband; but those who knew anything about her knew that she had never done exactly as other girls did. She had her own ways, her own freedoms, and her own scruples. Certainly he made the London weeks much richer than they had ever been for a subordinate young person; he put more things into them, so that they grew dense and complicated. This frightened her at moments, especially when she thought with compunction that she was deceiving her very friends. She didn't mind taking the vulgar world in, but there were people she hated not to enlighten, to reassure. She could undeceive no one now, and, indeed, she would have been ashamed. There were hours when she wanted to stop—she had such a dread of doing too much; hours when she thought with dismay that the fiction of the rupture was still to come, with its horrid train of new untrue things. She spoke of it repeatedly to her confederate, who only postponed and postponed, told her she would never dream of forsaking him if she measured the good she was doing him. She did measure it however when she met him in the great world; she was of course always meeting him: that was the only way appearances were kept up. There was a certain attitude she could allow him to take on these occasions; it covered and carried off their subterfuge. He could talk to her unmolested; for herself she never spoke of anything but the charming girls, everywhere present, among whom he could freely choose. He didn't protest, because to choose freely was what he wanted, and they discussed these young ladies one by one. Some she recommended, some she disparaged, but it was almost the only subject she tolerated. It was her system, in short, and she wondered he didn't get tired of it; she was so tired of it herself.

She tried other things that she thought he might find wearisome, but his good-humor was magnificent. He was now really for the first time enjoying his promotion, his wealth, his insight into the terms on which the world offered itself to the happy few, and these terms made a mixture healing to irritation. Once, at some glittering ball, he asked her if she should be jealous if he were to dance again with Lady Whiteroy, with whom he had danced already, and this was the only occasion on which he had come near making a joke of the wrong sort. She showed him what she thought of it and made him feel that the way to be forgiven was to spend the rest of the evening with that lovely creature. Now that the phalanx of the pressingly nubile was held in check there was accordingly nothing to prevent his passing his time pleasantly. Before he had taken this effective way the diplomatic mother, when she spied him flirting with a married woman, felt that in urging a virgin daughter's superior claims she worked for righteousness as well as for the poor girl. But Mary Gosselin protected these scandals practically by the still greater scandal of her indifference; so that he was in the odd position of having waited to be confined to know what it was to be at large. He had in other words the maximum of security with the minimum of privation. The lovely creatures of Lady Whiteroy's order thought Mary Gosselin charming, but they were the first to see through her falsity.

All this carried our precious pair to the middle of July; but nearly a month before that, one night under the summer stars, on the deck of the steamer that was to reach New York on the morrow, something had passed between Hugh Gosselin and his brooding American friend. The night was warm and splendid; these were their last hours at sea, and Hugh, who had been playing whist in the cabin, came up very late to take an observation before turning in. It was in this way that he chanced on his companion, who was leaning over the stern of the ship and gazing off, beyond its phosphorescent track, at the muffled, moaning ocean, the backward darkness, everything he had relinquished. Hugh stood by him for a moment and then asked him what he was thinking about. Bolton-Brown gave at first no answer; after which he turned round and, with his back against the guard of the deck, looked up at the multiplied stars. "He has it badly," Hugh Gosselin mentally commented. At last his friend replied: "About something you said yesterday."

"I forget what I said yesterday."

"You spoke of your sister's intended marriage; it was the only time you had spoken of it. You seemed to intimate that it might not after all take place."

Hugh hesitated a little. "Well, it *won't* take place. They're not engaged, not really. This is a secret, a preposterous secret. I wouldn't tell any one else, but I'm willing to tell *you*. It may make a difference to you."

Bolton-Brown turned his head; he looked at Hugh a minute through the fresh darkness. "It does make a difference to me. But I don't understand," he added.

"Neither do I. I don't like it. It's a pretence, a temporary make-believe, to help Beaupré through."

"Through what?"

"He's so run after."

The young American stared, ejaculated, mused. "Oh, yes—your mother told me."

"It's a sort of invention of my mother's and a notion of his own (very absurd, I think), till he can see his way. Mary serves as a kind of escort for these first exposed months. It's ridiculous, but I don't know that it hurts her."

"Oh!" said Bolton-Brown.

"I don't know either that it does her any good."

"No!" said Bolton-Brown. Then he added: "It's certainly very kind of her."

"It's a case of old friends," Hugh explained, inadequately as he felt. "He has always been in and out of our house."

"But how will it end?"

"I haven't the least idea."

Bolton-Brown was silent; he faced about to the stern again and stared at the rush of the ship. Then shifting his position once more: "Won't the engagement, before they've done, develop into the regular thing?"

Hugh felt as if his mother were listening. "I daresay not. If there were even a remote chance of that, Mary wouldn't have consented."

"But mayn't *he* easily find that—charming as she is—he's in love with her?"

"He's too much taken up with himself."

"That's just a reason," said Bolton-Brown. "Love is selfish." He considered a moment longer, then he went on: "And mayn't *she* find—"

"Find what?" said Hugh, as he hesitated.

"Why, that she likes him."

"She likes him, of course, else she wouldn't have come to his assistance. But her certainty about herself must have been just what made her not object to lending herself to the arrangement. She could do it decently because she doesn't seriously care for him. If she did—!" Hugh suddenly stopped.

"If she did?" his friend repeated.

"It would have been odious."

"I see," said Bolton-Brown, gently. "But how will they break off?"

"It will be Mary who'll break off."

"Perhaps she'll find it difficult."

"She'll require a pretext."

"I see," mused Bolton-Brown, shifting his position again.

"She'll find one," Hugh declared.

"I hope so," his companion responded.

For some minutes neither of them spoke; then Hugh asked: "Are you in love with her?"

"Oh, my dear fellow!" Bolton-Brown wailed. He instantly added, "Will it be any use for me to go back?"

Again Hugh felt as if his mother were listening; but he answered: "*Do* go back."

"It's awfully strange," said Bolton-Brown. "I'll go back."

"You had better wait a couple of months, you know."

"Mayn't I lose her then?"

"No; they'll drop it all."

"I'll go back," the American repeated, as if he hadn't heard. He was restless, agitated; he had evidently been much affected. He fidgeted away dimly, moved up the level length of the deck. Hugh Gosselin lingered longer at the stern; he fell into the attitude in which he had found the other, leaning over it and looking back at the great vague distance they had come. He thought of his mother.

VI.

To remind her fond parent of the vanity of certain expectations which she more than suspected her of entertaining, Mary Gosselin, while she felt herself intensely watched (it had all brought about a horrid new situation at home), produced every day some fresh illustration of the fact that people were no longer imposed upon. Moreover, these illustrations were not invented; the girl believed in them, and when once she had begun to note them she saw them multiply fast. Lady Whiteroy, for one, was distinctly suspicious; she had taken the liberty more than once of asking the future Lady Beaupré what in the world was the matter with her. Brilliant figure as she was and occupied with her own pleasures, which were of a very independent nature, she had nevertheless constituted herself Miss Gosselin's social sponsor: she took a particular interest in her marriage—an interest all the greater as it rested not only on a freely-professed regard for her, but on a keen sympathy with the other party to the transaction. Lady Whiteroy, who was very pretty and very clever and whom Mary secretly but profoundly mistrusted, delighted in them both in short; so much so that Mary judged herself happy to be in a false position, so certain should she have been to be jealous had she been in a true one. This charming woman threw out inquiries that made the girl not care to meet her eyes; and Mary ended by forming a theory of the sort of marriage for Lord Beaupré that Lady Whiteroy really would have appreciated. It would have been a marriage to a fool, a marriage to Maud Ashbury or to Charlotte Firminger. She would have her reasons for preferring that; and as regarded the actual prospect, she had only discovered that Mary was even more astute than herself.

It will be understood how much our young lady was on the crest of the wave when I mention that in spite of this complicated consciousness she was one of the ornaments (Guy Firminger was of course another) of the party entertained by her zealous friend and Lord Whiteroy during the Goodwood week. She came back to town with the firm intention of putting an end to a comedy which had more than ever become odious to her; in consequence of which she had on this subject with her fellow-comedian a scene—the scene she had dreaded—half pathetic, half ridiculous. He appealed to her, wrestled with her, took his usual ground that she was saving his life without really lifting a finger. He denied that the public was not satisfied with their pretexts for postponement, their explanations of delay; what else was expected of a man who would wish to celebrate his nuptials on a suitable scale, but who had the misfortune to have had, one after another, three grievous bereavements? He promised not to molest her for the next three months, to go away till his "mourning" was over, to go abroad, to let her do as she liked. He wouldn't come near her, he wouldn't even write (no one would know it), if she would let him keep up the mere form of their fiction; and he would let her off the very first instant he definitely perceived that this expedient had ceased to be effective. She couldn't judge of that—she must let *him* judge; and it was a matter in which she could surely trust to his honour.

Mary Gosselin trusted to it, but she insisted on his going away. When he took such a tone as that she couldn't help being moved; he breathed with such frank, generous lips on the irritation she had stored up against him. Guy Firminger went to Homburg; and if his confederate consented not to clip the slender thread by which this particular engagement still hung, she made very short work with every other. A dozen invitations, for Cowes, for the country, for Scotland, shimmered there before her, made a pathway of flowers, but she sent barbarous excuses. When her mother, aghast, said to her, "What then will you do?" she replied, in a very conclusive manner "I'll go home!" Mrs. Gosselin was wise enough not to struggle; she saw that the thread was delicate, that it must dangle in quiet air. She therefore travelled back with her daughter to homely Hampshire, feeling that they were people of less importance than they had been for many a week. On the August afternoons they sat again on the little lawn on which Guy Firminger had found them the day he first became eloquent about the perils of the desirable young bachelor; and it was on this very spot that, towards the end of the month, and with some surprise, they beheld Mr. Bolton-Brown once more approach. He had come back from America; he had arrived but a few days before; he was staying, of all places in the world, at the inn in the village.

His explanation of this caprice was of all explanations the oddest: he had come three thousand miles for the love of water-colour. There was nothing more sketchable than the sketchability of Hampshire—wasn't it celebrated, classic? and he was so good as to include Mrs. Gosselin's charming premises, and even their charming occupants, in his view of the field. He fell to work with speed, with a sort of feverish eagerness; he seemed possessed, indeed, by the frenzy of the brush. He sketched everything on the place, and when he had represented an object once he went straight at it again. His advent was soothing to Mary Gosselin, in spite of his nervous activity; it must be admitted indeed that at the moment he arrived she had already felt herself in quieter waters. The August afternoons, the relinquishment of London, the simplified life, had rendered her a service which, if she had freely qualified it, she would have described as a restoration of her self-respect. If poor Guy found any profit in such conditions as these, there was no great reason to repudiate him. She had so completely shaken off responsibility that she took scarcely more than a languid interest in the fact, communicated to her by Lady Whiteroy, that Charlotte Firminger had also, as the newspapers said, "proceeded" to Homburg. Lady Whiteroy knew, for Lady Whiteroy had "proceeded" as well; her physician had discovered in her constitution a pressing need for the comfort imbibed in dripping matutinal tumblers. She chronicled Charlotte's presence, and even to some extent her behavior, among the haunters of the spring, but it was not till some time afterwards that Mary learned how Miss Firminger's pilgrimage had been made under her ladyship's protection. This was a further sign that, like Mrs. Gosselin, Lady Whiteroy had ceased to struggle; she had, in town, only shrugged her shoulders ambiguously on being informed that Lord Beaupré's intended was going down to her stupid home.

The fulness of Mrs. Gosselin's renunciation was apparent during the stay of the young American in the neighborhood of that retreat. She occupied herself with her knitting, her garden, and the cares of a punctilious hospitality, but she had no appearance of any other occupation. When people came to tea Bolton-Brown was always there, and she had the self-control to attempt to say nothing that could assuage their natural surprise. Mrs. Ashbury came one day

with poor Maud, and the two elder ladies, as they had done more
than once before, looked for some moments into each other's eyes.
This time it was not a look of defiance, it was rather—or it would
have been for an observer completely in the secret—a look of
reciprocity, of fraternity, a look of arrangement. There was, however, no one completely in the secret save perhaps Mary, and Mary
didn't heed. The arrangement at any rate was ineffectual; Mrs.
Gosselin might mutely say, over the young American's eager, talkative shoulders, "Yes, you may have him if you can get him:" the
most rudimentary experiments demonstrated that he was not to be
got. Nothing passed on this subject between Mary and her mother,
whom the girl none the less knew to be holding her breath and
continuing to watch. She counted it more and more as one unpleasant result of her conspiracy with Guy Firminger, that it almost
poisoned a relation that had always been sweet. It was to show that
she was independent of it that she did as she liked now, which was
almost always as Bolton-Brown liked. When in the first days of
September—it was in the warm, clear twilight, and they happened,
amid the scent of fresh hay, to be leaning side by side on a stile—he
gave her a view of the fundamental and esoteric, as distinguished
from the convenient and superficial motive of his having come
back to England, she of course made no allusion to a prior tie. On
the other hand, she insisted on his going up to London by the first
train the next day. He was to wait—that was distinctly understood—
for his satisfaction.

She desired, meanwhile, to write immediately to Guy Firminger,
but as he had kept his promise of not complicating their contract
with letters she was uncertain as to his actual whereabouts; she was
only sure he would have left Homburg. Lady Whiteroy had become silent, so there were no more sidelights, and she was on the
point of telegraphing to London for an address when she received
a telegram from Bosco. The proprietor of that seat had arrived there
the day before, and he found he could make trains fit if she would
on the morrow allow him to come over and see her for a day or
two. He had returned sooner than their agreement allowed, but she
answered, "Come," and she showed his missive to her mother,
who at the sight of it wept with strange passion. Mary said to her,
"For Heaven's sake, don't let him see you!" She lost no time: she
told him on the morrow as soon as he entered the house that she
couldn't keep it up another hour.

"All right—it *is* no use," he conceded; "they're at it again !"

"You see you've gained nothing," she replied, triumphantly. She had instantly recognized that he was different, how much had happened.

"I've gained some of the happiest days of my life."

"Oh, that was not what you tried for!"

"Indeed it was, and I got exactly what I wanted," said Guy Firminger. They were in the cool little drawing-room where the morning light was dim. Guy Firminger had a sunburnt appearance, as in England people returning from other countries are apt to have, and Mary thought he had never looked so well. It was odd, but it was noticeable, that he had grown much handsomer since he had become a personage. He paused a moment, smiling at her while her mysterious eyes rested on him, and then he added: "Nothing ever worked better. It's no use now—people see. But I've got a start. I wanted to turn round and look about, and I *have* turned round and looked about. There are things I've escaped. I'm afraid you'll never understand how deeply I'm indebted to you."

"Oh, it's all right," said Mary Gosselin.

There was another short silence, after which he went on: "I've come back sooner than I promised, but only to be strictly fair. I began to see that we couldn't hold out, and that it was my duty to let you off. From that moment I was bound to put an end to your situation. I might have done so by letter, but that seemed scarcely decent. It's all I came back for, you know, and it's why I wired to you yesterday."

Mary hesitated an instant; she reflected intensely. What had happened, what would happen, was that if she didn't take care the signal for the end of their little arrangement would not have appeared to come from herself. She particularly wished it not to come from any one else, she had even a horror of that; so that after an instant she hastened to say: "I was on the very point of wiring to *you*—I was only waiting for your address."

"Wiring to me?" He seemed rather blank.

"To tell you that our absurd affair really, this time, can't go on another day—to put a complete stop to it."

"Oh!" said Guy Firminger.

"So it's all right."

"You've always hated it!" Guy laughed; and his laugh sounded slightly foolish to the girl.

"I found yesterday that I hated it more than ever."

Lord Beaupré showed a quickened attention. "For what reason—yesterday?"

"I would rather not tell you, please. Perhaps some time you'll find it out."

He continued to look at her brightly and fixedly, with his confused cheerfulness. Then he said, with a vague, courteous alacrity, "I see, I see!" She had an impression that he didn't see; but it didn't matter, she was nervous and quite preferred that he shouldn't. They both got up, and in a moment he exclaimed: "Well, I'm intensely sorry it's over! It has been so charming."

"You've been very good about it; I mean very reasonable," Mary said, to say something. Then she felt in her nervousness that this was just what she ought not to have said; it sounded ironical and provoking, whereas she had meant it as pure good-nature. "Of course you'll stay to luncheon?" she continued. She was bound in common hospitality to speak of that, and he answered that it would give him the greatest pleasure. After this her apprehension increased, and it was confirmed in particular by the manner in which he suddenly asked:

"By-the-way, what reason shall we give?"

"What reason?"

"For our rupture. Don't let us seem to have quarrelled."

"We can't help that," said Mary. "Nothing else will account for our behavior."

"Well, I sha'n't say anything about *you*."

"Do you mean you'll let people think it was yourself who were tired of it?"

"I mean I sha'n't *blame* you."

"You ought to behave as if you cared!" said Mary.

Guy Firminger laughed, but he looked worried, and he evidently was puzzled. "You must act as if you had jilted me."

"You're not the sort of person, unfortunately, that people jilt."

Lord Beaupré appeared to accept this statement as incontestable; not with elation, however, but with candid regret, the slightly embarrassed recognition of a fundamental obstacle. "Well, it's no one's business, at any rate, is it?"

"No one's, and that's what I shall say if people question me. Besides," Mary added, "they'll see for themselves."

"What will they see?"

"I mean they'll understand. And now we had better join mamma."

It was his evident inclination to linger in the room after he had said this that gave her complete alarm. Mrs. Gosselin was in another room, in which she sat in the morning, and Mary moved in that direction, pausing only in the hall for him to accompany her. She wished to get him into the presence of a third person. In the hall he joined her, and in doing so laid his hand gently on her arm. Then looking into her eyes with all the pleasantness of his honesty, he said: "It will be very easy for me to appear to care—for I *shall* care. I shall care immensely!" Lord Beaupré added, smiling.

Anything, it struck her, was better than that—than that he should say: "Well keep on, if you like, (*I* should!) only this time it will be serious. Hold me to it—do; don't let me go; lead me on to the altar, really!" Some such words as these, she believed, were rising to his lips, and she had an insurmountable horror of hearing them. It was as if, well enough meant on *his* part, they would do her a sort of dishonour, so that all her impulse was quickly to avert them. That was not the way she wanted to be asked in marriage. "Thank you very much," she said, "but it doesn't in the least matter. You will seem to have been jilted—so it's all right!"

"All right! You mean—?" He hesitated, he had colored a little; his eyes questioned her.

"I'm engaged to be married—in earnest."

"Oh!" said Lord Beaupré.

"You asked me just now if I had a special reason for having been on the point of telegraphing to you, and I said I had. That was my special reason."

"I see!" said Lord Beaupré. He looked grave for a few seconds, then he gave an awkward smile. But he behaved with perfect tact and discretion, didn't even ask her who the gentleman in the case might be. He congratulated her in the dark, as it were, and if the effect of this was indeed a little odd, she liked him for his quick perception of the fine fitness of pulling up short. Besides, he extracted the name of the gentleman soon enough from her mother, in whose company they now immediately found themselves. Mary left Guy Firminger with the good lady for half an hour before luncheon; and when the girl came back it was to observe that she had been crying again. It was dreadful—what she might have been saying. Their guest, however, at luncheon was not lachrymose; he was natural, but he was talkative and gay. Mary liked the way he now behaved, and more particularly the way he departed immediately after the meal. As soon as he was gone Mrs. Gosselin broke out, suppliantly: "Mary!" But her daughter replied:

"I know, mamma, perfectly what you're going to say, and if you attempt to say it I shall leave the room." With this threat (day after day, for the following time) she kept the terrible appeal unuttered until it was too late for an appeal to be of use. That afternoon she wrote to Bolton-Brown that she accepted his offer of marriage.

Guy Firminger departed altogether; he went abroad again, and to far countries. He was therefore not able to be present at the nuptials of Miss Gosselin and the young American whom he had entertained at Bosco, which took place in the middle of November. Had he been in England however he probably would have felt impelled by a due regard for past verisimilitude to abstain from giving his countenance to such an occasion. His absence from the country contributed to the needed even if astonishing effect of his having been jilted; so, likewise, did the reputed vastness of Bolton-Brown's young income, which in London was grossly exaggerated. Hugh Gosselin had perhaps a little to do with this; as he had sacrificed a part of his summer holiday, he got another month and came out to his sister's wedding. He took public comfort in his brother-in-law; nevertheless he listened with attention to a curious communication made him by his mother after the young couple had started for Italy; even to the point of bringing out the inquiry (in answer to her assertion that poor Guy had been ready to place everything he had at Mary's feet): "Then why the devil didn't he do it?"

"From simple delicacy! He didn't want to make her feel as if she had lent herself to an artifice only on purpose to get hold of him—to treat her as if she, too, had been at bottom one of the very harpies she helped him to elude."

Hugh thought a moment. "That *was* delicate."

"He's the dearest creature in the world. He's on his guard, he's prudent, he tested himself by separation. Then he came back to England in love with her. She might have had it all!"

"I'm glad she didn't get it *that* way."

"She had only to wait—to put an end to their artifice, harmless as it was, for the present, but still wait. She might have broken off in a way that would have made it come on again better."

"That's exactly what she didn't want."

"I mean as a quite separate incident," said Mrs. Gosselin.

"*I* loathed their artifice, harmless as it was!" her son observed.

Mrs. Gosselin for a moment made no answer; then she turned away from the fire, into which she had been pensively gazing, with the ejaculation, "Poor dear Guy!"

"I can't for the life of me see that he's to be pitied."

"He'll marry Charlotte Firminger."

"If he's such an ass as that, it's his own affair."

"Bessie Whiteroy will bring it about."

"What has *she* to do with it?"

"She wants to get hold of him."

"Then why will she marry him to another woman?"

"Because in that way she can select the other—a woman he won't care for. It will keep him from taking some one that's nicer."

Hugh Gosselin stared—he laughed aloud. "Lord, mamma, you're deep!"

"Indeed I am. I see much more."

"What do you see?"

"Mary won't in the least care for America. Don't tell me she will," Mrs. Gosselin added, "for you know perfectly you don't believe it."

"She'll care for her husband, she'll care for everything that concerns him."

"He's very nice; in his little way he's delightful. But as an alternative to Lord Beaupré, he's ridiculous!"

"Mary's in a position in which she has nothing to do with alternatives."

"For the present, yes, but not forever. She'll have enough of your New York; they'll come back here. I see the future dark," Mrs. Gosselin pursued, inexorably musing.

"Tell me then all you see."

"She'll find poor Guy wretchedly married, and she'll be very sorry for him."

"Do you mean that he'll make love to her? You give a queer account of your paragon."

"He'll value her sympathy. I see life as it is."

"You give a queer account of your daughter."

"I don't give *any* account. She'll behave perfectly," Mrs. Gosselin somewhat inconsequently subjoined.

"Then what are you afraid of?"

"She'll be sorry for him, and it will be all a worry."

"A worry to whom?"

The good lady was silent a moment. "To me," she replied. "And to you as well."

"Then they mustn't come back."

"That will be a greater worry still."

"Surely not a greater—a smaller. We'll put up with the lesser evil."

"Nothing will prevent her coming to a sense, eventually, of what *might* have been. And when they *both* recognize it—"

"It will be very dreadful!" Hugh exclaimed, completing gaily his mother's phrase. "I don't see, however," he added, "what in all this you do with Bessie Whiteroy."

"Oh, he'll be tired of her; she's hard, she'll have become despotic. I see life as it is," the good lady repeated.

"Then all I can say is that it's not very nice! But they sha'n't come back; I'll attend to that!" said Hugh Gosselin, who has attended to it up to this time successfully, though the rest of his mother's prophecy is so far accomplished (it was her second hit) as that Charlotte Firminger is now, strange as it may seem, Lady Beaupré.

THE REAL THING

I.

WHEN THE PORTER'S wife (she used to answer the house-bell), announced "A gentleman—with a lady, sir," I had, as I often had in those days, for the wish was father to the thought, an immediate vision of sitters. Sitters my visitors in this case proved to be; but not in the sense I should have preferred. However, there was nothing at first to indicate that they might not have come for a portrait. The gentleman, a man of fifty, very high and very straight, with a moustache slightly grizzled and a dark grey walking-coat admirably fitted, both of which I noted professionally—I don't mean as a barber or yet as a tailor—would have struck me as a celebrity if celebrities often were striking. It was a truth of which I had for some time been conscious that a figure with a good deal of frontage was, as one might say, almost never a public institution. A glance at the lady helped to remind me of this paradoxical law: she also looked too distinguished to be a "personality." Moreover one would scarcely come across two variations together.

Neither of the pair spoke immediately—they only prolonged the preliminary gaze which suggested that each wished to give the other a chance. They were visibly shy; they stood there letting me take them in—which, as I afterwards perceived, was the most practical thing they could have done. In this way their embarrassment served their cause. I had seen people painfully reluctant to mention that they desired anything so gross as to be represented on canvas; but the scruples of my new friends appeared almost insurmountable. Yet the gentleman might have said "I should like a portrait of my wife," and the lady might have said "I should like a portrait of my husband." Perhaps they were not husband and wife—this naturally would make the matter more delicate. Perhaps they wished to be done together—in which case they ought to have brought a third person to break the news.

"We come from Mr. Rivet," the lady said at last, with a dim smile which had the effect of a moist sponge passed over a "sunk" piece of painting, as well as of a vague allusion to vanished beauty. She was as tall and straight, in her degree, as her companion, and with ten years less to carry. She looked as sad as a woman could look whose face was not charged with expression; that is her tinted oval mask showed friction as an exposed surface shows it. The hand of time had played over her freely, but only to simplify. She was slim and stiff, and so well-dressed, in dark blue cloth, with lappets and pockets and buttons, that it was clear she employed the same tailor as her husband. The couple had an indefinable air of prosperous thrift—they evidently got a good deal of luxury for their money. If I was to be one of their luxuries it would behove me to consider my terms.

"Ah, Claude Rivet recommended me?" I inquired; and I added that it was very kind of him, though I could reflect that, as he only painted landscape, this was not a sacrifice.

The lady looked very hard at the gentleman, and the gentleman looked round the room. Then staring at the floor a moment and stroking his moustache, he rested his pleasant eyes on me with the remark: "He said you were the right one."

"I try to be, when people want to sit."

"Yes, we should like to," said the lady anxiously.

"Do you mean together?"

My visitors exchanged a glance. "If you could do anything with *me,* I suppose it would be double," the gentleman stammered.

"Oh yes, there's naturally a higher charge for two figures than for one."

"We should like to make it pay," the husband confessed.

"That's very good of you," I returned, appreciating so unwonted a sympathy—for I supposed he meant pay the artist.

A sense of strangeness seemed to dawn on the lady. "We mean for the illustrations—Mr. Rivet said you might put one in."

"Put one in—an illustration? "I was equally confused.

"Sketch her off, you know," said the gentleman, colouring.

It was only then that I understood the service Claude Rivet had rendered me; he had told them that I worked in black and white, for magazines, for story-books, for sketches of contemporary life, and consequently had frequent employment for models. These things were true, but it was not less true (I may confess it now—whether because the aspiration was to lead to everything or to nothing I leave the reader to guess), that I couldn't get the honours, to say nothing of the emoluments, of a great painter of portraits out of my head. My "illustrations" were my pot-boilers; I looked to a different branch of art (far and away the most interesting it had always seemed to me), to perpetuate my fame. There was no shame in looking to it also to make my fortune; but that fortune was by so much further from being made from the moment my visitors wished to be "done" for nothing. I was disappointed; for in the pictorial sense I had immediately *seen* them. I had seized their type—I had already settled what I would do with it. Something that wouldn't absolutely have pleased them, I afterwards reflected.

"Ah, you're—you're—a—?" I began, as soon as I had mastered my surprise. I couldn't bring out the dingy word "models"; it seemed to fit the case so little.

"We haven't had much practice," said the lady.

"We've got to *do* something, and we've thought that an artist in your line might perhaps make something of us," her husband threw off. He further mentioned that they didn't know many artists and that they had gone first, on the off-chance (he painted views of course, but sometimes put in figures—perhaps I remembered), to Mr. Rivet, whom they had met a few years before at a place in Norfolk where he was sketching.

"We used to sketch a little ourselves," the lady hinted.

"It's very awkward, but we absolutely *must* do something," her husband went on.

"Of course, we're not so *very* young," she admitted, with a wan smile.

With the remark that I might as well know something more about them, the husband had handed me a card extracted from a neat new pocket-book (their appurtenances were all of the freshest) and inscribed with the words "Major Monarch." Impressive as these words were they didn't carry my knowledge much further; but my visitor presently added: "I've left the army, and we've had the misfortune to lose our money. In fact our means are dreadfully small."

"It's an awful bore," said Mrs. Monarch.

They evidently wished to be discreet—to take care not to swagger because they were gentlefolks. I perceived they would have been willing to recognise this as something of a drawback, at the same time that I guessed at an underlying sense—their consolation in adversity—that they *had* their points. They certainly had; but these advantages struck me as preponderantly social; such for instance as would help to make a drawing-room look well. However, a drawing-room was always, or ought to be, a picture.

In consequence of his wife's allusion to their age Major Monarch observed: "Naturally, it's more for the figure that we thought of going in. We can still hold ourselves up." On the instant I saw that the figure was indeed their strong point. His "naturally" didn't sound vain, but it lighted up the question. "*She* has got the best," he continued, nodding at his wife, with a pleasant after-dinner absence of circumlocution. I could only reply, as if we were in fact sitting over our wine, that this didn't prevent his own from being very good; which led him in turn to rejoin: "We thought that if you ever have to do people like us, we might be something like it. *She,* particularly—for a lady in a book, you know."

I was so amused by them that, to get more of it, I did my best to take their point of view; and though it was an embarrassment to find myself appraising physically, as if they were animals on hire or useful blacks, a pair whom I should have expected to meet only in one of the relations in which criticism is tacit, I looked at Mrs. Monarch judicially enough to be able to exclaim, after a moment, with conviction: "Oh yes, a lady in a book!" She was singularly like a bad illustration.

"We'll stand up, if you like," said the Major; and he raised himself before me with a really grand air.

I could take his measure at a glance—he was six feet two and a perfect gentleman. It would have paid any club in process of formation and in want of a stamp to engage him at a salary to stand in the principal window. What struck me immediately was that in coming to me they had rather missed their vocation; they could surely have been turned to better account for advertising purposes. I couldn't of course see the thing in detail, but I could see them make someone's fortune—I don't mean their own. There was something in them for a waistcoat-maker, an hotel-keeper or a soap-vendor. I could imagine "We always use it" pinned on their bosoms with the greatest effect; I had a vision of the promptitude with which they would launch a table d'hôte.

Mrs. Monarch sat still, not from pride but from shyness, and presently her husband said to her: "Get up my dear and show how smart you are." She obeyed, but she had no need to get up to show it. She walked to the end of the studio, and then she came back blushing, with her fluttered eyes on her husband. I was reminded of an incident I had accidentally had a glimpse of in Paris—being with a friend there, a dramatist about to produce a play—when an actress came to him to ask to be intrusted with a part. She went through her paces before him, walked up and down as Mrs. Monarch was doing. Mrs. Monarch did it quite as well, but I abstained from applauding. It was very odd to see such people apply for such poor pay. She looked as if she had ten thousand a year. Her husband had used the word that described her: she was, in the London current jargon, essentially and typically "smart." Her figure was, in the same order of ideas, conspicuously and irreproachably "good." For a woman of her age her waist was surprisingly small; her elbow moreover had the orthodox crook. She held her head at the conventional angle; but why did she come to *me?* She ought to have tried on jackets at a big shop. I feared my visitors were not only destitute, but "artistic"—which would be a great complication. When she sat down again I thanked her, observing that what a draughtsman most valued in his model was the faculty of keeping quiet.

"Oh, *she* can keep quiet," said Major Monarch. Then he added, jocosely: "I've always kept her quiet."

"I'm not a nasty fidget, am I?" Mrs. Monarch appealed to her husband.

He addressed his answer to me. "Perhaps it isn't out of place to mention—because we ought to be quite business-like, oughtn't we?—that when I married her she was known as the Beautiful Statue."

"Oh dear! "said Mrs. Monarch, ruefully.

"Of course I should want a certain amount of expression," I rejoined.

"Of *course!*" they both exclaimed.

"And then I suppose you know that you'll get awfully tired."

"Oh, we *never* get tired!" they eagerly cried.

"Have you had any kind of practice?"

They hesitated—they looked at each other. "We've been photographed, *immensely,*" said Mrs. Monarch.

"She means the fellows have asked us," added the Major.

"I see—because you're so good-looking."

"I don't know what they thought, but they were always after us."

"We always got our photographs for nothing," smiled Mrs. Monarch.

"We might have brought some, my dear," her husband remarked.

"I'm not sure we have any left. We've given quantities away," she explained to me.

"With our autographs and that sort of thing," said the Major.

"Are they to be got in the shops?" I inquired, as a harmless pleasantry.

"Oh, yes; *hers*—they used to be."

"Not now," said Mrs. Monarch, with her eyes on the floor.

II.

I COULD fancy the "sort of thing" they put on the presentation-copies of their photographs, and I was sure they wrote a beautiful hand. It was odd how quickly I was sure of everything that concerned them. If they were now so poor as to have to earn shillings and pence, they never had had much of a margin. Their good looks had been their capital, and they had good-humouredly made the most of the career that this resource marked out for them. It was in their faces, the blankness, the deep intellectual repose of the twenty years of country-house visiting which had given them pleasant intonations. I could see the sunny drawing-rooms, sprinkled with periodicals she didn't read, in which Mrs. Monarch had continuously sat; I could see the wet shrubberies in which she had walked, equipped to admiration for either exercise. I could see the rich covers the Major had helped to shoot and the wonderful garments in which, late at night, he repaired to the smoking-room to talk about them. I could imagine their leggings and waterproofs, their knowing tweeds and rugs, their rolls of sticks and cases of tackle and neat umbrellas; and I could evoke the exact appearance of their servants and the compact variety of their luggage on the platforms of country stations.

They gave small tips, but they were liked; they didn't do anything themselves, but they were welcome. They looked so well everywhere; they gratified the general relish for stature, complexion and "form." They knew it without fatuity or vulgarity, and they respected themselves in consequence. They were not superficial; they were thorough and kept themselves up—it had been their line. People with such a taste for activity had to have some line. I could feel how, even in a dull house, they could have been counted upon for cheerfulness. At present something had happened—it didn't matter what, their little income had grown less, it had grown least—and they had to do something for pocket-money. Their friends liked them, but didn't like to support them. There was something about them that represented credit—their clothes, their manners, their type; but if credit is a large empty pocket in which an occasional chink reverberates, the chink at least must be audible. What they wanted of me was to help to make it so. Fortunately they had no children—I soon divined that. They would also perhaps wish our relations to be kept secret: this was why it was "for the figure"—the reproduction of the face would betray them.

I liked them—they were so simple; and I had no objection to them if they would suit. But, somehow, with all their perfections I didn't easily believe in them. After all they were amateurs, and the ruling passion of my life was the detestation of the amateur. Combined with this was another perversity—an innate preference for the represented subject over the real one: the defect of the real one was so apt to be a lack of representation. I liked things that appeared; then one was sure. Whether they *were* or not was a subordinate and almost always a profitless question. There were other considerations, the first of which was that I already had two or three people in use, notably a young person with big feet, in alpaca, from Kilburn, who for a couple of years had come to me regularly for my illustrations and with whom I was still—perhaps ignobly—satisfied. I frankly explained to my visitors how the case stood; but they had taken more precautions than I supposed. They had reasoned out their opportunity, for Claude Rivet had told them of the projected *édition de luxe* of one of the writers of our day—the rarest of the novelists—who, long neglected by the multitudinous vulgar and dearly prized by the attentive (need I mention Philip Vincent?) had had the happy fortune of seeing, late in life, the dawn and then the full light of a higher criticism—an estimate in which, on the part of the public, there was something really of expiation. The edition in question, planned by a publisher of taste, was practically an act of high reparation; the wood-cuts with which it was to be enriched were the homage of English art to one of the most independent representatives of English letters. Major and Mrs. Monarch confessed to me that they had hoped I might be able to work *them* into my share of the enterprise. They knew I was to do the first of the books, "Rutland Ramsay," but I had to make clear to them that my participation in the rest of the affair—this first book was to be a test—was to depend on the satisfaction I should give. If this should be limited my employers would drop me without a scruple. It was therefore a crisis for me, and naturally I was making special preparations, looking about for new people, if they should be necessary, and securing the best types. I admitted however that I should like to settle down to two or three good models who would do for everything.

"Should we have often to—a—put on special clothes?" Mrs. Monarch timidly demanded.

"Dear, yes—that's half the business."

"And should we be expected to supply our own costumes?"

"Oh, no; I've got a lot of things. A painter's models put on—or put off—anything he likes."

"And do you mean—a—the same?"

"The same?"

Mrs. Monarch looked at her husband again.

"Oh, she was just wondering," he explained, "if the costumes are in *general* use." I had to confess that they were, and I mentioned further that some of them (I had a lot of genuine, greasy last-century things), had served their time, a hundred years ago, on living, world-stained men and women. "We'll put on anything that *fits*," said the Major.

"Oh, I arrange that—they fit in the pictures."

"I'm afraid I should do better for the modern books. I would come as you like," said Mrs. Monarch.

"She has got a lot of clothes at home: they might do for contemporary life," her husband continued.

"Oh, I can fancy scenes in which you'd be quite natural." And indeed I could see the slipshod rearrangements of stale properties—the stories I tried to produce pictures for without the exasperation of reading them—whose sandy tracts the good lady might help to people. But I had to return to the fact that for this sort of work—the daily mechanical grind—I was already equipped; the people I was working with were fully adequate.

"We only thought we might be more like *some* characters," said Mrs. Monarch mildly, getting up.

Her husband also rose; he stood looking at me with a dim wistfulness that was touching in so fine a man. "Wouldn't it be rather a pull sometimes to have—a—to have—?" He hung fire; he wanted me to help him by phrasing what he meant. But I couldn't—I didn't know. So he brought it out, awkwardly: "The *real* thing; a gentleman, you know, or a lady." I was quite ready to give a general assent—I admitted that there was a great deal in that. This encouraged Major Monarch to say, following up his appeal with an unacted gulp: "It's awfully hard—we've tried everything." The gulp was communicative; it proved too much for his wife. Before I knew it Mrs. Monarch had dropped again upon a divan and burst into tears. Her husband sat down beside her, holding one of her hands; whereupon she quickly dried her eyes with the other, while I felt embarrassed as she looked up at me. "There isn't a confounded job I haven't applied for—waited for—prayed for. You can fancy we'd be pretty bad first. Secretaryships and that sort of thing? You might as well ask for a peerage. I'd be *anything*—I'm strong; a messenger or a coalheaver. I'd put on a gold-laced cap and open carriage-doors in front of the haberdasher's; I'd hang about a station, to carry portmanteaus; I'd be a postman. But they won't *look* at you; there are thousands, as good as yourself, already on the ground. *Gentlemen,* poor beggars, who have drunk their wine, who have kept their hunters!"

I was as reassuring as I knew how to be, and my visitors were presently on their feet again while, for the experiment, we agreed on an hour. We were discussing it when the door opened and Miss Churm came in with a wet umbrella. Miss Churm had to take the omnibus to Maida Vale and then walk half-a-mile. She looked a trifle blowsy and slightly splashed. I scarcely ever saw her come in without thinking afresh how odd it was that, being so little in herself, she should yet be so much in others. She was a meagre little Miss Churm, but she was an ample heroine of romance. She was only a freckled cockney, but she could represent everything, from a fine lady to a shepherdess; she had the faculty, as she might have had a fine voice or long hair. She couldn't spell, and she loved beer, but she had two or three "points," and practice, and a knack, and mother-wit, and a kind of whimsical sensibility, and a love of the theatre, and seven sisters, and not an ounce of respect, especially for the *h*. The first thing my visitors saw was that her umbrella was wet, and in their spotless perfection they visibly winced at it. The rain had come on since their arrival.

"I'm all in a soak; there *was* a mess of people in the 'bus. I wish you lived near a stytion," said Miss Churm. I requested her to get ready as quickly as possible, and she passed into the room in which she always changed her dress. But before going out she asked me what she was to get into this time.

"It's the Russian princess, don't you know?" I answered; "the one with the 'golden eyes,' in black velvet, for the long thing in the *Cheapside*."

"Golden eyes? I *say!*" cried Miss Churm, while my companions watched her with intensity as she withdrew. She always arranged herself, when she was late, before I could turn round; and I kept my visitors a little, on purpose, so that they might get an idea, from seeing her, what would be expected of themselves. I mentioned that she was quite my notion of an excellent model—she was really very clever.

"Do you think she looks like a Russian princess?" Major Monarch asked, with lurking alarm.

"When I make her, yes."

"Oh, if you have to *make* her—! "he reasoned, acutely.

"That's the most you can ask. There are so many that are not makeable."

"Well now, *here's* a lady"—and with a persuasive smile he passed his arm into his wife's—"who's already made!"

"Oh, I'm not a Russian princess," Mrs. Monarch protested, a little coldly. I could see that she had known some and didn't like them. There, immediately, was a complication of a kind that I never had to fear with Miss Churm.

This young lady came back in black velvet—the gown was rather rusty and very low on her lean shoulders—and with a Japanese fan in her red hands. I reminded her that in the scene I was doing she had to look over someone's head. "I forget whose it is; but it doesn't matter. Just look over a head."

"I'd rather look over a stove," said Miss Churm; and she took her station near the fire. She fell into position, settled herself into a tall attitude, gave a certain backward inclination to her head and a certain forward droop to her fan, and looked, at least to my prejudiced sense, distinguished and charming, foreign and dangerous.

We left her looking so, while I went down-stairs with Major and Mrs. Monarch.

"I think I could come about as near it as that," said Mrs. Monarch.

"Oh, you think she's shabby, but you must allow for the alchemy of art."

However, they went off with an evident increase of comfort, founded on their demonstrable advantage in being the real thing. I could fancy them shuddering over Miss Churm. She was very droll about them when I went back, for I told her what they wanted.

"Well, if *she* can sit I'll tyke to bookkeeping," said my model.

"She's very lady-like," I replied, as an innocent form of aggravation.

"So much the worse for *you*. That means she can't turn round."

"She'll do for the fashionable novels."

"Oh yes, she'll *do* for them! "my model humorously declared. "Ain't they bad enough without her?" I had often sociably denounced them to Miss Churm.

III.

IT was for the elucidation of a mystery in one of these works that I first tried Mrs. Monarch. Her husband came with her, to be useful if necessary—it was sufficiently clear that as a general thing he would prefer to come with her. At first I wondered if this were for " propriety's" sake—if he were going to be jealous and meddling. The idea was too tiresome, and if it had been confirmed it would speedily have brought our acquaintance to a close. But I soon saw there was nothing in it and that if he accompanied Mrs. Monarch it was (in addition to the chance of being wanted), simply because he had nothing else to do. When she was away from him his occupation was gone—she never *had* been away from him. I judged, rightly, that in their awkward situation their close union was their main comfort and that this union had no weak spot. It was a real marriage, an encouragement to the hesitating, a nut for pessimists to crack. Their address was humble (I remember afterwards thinking it had been the only thing about them that was really professional), and I could fancy the lamentable lodgings in which the Major would have been left alone. He could bear them with his wife—he couldn't bear them without her.

He had too much tact to try and make himself agreeable when he couldn't be useful; so he simply sat and waited, when I was too absorbed in my work to talk. But I liked to make him talk—it made my work, when it didn't interrupt it, less sordid, less special. To listen to him was to combine the excitement of going out with the economy of staying at home. There was only one hindrance: that I seemed not to know any of the people he and his wife had known. I think he wondered extremely, during the term of our intercourse, whom the deuce I *did* know. He hadn't a stray sixpence of an idea to fumble for; so we didn't spin it very fine—we confined ourselves to questions of leather and even of liquor (saddlers and breeches-makers and how to get good claret cheap), and matters like "good trains" and the habits of small game. His lore on these last subjects was astonishing, he managed to interweave the station-master with the ornithologist. When he couldn't talk about greater things he could talk cheerfully about smaller, and since I couldn't accompany him into reminiscences of the fashionable world he could lower the conversation without a visible effort to my level.

So earnest a desire to please was touching in a man who could so easily have knocked one down. He looked after the fire and had an opinion on the draught of the stove, without my asking him, and I could see that he thought many of my arrangements not half clever enough. I remember telling him that if I were only rich I would offer him a salary to come and teach me how to live. Sometimes he gave a random sigh, of which the essence was: "Give me even such a bare old barrack as *this,* and I'd do something with it!" When I wanted to use him he came alone; which was an illustration of the superior courage of women. His wife could bear her solitary second floor, and she was in general more discreet; showing by various small reserves that she was alive to the propriety of keeping our relations markedly professional—not letting them slide into sociability. She wished it to remain clear that she and the Major were employed, not cultivated, and if she approved of me as a superior, who could be kept in his place, she never thought me quite good enough for an equal.

She sat with great intensity, giving the whole of her mind to it, and was capable of remaining for an hour almost as motionless as if she were before a photographer's lens. I could see she had been photographed often, but somehow the very habit that made her good for that purpose unfitted her for mine. At first I was extremely pleased with her lady-like air, and it was a satisfaction, on coming to follow her lines, to see how good they were and how far they could lead the pencil. But after a few times I began to find her too insurmountably stiff; do what I would with it my drawing looked like a photograph or a copy of a photograph. Her figure had no variety of expression—she herself had no sense of variety. You may say that this was my business, was only a question of placing her. I placed her in every conceivable position, but she managed to obliterate their differences. She was always a lady certainly, and into the bargain was always the same lady. She was the real thing, but always the same thing. There were moments when I was oppressed by the serenity of her confidence that she *was* the real thing. All her dealings with me and all her husband's were an implication that this was lucky for *me*. Meanwhile I found myself trying to invent types that approached her own, instead of making her own transform itself—in the clever way that was not impossible, for instance, to poor Miss Churm. Arrange as I would and take the precautions I would, she always, in my pictures, came out too tall—landing me in the dilemma of having represented a fascinating woman as seven feet high, which, out of respect perhaps to my own very much scantier inches, was far from my idea of such a personage.

The case was worse with the Major—nothing I could do would keep *him* down, so that he became useful only for the representation of brawny giants. I adored variety and range, I cherished human accidents, the illustrative note; I wanted to characterise closely, and the thing in the world I most hated was the danger of being ridden by a type. I had quarrelled with some of my friends about it—I had parted company with them for maintaining that one *had* to be, and that if the type was beautiful (witness Raphael and Leonardo), the servitude was only a gain. I was neither Leonardo nor Raphael; I might only be a presumptuous young modern searcher, but I held that everything was to be sacrificed sooner than character. When they averred that the haunting type in question could easily *be* character, I retorted, perhaps superficially: "Whose?" It couldn't be everybody's—it might end in being nobody's.

After I had drawn Mrs. Monarch a dozen times I perceived more clearly than before that the value of such a model as Miss Churm resided precisely in the fact that she had no positive stamp, combined of course with the other fact that what she did have was a curious and inexplicable talent for imitation. Her usual appearance was like a curtain which she could draw up at request for a capital performance. This performance was simply suggestive; but it was a word to the wise—it was vivid and pretty. Sometimes, even, I thought it, though she was plain herself, too insipidly pretty; I made it a reproach to her that the figures drawn from her were monotonously (*bêtement,* as we used to say) graceful. Nothing made her more angry: it was so much her pride to feel that she could sit for characters that had nothing in common with each other. She would accuse me at such moments of taking away her "reputytion."

It suffered a certain shrinkage, this queer quantity, from the repeated visits of my new friends. Miss Churm was greatly in demand, never in want of employment, so I had no scruple in putting her off occasionally, to try them more at my ease. It was certainly amusing at first to do the real thing—it was amusing to do Major Monarch's trousers. They *were* the real thing, even if he did come out colossal. It was amusing to do his wife's back hair (it was so mathematically neat) and the particular "smart" tension of her tight stays. She lent herself especially to positions in which the face was somewhat averted or blurred; she abounded in lady-like back views and *profits perdus.* When she stood erect she took naturally one of the attitudes in which court-painters represent queens and princesses; so that I found myself wondering whether, to draw out this accomplishment, I couldn't get the editor of the *Cheapside* to publish a really royal romance, "A Tale of Buckingham Palace." Sometimes, however, the real thing and the make-believe came into contact; by which I mean that Miss Churm, keeping an appointment or coming to make one on days when I had much work in hand, encountered her invidious rivals. The encounter was not on their part, for they noticed her no more than if she had been the housemaid; not from intentional loftiness, but simply because, as yet, professionally, they didn't know how to fraternise, as I could guess that they would have liked—or at least that the Major would. They couldn't talk about the omnibus—they always walked; and they didn't know what else to try—she wasn't interested in good trains or cheap claret. Besides, they must have felt—in the air—that she was amused at them, secretly derisive of their ever knowing how. She was not a person to conceal her scepticism if she had had a chance to show it. On the other hand Mrs. Monarch didn't think her tidy; for why else did she take pains to say to me (it was going out of the way, for Mrs. Monarch), that she didn't like dirty women? One day when my young lady happened to be present with my other sitters (she even dropped in, when it was convenient, for a chat), I asked her to be so good as to lend a hand in getting tea—a service with which she was familiar and which was one of a class that, living as I did in a small way, with slender domestic resources, I often appealed to my models to render. They liked to lay hands on my property, to break the sitting, and sometimes the china—I made them feel Bohemian. The next time I saw Miss Churm after this incident she surprised me greatly by making a scene about it—she accused me of having wished to humiliate her. She had not resented the outrage at the time, but had seemed obliging and amused, enjoying the comedy of asking Mrs. Monarch, who sat vague and silent, whether she would have cream and sugar, and putting an exaggerated simper into the question. She had tried intonations—as if she too wished to pass for the real thing; till I was afraid my other visitors would take offence.

Oh, *they* were determined not to do this; and their touching patience was the measure of their great need. They would sit by the hour, uncomplaining, till I was ready to use them; they would come back on the chance of being wanted and would walk away cheerfully if they were not. I used to go to the door with them to see in what magnificent order they retreated. I tried to find other employment for them—I introduced them to several artists. But they didn't "take," for reasons I could appreciate, and I became conscious, rather anxiously, that after such disappointments they fell back upon me with a heavier weight. They did me the honour to think that it was I who was most *their* form. They were not picturesque enough for the painters, and in those days there were not so many serious workers in black and white. Besides, they had an eye to the great job I had mentioned to them—they had secretly set their hearts on supplying the right essence for my pictorial vindication of our fine novelist. They knew that for this undertaking I should want no costume-effects, none of the frippery of past ages—that it was a case in which everything would be contemporary and satirical and, presumably, genteel. If I could work them into it their future would be assured, for the labour would of course be long and the occupation steady.

One day Mrs. Monarch came without her husband—she explained his absence by his having had to go to the City. While she sat there in her usual anxious stiffness there came, at the door, a knock which I immediately recognised as the subdued appeal of a model out of work. It was followed by the entrance of a young man whom I easily perceived to be a foreigner and who proved in fact an Italian acquainted with no English word but my name, which he uttered in a way that made it seem to include all others. I had not then visited his country, nor was I proficient in his tongue; but as he was not so meanly constituted—what Italian is?—as to depend only on that member for expression he conveyed to me, in familiar but graceful mimicry, that he was in search of exactly the employment in which the lady before me was engaged. I was not struck with him at first, and while I continued to draw I emitted rough sounds of discouragement and dismissal. He stood his ground, however, not importunately, but with a dumb, dog-like fidelity in his eyes which amounted to innocent impudence—the manner of a devoted servant (he might have been in the house for years), unjustly suspected. Suddenly I saw that this very attitude and expression made a picture, whereupon I told him to sit down and wait till I should be free. There was another picture in the way he obeyed me, and I observed as I worked that there were others still in the way he looked wonderingly, with his head thrown back, about the high studio. He might have been crossing himself in St. Peter's. Before I finished I said to myself: "The fellow's a bankrupt orange-monger, but he's a treasure."

When Mrs. Monarch withdrew he passed across the room like a flash to open the door for her, standing there with the rapt, pure gaze of the young Dante spellbound by the young Beatrice. As I never insisted, in such situations, on the blankness of the British domestic, I reflected that he had the making of a servant (and I needed one, but couldn't pay him to be only that), as well as of a model; in short I made up my mind to adopt my bright adventurer if he would agree to officiate in the double capacity. He jumped at my offer, and in the event my rashness (for I had known nothing about him), was not brought home to me. He proved a sympathetic though a desultory ministrant, and had in a wonderful degree the *sentiment de la pose*. It was uncultivated, instinctive; a part of the happy instinct which had guided him to my door and helped him to spell out my name on the card nailed to it. He had had no other introduction to me than a guess, from the shape of my high north window, seen outside, that my place was a studio and that as a studio it would contain an artist. He had wandered to England in search of fortune, like other itinerants, and had embarked, with a partner and a small green handcart, on the sale of penny ices. The ices had melted away and the partner had dissolved in their train. My young man wore tight yellow trousers with reddish stripes and his name was Oronte. He was sallow but fair, and when I put him into some old clothes of my own he looked like an Englishman. He was as good as Miss Churm, who could look, when required, like an Italian.

IV.

I THOUGHT Mrs. Monarch's face slightly convulsed when, on her coming back with her husband, she found Oronte installed. It was strange to have to recognise in a scrap of a lazzarone a competitor to her magnificent Major. It was she who scented danger first, for the Major was anecdotically unconscious. But Oronte gave us tea, with a hundred eager confusions (he had never seen such a queer process), and I think she thought better of me for having at last an "establishment." They saw a couple of drawings that I had made of the establishment, and Mrs. Monarch hinted that it never would have struck her that he had sat for them. "Now the drawings you make from *us,* they look exactly like us," she reminded me, smiling in triumph; and I recognised that this was indeed just their defect. When I drew the Monarchs I couldn't, somehow, get away from them—get into the character I wanted to represent; and I had not the least desire my model should be discoverable in my picture. Miss Churm never was, and Mrs. Monarch thought I hid her, very properly, because she was vulgar; whereas if she was lost it was only as the dead who go to heaven are lost—in the gain of an angel the more.

By this time I had got a certain start with "Rutland Ramsay," the first novel in the great projected series; that is I had produced a dozen drawings, several with the help of the Major and his wife, and I had sent them in for approval. My understanding with the publishers, as I have already hinted, had been that I was to be left to do my work, in this particular case, as I liked, with the whole book committed to me; but my connection with the rest of the series was only contingent. There were moments when, frankly, it *was* a comfort to have the real thing under one's hand; for there were characters in "Rutland Ramsay "that were very much like it. There were people presumably as straight as the Major and women of as good a fashion as Mrs. Monarch. There was a great deal of country-house life—treated, it is true, in a fine, fanciful, ironical, generalised way—and there was a considerable implication of knickerbockers and kilts. There were certain things I had to settle at the outset; such things for instance as the exact appearance of the hero, the particular bloom of the heroine. The author of course gave me a lead, but there was a margin for interpretation. I took the Monarchs into my confidence, I told them frankly what I was about, I mentioned my embarrassments and alternatives. "Oh, take *him!*" Mrs. Monarch murmured sweetly, looking at her husband; and "What could you want better than my wife? "the Major inquired, with the comfortable candour that now prevailed between us.

I was not obliged to answer these remarks—I was only obliged to place my sitters. I was not easy in mind, and I postponed, a little timidly perhaps, the solution of the question. The book was a large canvas, the other figures were numerous, and I worked off at first some of the episodes in which the hero and the heroine were not concerned. When once I had set *them* up I should have to stick to them—I couldn't make my young man seven feet high in one place and five feet nine in another. I inclined on the whole to the latter measurement, though the Major more than once reminded me that *he* looked about as young as anyone. It was indeed quite possible to arrange him, for the figure, so that it would have been difficult to detect his age. After the spontaneous Oronte had been with me a month, and after I had given him to understand several different times that his native exuberance would presently constitute an insurmountable barrier to our further intercourse, I waked to a sense of his heroic capacity. He was only five feet seven, but the remaining inches were latent. I tried him almost secretly at first, for I was really rather afraid of the judgment my other models would pass on such a choice. If they regarded Miss Churm as little better than a snare, what would they think of the representation by a person so little the real thing as an Italian street-vendor of a protagonist formed by a public school?

If I went a little in fear of them it was not because they bullied me, because they had got an oppressive foothold, but because in their really pathetic decorum and mysteriously permanent newness they counted on me so intensely. I was therefore very glad when Jack Hawley came home: he was always of such good counsel. He painted badly himself, but there was no one like him for putting his finger on the place. He had been absent from England for a year; he had been somewhere—I don't remember where—to get a fresh eye. I was in a good deal of dread of any such organ, but we were old friends; he had been away for months and a sense of emptiness was creeping into my life. I hadn't dodged a missile for a year.

He came back with a fresh eye, but with the same old black velvet blouse, and the first evening he spent in my studio we smoked cigarettes till the small hours. He had done no work himself, he had only got the eye; so the field was clear for the production of my little things. He wanted to see what I had done for the *Cheapside,* but he was disappointed in the exhibition. That at least seemed the meaning of two or three comprehensive groans which, as he lounged on my big divan, on a folded leg, looking at my latest drawings, issued from his lips with the smoke of the cigarette.

"What's the matter with you?" I asked.

"What's the matter with *you?*"

"Nothing save that I'm mystified."

"You are indeed. You're quite off the hinge. What's the meaning of this new fad?" And he tossed me, with visible irreverence, a drawing in which I happened to have depicted both my majestic models. I asked if he didn't think it good, and he replied that it struck him as execrable, given the sort of thing I had always represented myself to him as wishing to arrive at; but I let that pass, I was so anxious to see exactly what he meant. The two figures in the picture looked colossal, but I supposed this was *not* what he meant, inasmuch as, for aught he knew to the contrary, I might have been trying for that. I maintained that I was working exactly in the same way as when he last had done me the honour to commend me. "Well, there's a big hole somewhere," he answered; "wait a bit and I'll discover it." I depended upon him to do so: where else was the fresh eye? But he produced at last nothing more luminous than "I don't know—I don't like your types." This was lame, for a critic who had never consented to discuss with me anything but the question of execution, the direction of strokes and the mystery of values.

"In the drawings you've been looking at I think my types are very handsome."

"Oh, they won't do! "

"I've had a couple of new models."

"I see you have. *They* won't do."

"Are you very sure of that?"

"Absolutely—they're stupid."

"You mean *I* am—for I ought to get round that."

"You *can't*—with such people. Who are they?"

I told him, as far as was necessary, and he declared, heartlessly: "*Ce sont des gens qu'il faut mettre à la porte.*"

"You've never seen them; they're awfully good," I compassionately objected.

"Not seen them? Why, all this recent work of yours drops to pieces with them. It's all I want to see of them."

"No one else has said anything against it—the *Cheapside* people are pleased."

"Everyone else is an ass, and the *Cheapside* people the biggest asses of all. Come, don't pretend, at this time of day, to have pretty illusions about the public, especially about publishers and editors. It's not for *such* animals you work—it's for those who know, *coloro che sanno;* so keep straight for *me* if you can't keep straight for yourself. There's a certain sort of thing you tried for from the first—and a very good thing it is. But this twaddle isn't *in* it." When I talked with Hawley later about "Rutland Ramsay "and its possible successors he declared that I must get back into my boat again or I would go to the bottom. His voice in short was the voice of warning. I noted the warning, but I didn't turn my friends out of doors. They bored me a good deal; but the very fact that they bored me admonished me not to sacrifice them—if there was anything to be done with them—simply to irritation. As I look back at this phase they seem to me to have pervaded my life not a little. I have a vision of them as most of the time in my studio, seated, against the wall, on an old velvet bench to be out of the way, and looking like a pair of patient courtiers in a royal ante-chamber. I am convinced that during the coldest weeks of the winter they held their ground because it saved them fire. Their newness was losing its gloss, and it was impossible not to feel that they were objects of charity. Whenever Miss Churm arrived they went away, and after I was fairly launched in "Rutland Ramsay" Miss Churm arrived pretty often. They managed to express to me tacitly that they supposed I wanted her for the low life of the book, and I let them suppose it, since they had attempted to study the work—it was lying about the studio—without discovering that it dealt only with the highest circles. They had dipped into the most brilliant of our novelists without deciphering many passages. I still took an hour from them, now and again, in spite of Jack Hawley's warning: it would be time enough to dismiss them, if dismissal should be necessary, when the rigour of the season was over. Hawley had made their acquaintance—he had met them at my fireside—and thought them a ridiculous pair. Learning that he was a painter they tried to approach him, to show him too that they were the real thing; but he looked at them, across the big room, as if they were miles away: they were a compendium of everything that he most objected to in the social system of his country. Such people as that, all convention and patent-leather, with ejaculations that stopped conversation, had no business in a studio. A studio was a place to learn to see, and how could you see through a pair of feather beds?

The main inconvenience I suffered at their hands was that, at first, I was shy of letting them discover how my artful little servant had begun to sit to me for "Rutland Ramsay." They knew that I had been odd enough (they were prepared by this time to allow oddity to artists,) to pick a foreign vagabond out of the streets, when I might have had a person with whiskers and credentials; but it was some time before they learned how high I rated his accomplishments. They found him in an attitude more than once, but they never doubted I was doing him as an organ-grinder. There were several things they never guessed, and one of them was that for a striking scene in the novel, in which a footman briefly figured, it occurred to me to make use of Major Monarch as the menial. I kept putting this off, I didn't like to ask him to don the livery—besides the difficulty of finding a livery to fit him. At last, one day late in the winter, when I was at work on the despised Oronte (he caught one's idea in an instant), and was in the glow of feeling that I was going very straight, they came in, the Major and his wife, with their society laugh about nothing (there was less and less to laugh at), like country-callers—they always reminded me of that—who have walked across the park after church and are presently persuaded to stay to luncheon. Luncheon was over, but they could stay to tea—I knew they wanted it. The fit was on me, however, and I couldn't let my ardour cool and my work wait, with the fading daylight, while my model prepared it. So I asked Mrs. Monarch if she would mind laying it out—a request which, for an instant, brought all the blood to her face. Her eyes were on her husband's for a second, and some mute telegraphy passed between them. Their folly was over the next instant; his cheerful shrewdness put an end to it. So far from pitying their wounded pride, I must add, I was moved to give it as complete a lesson as I could. They bustled about together and got out the cups and saucers and made the kettle boil. I know they felt as if they were waiting on my servant, and when the tea was prepared I said: "He'll have a cup, please— he's tired." Mrs. Monarch brought him one where he stood, and he took it from her as if he had been a gentleman at a party, squeezing a crush-hat with an elbow.

Then it came over me that she had made a great effort for me— made it with a kind of nobleness—and that I owed her a compensation. Each time I saw her after this I wondered what the compensation could be. I couldn't go on doing the wrong thing to oblige them. Oh, it *was* the wrong thing, the stamp of the work for which they sat—Hawley was not the only person to say it now. I sent in a large number of the drawings I had made for "Rutland Ramsay," and I received a warning that was more to the point than Hawley's. The artistic adviser of the house for which I was working was of opinion that many of my illustrations were not what had been looked for. Most of these illustrations were the subjects in which the Monarchs had figured. Without going into the question of what *had* been looked for, I saw at this rate I shouldn't get the other books to do. I hurled myself in despair upon Miss Churm, I put her through all her paces. I not only adopted Oronte publicly as my hero, but one morning when the Major looked in to see if I didn't require him to finish a figure for the *Cheapside,* for which he had begun to sit the week before, I told him that I had changed my mind—I would do the drawing from my man. At this my visitor turned pale and stood looking at me. "Is *he* your idea of an English gentleman?" he asked.

I was disappointed, I was nervous, I wanted to get on with my work; so I replied with irritation: "Oh, my dear Major—I can't be ruined for *you!*"

He stood another moment; then, without a word, he quitted the studio. I drew a long breath when he was gone, for I said to myself that I shouldn't see him again. I had not told him definitely that I was in danger of having my work rejected, but I was vexed at his not having felt the catastrophe in the air, read with me the moral of our fruitless collaboration, the lesson that, in the deceptive atmosphere of art, even the highest respectability may fail of being plastic.

I didn't owe my friends money, but I did see them again. They re-appeared together, three days later, and under the circumstances there was something tragic in the fact. It was a proof to me that they could find nothing else in life to do. They had threshed the matter out in a dismal conference—they had digested the bad news that they were not in for the series. If they were not useful to me even for the *Cheapside* their function seemed difficult to determine, and I could only judge at first that they had come, forgivingly, decorously, to take a last leave. This made me rejoice in secret that I had little leisure for a scene; for I had placed both my other models in position together and I was pegging away at a drawing from which I hoped to derive glory. It had been suggested by the passage in which Rutland Ramsay, drawing up a chair to Artemisia's piano-stool, says extraordinary things to her while she ostensibly fingers out a difficult piece of music. I had done Miss Churm at the piano before—it was an attitude in which she knew how to take on an absolutely poetic grace. I wished the two figures to "compose" together, intensely, and my little Italian had entered perfectly into my conception. The pair were vividly before me, the piano had been pulled out; it was a charming picture of blended youth and murmured love, which I had only to catch and keep. My visitors stood and looked at it, and I was friendly to them over my shoulder.

They made no response, but I was used to silent company and went on with my work, only a little disconcerted (even though exhilarated by the sense that *this* was at least the ideal thing), at not having got rid of them after all. Presently I heard Mrs. Monarch's sweet voice beside, or rather above me: "I wish her hair was a little better done." I looked up and she was staring with a strange fixedness at Miss Churm, whose back was turned to her. "Do you mind my just touching it?" she went on—a question which made me spring up for an instant, as with the instinctive fear that she might do the young lady a harm. But she quieted me with a glance I shall never forget—I confess I should like to have been able to paint *that*—and went for a moment to my model. She spoke to her softly, laying a hand upon her shoulder and bending over her; and as the girl, understanding, gratefully assented, she disposed her rough curls, with a few quick passes, in such a way as to make Miss Churm's head twice as charming. It was one of the most heroic personal services I have ever seen rendered. Then Mrs. Monarch turned away with a low sigh and, looking about her as if for something to do, stooped to the floor with a noble humility and picked up a dirty rag that had dropped out of my paint-box.

The Major meanwhile had also been looking for something to do and, wandering to the other end of the studio, saw before him my breakfast things, neglected, unremoved. "I say, can't I be useful *here?*" he called out to me with an irrepressible quaver. I assented with a laugh that I fear was awkward and for the next ten minutes, while I worked, I heard the light clatter of china and the tinkle of spoons and glass. Mrs. Monarch assisted her husband—they washed up my crockery, they put it away. They wandered off into my little scullery, and I afterwards found that they had cleaned my knives and that my slender stock of plate had an unprecedented surface. When it came over me, the latent eloquence of what they were doing, I confess that my drawing was blurred for a moment—the picture swam. They had accepted their failure, but they couldn't accept their fate. They had bowed their heads in bewilderment to the perverse and cruel law in virtue of which the real thing could be so much less precious than the unreal; but they didn't want to starve. If my servants were my models, my models might be my servants. They would reverse the parts—the others would sit for the ladies and gentlemen, and *they* would do the work. They would still be in the studio—it was an intense dumb appeal to me not to turn them out. "Take us on," they wanted to say—"we'll do *anything.*"

When all this hung before me the *afflatus* vanished—my pencil dropped from my hand. My sitting was spoiled and I got rid of my sitters, who were also evidently rather mystified and awestruck. Then, alone with the Major and his wife, I had a most uncomfortable moment. He put their prayer into a single sentence: "I say, you know—just let *us* do for you, can't you?" I couldn't—it was dreadful to see them emptying my slops; but I pretended I could, to oblige them, for about a week. Then I gave them a sum of money to go away; and I never saw them again. I obtained the remaining books, but my friend Hawley repeats that Major and Mrs. Monarch did me a permanent harm, got me into a second-rate trick. If it be true I am content to have paid the price—for the memory.

THE MIDDLE YEARS

THE APRIL DAY was soft and bright, and poor Dencombe, happy in the conceit of reasserted strength, stood in the garden of the hotel, comparing, with a deliberation in which, however, there was still something of languor, the attractions of easy strolls. He liked the feeling of the south, so far as you could have it in the north, he liked the sandy cliffs and the clustered pines, he liked even the colourless sea. "Bournemouth as a health-resort" had sounded like a mere advertisement, but now he was reconciled to the prosaic. The sociable country postman, passing through the garden, had just given him a small parcel, which he took out with him, leaving the hotel to the right and creeping to a convenient bench that he knew of, a safe recess in the cliff. It looked to the south, to the tinted walls of the Island, and was protected behind by the sloping shoulder of the down. He was tired enough when he reached it, and for a moment he was disappointed; he was better, of course, but better, after all, than what? He should never again, as at one or two great moments of the past, be better than himself. The infinite of life had gone, and what was left of the dose was a small glass engraved like a thermometer by the apothecary. He sat and stared at the sea, which appeared all surface and twinkle, far shallower than the spirit of man. It was the abyss of human illusion that was the real, the tideless deep. He held his packet, which had come by book-post, unopened on his knee, liking, in the lapse of so many joys (his illness had made him feel his age), to know that it was there, but taking for granted there could be no complete renewal of the pleasure, dear to young experience, of seeing one's self "just out." Dencombe, who had a reputation, had come out too often and knew too well in advance how he should look.

His postponement associated itself vaguely, after a little, with a group of three persons, two ladies and a young man, whom, beneath him, straggling and seemingly silent, he could see move slowly together along the sands. The gentleman had his head bent over a book and was occasionally brought to a stop by the charm of this volume, which, as Dencombe could perceive even at a distance, had a cover alluringly red. Then his companions, going a little further, waited for him to come up, poking their parasols into the beach, looking around them at the sea and sky and clearly sensible of the beauty of the day. To these things the young man with the book was still more clearly indifferent; lingering, credulous, absorbed, he was an object of envy to an observer from whose connection with literature all such artlessness had faded. One of the ladies was large and mature; the other had the spareness of comparative youth and of a social situation possibly inferior. The large lady carried back Dencombe's imagination to the age of crinoline; she wore a hat of the shape of a mushroom, decorated with a blue veil, and had the air, in her aggressive amplitude, of clinging to a vanished fashion or even a lost cause. Presently her companion produced from under the folds of a mantle a limp, portable chair which she stiffened out and of which the large lady took possession. This act, and something in the movement of either party, instantly characterised the performers—they performed for Dencombe's recreation—as opulent matron and humble dependant. What, moreover, was the use of being an approved novelist if one couldn't establish a relation between such figures; the clever theory, for instance, that the young man was the son of the opulent matron, and that the humble dependant, the daughter of a clergyman or an officer, nourished a secret passion for him? Was that not visible from the way she stole behind her protectress to look back at him?—back to where he had let himself come to a full stop when his mother sat down to rest. His book was a novel; it had the catchpenny cover, and while the romance of life stood neglected at his side he lost himself in that of the circulating library. He moved mechanically to where the sand was softer, and ended by plumping down in it to finish his chapter at his ease. The humble dependant, discouraged by his remoteness, wandered, with a martyred droop of the head, in another direction, and the exorbitant lady, watching the waves, offered a confused resemblance to a flying-machine that had broken down.

When his drama began to fail Dencombe remembered that he had, after all, another pastime. Though such promptitude on the part of the publisher was rare, he was already able to draw from its wrapper his "latest," perhaps his last. The cover of "The Middle Years" was duly meretricious, the smell of the fresh pages the very odour of sanctity; but for the moment he went no further—he had become conscious of a strange alienation. He had forgotten what his book was about. Had the assault of his old ailment, which he had so fallaciously come to Bournemouth to ward off, interposed utter blankness as to what had preceded it? He had finished the revision of proof before quitting London, but his subsequent fortnight in bed had passed the sponge over colour. He couldn't have chanted to himself a single sentence, couldn't have turned with curiosity or confidence to any particular page. His subject had already gone from him, leaving scarcely a superstition behind. He uttered a low moan as he breathed the chill of this dark void, so desperately it seemed to represent the completion of a sinister process. The tears filled his mild eyes; something precious had passed away. This was the pang that had been sharpest during the last few years—the sense of ebbing time, of shrinking opportunity; and now he felt not so much that his last chance was going as that it was gone indeed. He had done all that he should ever do, and yet he had not done what he wanted. This was the laceration—that practically his career was over: it was as violent as a rough hand at his throat. He rose from his seat nervously, like a creature hunted by a dread; then he fell back in his weakness and nervously opened his book. It was a single volume; he preferred single volumes and aimed at a rare compression. He began to read, and little by little, in this occupation, he was pacified and reassured. Everything came back to him, but came back with a wonder, came back, above all, with a high and magnificent beauty. He read his own prose, he turned his own leaves, and had, as. he sat there with the spring sunshine on the page, an emotion peculiar and intense. His career was over, no doubt, but it was over, after all, with *that*.

He had forgotten during his illness the work of the previous year; but what he had chiefly forgotten was that it was extraordinarily good. He lived once more into his story and was drawn down, as by a siren's hand, to where, in the dim underworld of fiction, the great glazed tank of art, strange silent subjects float. He recognised his motive and surrendered to his talent. Never, probably, had that talent, such as it was, been so fine. His difficulties were still there, but what was also there, to his perception, though probably, alas! to nobody's else, was the art that in most cases had surmounted them. In his surprised enjoyment of this ability he had a glimpse of a possible reprieve. Surely its force was not spent—there was life and service in it yet. It had not come to him easily, it had been backward and roundabout. It was the child of time, the nursling of delay; he had struggled and suffered for it, making sacrifices not to be counted, and now that it was really mature was it to cease to yield, to confess itself brutally beaten? There was an infinite charm for Dencombe in feeling as he had never felt before that diligence *vincit omnia*. The result produced in his little book was somehow a result beyond his conscious intention: it was as if he had planted his genius, had trusted his method, and they had grown up and flowered with this sweetness. If the achievement had been real, however, the process had been manful enough. What he saw so intensely to-day, what he felt as a nail driven in, was that only now, at the very last, had he come into possession. His development had been abnormally slow, almost grotesquely gradual. He had been hindered and retarded by experience, and for long periods had only groped his way. It had taken too much of his life to produce too little of his art. The art had come, but it had come after everything else. As such a rate a first existence was too short—long enough only to collect material; so that to fructify, to use the material, one must have a second age, an extension. This extension was what poor Dencombe sighed for. As he turned the last leaves of his volume he murmured: "Ah for another go!—ah for a better chance!"

The three persons he had observed on the sands had vanished and then reappeared; they had now wandered up a path, an artificial and easy ascent, which led to the top of the cliff. Dencombe's bench was half-way down, on a sheltered ledge, and the large lady, a massive, heterogeneous person, with bold black eyes and kind red cheeks, now took a few moments to rest. She wore dirty gauntlets and immense diamond ear-rings; at first she looked vulgar, but she contradicted this announcement in an agreeable off-hand tone. While her companions stood waiting for her she spread her skirts on the end of Dencombe's seat. The young man had gold spectacles, through which, with his finger still in his red-covered book, he glanced at the volume, bound in the same shade of the same colour, lying on the lap of the original occupant of the bench. After

an instant Dencombe understood that he was struck with a resemblance, had recognised the gilt stamp on the crimson cloth, was
reading "The Middle Years," and now perceived that somebody
else had kept pace with him. The stranger was startled, possibly
even a little ruffled, to find that he was not the only person who
had been favoured with an early copy. The eyes of the two propri-
etors met for a moment, and Dencombe borrowed amusement
from the expression of those of his competitor, those, it might even
be inferred, of his admirer. They confessed to some resentment—
they seemed to say: "Hang it, has he got it *already*?—Of course he's
a brute of a reviewer!" Dencombe shuffled his copy out of sight
while the opulent matron, rising from her repose, broke out: "I feel
already the good of this air!"

"I can't say I do," said the angular lady. "I find myself quite let
down."

"I find myself horribly hungry. At what time did you order
lunch?" her protectress pursued.

The young person put the question by. "Doctor Hugh always
orders it."

"I ordered nothing to-day I'm going to make you diet," said
their comrade.

"Then I shall go home and sleep. *Qui dort dine!*"

"Can I trust you to Miss Vernham?" asked Doctor Hugh of his
elder companion.

"Don't I trust *you*?" she archly inquired.

"Not too much!" Miss Vernham, with her eyes on the ground,
permitted herself to declare. "You must come with us at least to the
house," she went on, while the personage on whom they appeared
to be in attendance began to mount higher. She had got a little out
of ear-shot; nevertheless Miss Vernham became, so far as Dencombe
was concerned, less distinctly audible to murmur to the young man:
"I don't think you realise all you owe the Countess!"

Absently, a moment, Doctor Hugh caused his gold-rimmed
spectacles to shine at her.

"Is that the way I strike you? I see—I see!"

"She's awfully good to us," continued Miss Vernham, compelled
by her interlocutor's immovability to stand there in spite of his
discussion of private matters. Of what use would it have been that
Dencombe should be sensitive to shades had he not declared in that
immovability a strange influence from the quiet old convalescent in

the great tweed cape? Miss Vernham appeared suddenly to become aware of some such connection, for she added in a moment: "If you want to sun yourself here you can come back after you've seen us home."

Doctor Hugh, at this, hesitated, and Dencombe, in spite of a desire to pass for unconscious, risked a covert glance at him. What his eyes met this time, as it happened, was on the part of the young lady a queer stare, naturally vitreous, which made her aspect remind him of some figure (he couldn't name it) in a play or a novel, some sinister governess or tragic old maid. She seemed to scrutinise him, to challenge him, to say, from general spite: "What have you got to do with us?" At the same instant the rich humour of the Countess reached them from above: "Come, come, my little lambs, you should follow your old *bergère*!" Miss Vernham turned away at this, pursuing the ascent, and Doctor Hugh, after another mute appeal to Dencombe and a moment's evident demur, deposited his book on the bench, as if to keep his place or even as a sign that he would return, and bounded without difficulty up the rougher part of the cliff.

Equally innocent and infinite are the pleasures of observation and the resources engendered by the habit of analysing life. It amused poor Dencombe, as he dawdled in his tepid air-bath, to think that he was waiting for a revelation of something at the back of a fine young mind. He looked hard at the book on the end of the bench, but he wouldn't have touched it for the world. It served his purpose to have a theory which should not be exposed to refutation. He already felt better of his melancholy; he had, according to his old formula, put his head at the window. A passing Countess could draw off the fancy when, like the elder of the ladies who had just retreated, she was as obvious as the giantess of a caravan. It was indeed general views that were terrible; short ones, contrary to an opinion sometimes expressed, were the refuge, were the remedy. Doctor Hugh couldn't possibly be anything but a reviewer who had understandings for early copies with publishers or with newspapers. He reappeared in a quarter of an hour, with visible relief at finding Dencombe on the spot, and the gleam of white teeth in an embarrassed but generous smile. He was perceptibly disappointed at the eclipse of the other copy of the book; it was a pretext the less for speaking to the stranger. But he spoke notwithstanding; he held up his own copy and broke out pleadingly:

"*Do* say, if you have occasion to speak of it, that it's the best thing he has done yet!"

Dencombe responded with a laugh: "Done yet" was so amusing to him, made such a grand avenue of the future. Better still, the young man took *him* for a reviewer. He pulled out "The Middle Years" from under his cape, but instinctively concealed any tell-tale look of fatherhood. This was partly because a person was always a fool for calling attention to his work. "Is that what you're going to say yourself?" he inquired of his visitor.

"I'm not quite sure I shall write anything. I don't, as a regular thing—I enjoy in peace. But it's awfully fine."

Dencombe debated a moment. If his interlocutor had begun to abuse him he would have confessed on the spot to his identity, but there was no harm in drawing him on a little to praise. He drew him on with such success that in a few moments his new acquaintance, seated by his side, was confessing candidly that Dencombe's novels were the only ones he could read a second time. He had come the day before from London, where a friend of his, a journalist, had lent him his copy of the last—the copy sent to the office of the journal and already the subject of a "notice" which, as was pretended there (but one had to allow for "swagger") it had taken a full quarter of an hour to prepare. He intimated that he was ashamed for his friend, and in the case of a work demanding and repaying study, of such inferior manners; and, with his fresh appreciation and inexplicable wish to express it, he speedily became for poor Dencombe a remarkable, a delightful apparition. Chance had brought the weary man of letters face to face with the greatest admirer in the new generation whom it was supposable he possessed. The admirer, in truth, was mystifying, so rare a case was it to find a bristling young doctor—he looked like a German physiologist—enamoured of literary form. It was an accident, but happier than most accidents, so that Dencombe, exhilarated as well as confounded, spent half an hour in making his visitor talk while he kept himself quiet. He explained his premature possession of "The Middle Years" by an allusion to the friendship of the publisher, who, knowing he was at Bournemouth for his health, had paid him this graceful attention. He admitted that he had been ill, for Doctor Hugh would infallibly have guessed it; he even went so far as to wonder whether he mightn't look for some hygenic "tip" from a personage combining so bright an enthusiasm with a presumable knowledge of the remedies now in vogue. It would shake his faith a little perhaps to have to take a doctor seriously who could take *him* so seriously, but he enjoyed this gushing modern youth and he felt with an acute pang that there would still be work to do in a world in which such odd combinations were presented. It was not true, what he had tried for renunciation's sake to believe, that all the combinations were exhausted. They were not, they were not—they were infinite: the exhaustion was in the miserable artist.

Doctor Hugh was an ardent physiologist, saturated with the spirit of the age—in other words he had just taken his degree; but he was independent and various, he talked like a man who would have preferred to love literature best. He would fain have made fine phrases, but nature had denied him the trick. Some of the finest in "The Middle Years" had struck him inordinately, and he took the liberty of reading them to Dencombe in support of his plea. He grew vivid, in the balmy air, to his companion, for whose deep refreshment he seemed to have been sent; and was particularly ingenuous in describing how recently he had become acquainted, and how instantly infatuated, with the only man who had put flesh between the ribs of an art that was starving on superstitions. He had not yet written to him—he was deterred by a sentiment of respect. Dencombe at this moment felicitated himself more than ever on having never answered the photographers. His visitor's attitude promised him a luxury of intercourse, but he surmised that a certain security in it, for Doctor Hugh, would depend not a little on the Countess. He learned without delay with what variety of Countess they were concerned, as well as the nature of the tie that united the curious trio. The large lady, an Englishwoman by birth and the daughter of a celebrated baritone, whose taste, without his talent, she had inherited, was the widow of a French nobleman and mistress of all that remained of the handsome fortune, the fruit of her father's earnings, that had constituted her dower. Miss Vernham, an odd creature but an accomplished pianist, was attached to her person at a salary. The Countess was generous, independent, eccentric; she travelled with her minstrel and her medical man. Ignorant and passionate, she had nevertheless moments in which she was almost irresistible. Dencombe saw her sit for her portrait in Doctor Hugh's free sketch, and felt the picture of his young friend's relation to her frame itself in his mind. This young friend, for a representative of the new psychology, was himself easily hypnotised, and if he became abnormally communicative it was only a sign of his real subjection. Dencombe did accordingly what he wanted with him, even without being known as Dencombe.

Taken ill on a journey in Switzerland the Countess had picked him up at an hotel, and the accident of his happening to please her had made her offer him, with her imperious liberality, terms that couldn't fail to dazzle a practitioner without patients and whose resources had been drained dry by his studies. It was not the way he would have elected to spend his time, but it was time that would pass quickly, and meanwhile she was wonderfully kind. She exacted perpetual attention, but it was impossible not to like her. He gave details about his queer patient, a "type" if there ever was one, who had in connection with her flushed obesity and in addition to the morbid strain of a violent and aimless will a grave organic disorder; but he came back to his loved novelist, whom he was so good as to pronounce more essentially a poet than many of those who went in for verse, with a zeal excited, as all his indiscretion had been excited, by the happy chance of Dencombe's sympathy and the coincidence of their occupation. Dencombe had confessed to a slight personal acquaintance with the author of "The Middle Years," but had not felt himself as ready as he could have wished when his companion, who had never yet encountered a being so privileged, began to be eager for particulars. He even thought that Doctor Hugh's eye at that moment emitted a glimmer of suspicion. But the young man was too inflamed to be shrewd and repeatedly caught up the book to exclaim: "Did you notice this?" or "Weren't you immensely struck with that?" "There's a beautiful passage toward the end," he broke out; and again he laid his hand upon the volume. As he turned the pages he came upon something else, while Dencombe saw him suddenly change colour. He had taken up, as it lay on the bench, Dencombe's copy instead of his own, and his neighbour immediately guessed the reason of his start. Doctor Hugh looked grave an instant; then he said: "I see you've been altering the text!" Dencombe was a passionate corrector, a fingerer of style; the last thing he ever arrived at was a form final for himself. His ideal would have been to publish secretly, and then, on the published text, treat himself to the terrified revise, sacrificing always a first edition and beginning for posterity and even for the collectors, poor dears, with a second. This morning, in "The Middle Years," his pencil had pricked a dozen lights. He was amused at the effect of the young man's reproach; for an instant it made him change colour. He stammered, at any rate, ambiguously; then, through a blur of ebbing consciousness, saw Doctor Hugh's mystified eyes. He only had time to feel he was about to be ill again—that emotion, excitement, fatigue, the heat of the sun, the solicitation of the air, had combined to play him a trick, before, stretching out a hand to his visitor with a plaintive cry, he lost his senses altogether.

Later he knew that he had fainted and that Doctor Hugh had got him home in a bath-chair, the conductor of which, prowling within hail for custom, had happened to remember seeing him in the garden of the hotel. He had recovered his perception in the transit, and had, in bed, that afternoon, a vague recollection of Doctor Hugh's young face, as they went together, bent over him in a comforting laugh and expressive of something more than a suspicion of his identity. That identity was ineffaceable now, and all the more that he was disappointed, disgusted. He had been rash, been stupid, had gone out too soon, stayed out too long. He oughtn't to have exposed himself to strangers, he ought to have taken his servant. He felt as if he had fallen into a hole too deep to descry any little patch of heaven. He was confused about the time that had elapsed—he pieced the fragments together. He had seen his doctor, the real one, the one who had treated him from the first and who had again been very kind. His servant was in and out on tiptoe, looking very wise after the fact. He said more than once something about the sharp young gentleman. The rest was vagueness, in so far as it wasn't despair. The vagueness, however, justified itself by dreams, dozing anxieties from which he finally emerged to the consciousness of a dark room and a shaded candle.

"You'll be all right again—I know all about you now," said a voice near him that he knew to be young. Then his meeting with Doctor Hugh came back. He was too discouraged to joke about it yet, but he was able to perceive, after a little, that the interest of it was intense for his visitor. "Of course I can't attend you professionally—you've got your own man, with whom I've talked and who's excellent," Doctor Hugh went on. "But you must let me come to see you as a good friend. I've just looked in before going to bed. You're doing beautifully, but it's a good job I was with you on the cliff. I shall come in early to-morrow. I want to do something for you. I want to do everything. You've done a tremendous lot for me." The young man held his hand, hanging over him, and poor Dencombe, weakly aware of this living pressure, simply lay there and accepted his devotion. He couldn't do anything less—he needed help too much.

The idea of the help he needed was very present to him that night, which he spent in a lucid stillness, an intensity of thought that constituted a reaction from his hours of stupor. He was lost, he was lost—he was lost if he couldn't be saved. He was not afraid of suffering, of death; he was not even in love with life; but he had had a deep demonstration of desire. It came over him in the long, quiet hours that only with "The Middle Years" had he taken his flight; only on that day, visited by soundless processions, had he recognised his kingdom. He had had a revelation of his range. What he dreaded was the idea that his reputation should stand on the unfinished. It was not with his past but with his future that it should properly be concerned. Illness and age rose before him like spectres with pitiless eyes: how was he to bribe such fates to give him the second chance? He had had the one chance that all men have—he had had the chance of life. He went to sleep again very late, and when he awoke Doctor Hugh was sitting by his head. There was already, by this time, something beautifully familiar in him.

"Don't think I've turned out your physician," he said; "I'm acting with his consent. He has been here and seen you. Somehow he seems to trust me. I told him how we happened to come together yesterday, and he recognises that I've a peculiar right."

Dencombe looked at him with a calculating earnestness. "How have you squared the Countess?"

The young man blushed a little, but he laughed. "Oh, never mind the Countess!"

"You told me she was very exacting."

Doctor Hugh was silent a moment. "So she is."

"And Miss Vernham's an *intrigante*."

"How do you know that?"

"I know everything. One *has* to, to write decently!"

"I think she's mad," said limpid Doctor Hugh.

"Well, don't quarrel with the Countess—she's a present help to you."

"I don't quarrel," Doctor Hugh replied. "But I don't get on with silly women." Presently he added: "You seem very much alone."

"That often happens at my age. I've outlived, I've lost by the way."

Doctor Hugh hesitated; then surmounting a soft scruple: "Whom have you lost?"

"Every one."

"Ah, no," the young man murmured, laying a hand on his arm.

"I once had a wife—I once had a son. My wife died when my child was born, and my boy, at school, was carried off by typhoid."

"I wish I'd been there!" said Doctor Hugh simply.

"Well—if you're here!" Dencombe answered, with a smile that, in spite of dimness, showed how much he liked to be sure of his companion's whereabouts.

"You talk strangely of your age. You're not old."

"Hypocrite—so early!"

"I speak physiologically."

"That's the way I've been speaking for the last five years, and it's exactly what I've been saying to myself. It isn't till we are old that we begin to tell ourselves we're not!"

"Yet I know I myself am young," Doctor Hugh declared.

"Not so well as I!" laughed his patient, whose visitor indeed would have established the truth in question by the honesty with which he changed the point of view, remarking that it must be one of the charms of age—at any rate in the case of high distinction—to feel that one has laboured and achieved. Doctor Hugh employed the common phrase about earning one's rest, and it made poor Dencombe, for an instant, almost angry. He recovered himself, however, to explain, lucidly enough, that if he, ungraciously, knew nothing of such a balm, it was doubtless because he had wasted inestimable years. He had followed literature from the first, but he had taken a lifetime to get alongside of her. Only to-day, at last, had he begun to see, so that what he had hitherto done was a movement without a direction. He had ripened too late and was so clumsily constituted that he had had to teach himself by mistakes.

"I prefer your flowers, then, to other people's fruit, and your mistakes to other people's successes," said gallant Doctor Hugh. "It's for your mistakes I admire you."

"You're happy—you don't know," Dencombe answered. Looking at his watch the young man had got up; he named the hour of the afternoon at which he would return. Dencombe warned him against committing himself too deeply, and expressed again all his dread of making him neglect the Countess—perhaps incur her displeasure.

"I want to be like you—I want to learn by mistakes!" Doctor Hugh laughed.

"Take care you don't make too grave a one! But do come back," Dencombe added, with the glimmer of a new idea.

"You should have had more vanity!" Doctor Hugh spoke as if he knew the exact amount required to make a man of letters normal.

"No, no—I only should have had more time. I want another go."

"Another go?"

"1 want an extension."

"An extension?" Again Doctor Hugh repeated Dencombe's words, with which he seemed to have been struck.

"Don't you know?—I want to what they call 'live.'"

The young man, for good-bye, had taken his hand, which closed with a certain force. They looked at each other hard a moment. "You *will* live," said Doctor Hugh.

"Don't be superficial. It's too serious!"

"You *shall* live!" Dencombe's visitor declared, turning pale.

"Ah, that's better!" And as he retired the invalid, with a troubled laugh, sank gratefully back.

All that day and all the following night he wondered if it mightn't be arranged. His doctor came again, his servant was attentive, but it was to his confident young friend that he found himself mentally appealing. His collapse on the cliff was plausibly explained, and his liberation, on a better basis, promised for the morrow; meanwhile, however, the intensity of his meditations kept him tranquil and made him indifferent. The idea that occupied him was none the less absorbing because it was a morbid fancy. Here was a clever son of the age, ingenious and ardent, who happened to have set him up for connoisseurs to worship. This servant of his altar had all the new learning in science and all the old reverence in faith; wouldn't he therefore put his knowledge at the disposal of his sympathy, his craft at the disposal of his love? Couldn't he be trusted to invent a remedy for a poor artist to whose art he had paid a tribute? If he couldn't, the alternative was hard: Dencombe would have to surrender to silence, unvindicated and undivined. The rest of the day and all the next he toyed in secret with this sweet futility. Who would work the miracle for him but the young man who could combine such lucidity with such passion? He thought of the fairy-tales of science and charmed himself into forgetting that he looked for a magic that was not of this world. Doctor Hugh was an apparition, and that placed him above the law. He came and went while his patient, who sat up, followed him with supplicating eyes. The interest of knowing the great author had made the young man begin "The Middle Years" afresh, and would help him to find a deeper meaning in its pages. Dencombe had told him what he "tried for;" with all his intelligence, on a first perusal, Doctor Hugh had failed to guess it. The baffled celebrity wondered then who in the world would guess it: he was amused once more at the fine, full way with which an intention could be missed. Yet he wouldn't rail at the general mind to-day—consoling as that ever had been: the revelation of his own slowness had seemed to make all stupidity sacred.

Doctor Hugh, after a little, was visibly worried, confessing, on inquiry, to a source of embarrassment at home. "Stick to the Countess—don't mind me," Dencombe said, repeatedly; for his companion was frank enough about the large lady's attitude. She was so jealous that she had fallen ill—she resented such a breach of allegiance. She paid so much for his fidelity that she must have it all: she refused him the right to other sympathies, charged him with scheming to make her die alone, for it was needless to point out how little Miss Vernham was a resource in trouble. When Doctor Hugh mentioned that the Countess would already have left Bournemouth if he hadn't kept her in bed, poor Dencombe held his arm tighter and said with decision: "Take her straight away." They had gone out together, walking back to the sheltered nook in which, the other day, they had met. The young man, who had given his companion a personal support, declared with emphasis that his conscience was clear—he could ride two horses at once. Didn't he dream, for his future, of a time when he should have to ride five hundred? Longing equally for virtue, Dencombe replied that in that golden age no patient would pretend to have contracted with him for his whole attention. On the part of the Countess was not such an avidity lawful? Doctor Hugh denied it, said there was no contract but only a free understanding, and that a sordid servitude was impossible to a generous spirit; he liked moreover to talk about art, and that was the subject on which, this time, as they sat together on the sunny bench, he tried most to engage the author of "The Middle Years." Dencombe, soaring again a little on the weak wings of convalescence and still haunted by that happy notion of an organised rescue, found another strain of eloquence to plead the cause of a certain splendid "last manner," the very citadel, as it would prove, of his reputation, the stronghold into which his real treasure would be gathered. While his listener gave up the morning and the great still sea appeared to wait, he had a wonderful explanatory hour. Even for himself he was inspired as he told of what his treasure would consist—the precious metals he would dig from the mine, the jewels rare, strings of pearls, he would hang between the columns of his temple. He was wonderful for himself, so thick his convictions crowded; but he was still more wonderful for Doctor Hugh, who assured him, none the less, that the very pages he had just published were already encrusted with gems. The young man, however, panted for the combinations to come, and, before the face of the beautiful day, renewed to Dencombe his guarantee that his profession would hold itself responsible for such a life. Then he suddenly clapped his hand upon his watch-pocket and asked leave to absent himself for half an hour. Dencombe waited there for his return, but was at last recalled to the actual by the fall of a shadow across the ground. The shadow darkened into that of Miss Vernham, the young lady in attendance on the Countess; whom Dencombe, recognising her, perceived so clearly to have come to speak to him that he rose from his bench to acknowledge the civility. Miss Vernham indeed proved not particularly civil; she looked strangely agitated, and her type was now unmistakable.

"Excuse me if I inquire," she said, "whether it's too much to hope that you may be induced to leave Doctor Hugh alone." Then, before Dencombe, greatly disconcerted, could protest: "You ought to be informed that you stand in his light; that you may do him a terrible injury."

"Do you mean by causing the Countess to dispense with his services?"

"By causing her to disinherit him." Dencombe stared at this, and Miss Vernham pursued, in the gratification of seeing she could produce an impression: "It has depended on himself to come into something very handsome. He has had a magnificent prospect, but I think you've succeeded in spoiling it."

"Not intentionally, I assure you. Is there no hope the accident may be repaired?" Dencombe asked.

"She was ready to do anything for him. She takes great fancies, she lets herself go—it's her way. She has no relations, she's free to dispose of her money, and she's very ill."

"I'm very sorry to hear it," Dencombe stammered.

"Wouldn't it be possible for you to leave Bournemouth? That's what I've come to ask you."

Poor Dencombe sank down on his bench. "I'm very ill myself, but I'll try!"

Miss Vernham still stood there with her colourless eyes and the brutality of her good conscience. "Before it's too late, please!" she said; and with this she turned her back, in order, quickly, as if it had been a business to which she could spare but a precious moment, to pass out of his sight.

Oh, yes, after this Dencombe was certainly very ill. Miss Vernham had upset him with her rough, fierce news; it was the sharpest shock to him to discover what was at stake for a penniless young man of fine parts. He sat trembling on his bench, staring at the waste of waters, feeling sick with the directness of the blow. He was indeed too weak, too unsteady, too alarmed; but he would make the effort to get away, for he couldn't accept the guilt of interference, and his honour was really involved. He would hobble home, at any rate, and then he would think what was to be done. He made his way back to the hotel and, as he went, had a characteristic vision of Miss Vernham's great motive. The Countess hated women, of course; Dencombe was lucid about that; so the hungry pianist had no personal hopes and could only console herself with the bold conception of helping Doctor Hugh in order either to marry him after he should get his money or to induce him to recognise her title to compensation and buy her off. If she had befriended him at a fruitful crisis he would really, as a man of delicacy, and she knew what to think of that point, have to reckon with her.

At the hotel Dencombe's servant insisted on his going back to bed. The invalid had talked about catching a train and had begun with orders to pack; after which his humming nerves had yielded to a sense of sickness. He consented to see his physician, who immediately was sent for, but he wished it to be understood that his door was irrevocably closed to Doctor Hugh. He had his plan, which was so fine that he rejoiced in it after getting back to bed.

Doctor Hugh, suddenly finding himself snubbed without mercy, would, in natural disgust and to the joy of Miss Vernham, renew his allegiance to the Countess. When his physician arrived Dencombe learned that he was feverish and that this was very wrong: he was to cultivate calmness and try, if possible, not to think. For the rest of the day he wooed stupidity; but there was an ache that kept him sentient, the probable sacrifice of his "extension," the limit of his course. His medical adviser was anything but pleased; his successive relapses were ominous. He charged this personage to put out a strong hand and take Doctor Hugh off his mind—it would contribute so much to his being quiet. The agitating name, in his room, was not mentioned again, but his security was a smothered fear, and it was not confirmed by the receipt, at ten o'clock that evening, of a telegram which his servant opened and read for him and to which, with an address in London, the signature of Miss Vernham was attached. "Beseech you to use all influence to make our friend join us here in the morning. Countess much the worse for dreadful journey, but everything may still be saved." The two ladies had gathered themselves up and had been capable in the afternoon of a spiteful revolution. They had started for the capital, and if the elder one, as Miss Vernham had announced, was very ill, she had wished to make it clear that she was proportionately reckless. Poor Dencombe, who was not reckless and who only desired that everything should indeed be "saved," sent this missive straight off to the young man's lodging and had on the morrow the pleasure of knowing that he had quitted Bournemouth by an early train.

Two days later he pressed in with a copy of a literary journal in his hand. He had returned because he was anxious and for the pleasure of flourishing the great review of "The Middle Years." Here at least was something adequate—it rose to the occasion; it was an acclamation, a reparation, a critical attempt to place the author in the niche he had fairly won. Dencombe accepted and submitted; he made neither objection nor inquiry, for old complications had returned and he had had two atrocious days. He was convinced not only that he should never again leave his bed, so that his young friend might pardonably remain, but that the demand he should make on the patience of beholders would be very moderate indeed. Doctor Hugh had been to town, and he tried to find in his eyes some confession that the Countess was pacified and his legacy clinched; but all he could see there was the light of his juvenile joy in two or three of the phrases of the newspaper. Dencombe couldn't read them, but when his visitor had insisted on repeating them more than once he was able to shake an unintoxicated head. "Ah, no; but they would have been true of what I *could* have done!"

"What people 'could have done' is mainly what they've in fact done," Doctor Hugh contended.

"Mainly, yes; but I've been an idiot!" said Dencombe.

Doctor Hugh did remain; the end was coming fast. Two days later Dencombe observed to him, by way of the feeblest of jokes, that there would now be no question whatever of a second chance. At this the young man stared; then he exclaimed: "Why, it has come to pass—it has come to pass! The second chance has been the public's—the chance to find the point of view, to pick up the pearl!"

"Oh, the pearl!" poor Dencombe uneasily sighed. A smile as cold as a winter sunset flickered on his drawn lips as he added: "The pearl is the unwritten—the pearl is the unalloyed, the *rest*, the lost!"

From that moment he was less and less present, heedless to all appearance of what went on around him. His disease was definitely mortal, of an action as relentless, after the short arrest that had enabled him to fall in with Doctor Hugh, as a leak in a great ship. Sinking steadily, though this visitor, a man of rare resources, now cordially approved by his physician, showed endless art in guarding him from pain, poor Dencombe kept no reckoning of favour or neglect, betrayed no symptom of regret or speculation. Yet toward the last he gave a sign of having noticed that for two days Doctor Hugh had not been in his room, a sign that consisted of his suddenly opening his eyes to ask of him if had spent the interval with the Countess.

"The Countess is dead," said Doctor Hugh. "I knew that in a particular contingency she wouldn't resist. I went to her grave."

Dencombe's eyes opened wider. "She left you 'something handsome'?"

The young man gave a laugh almost too light for a chamber of woe. "Never a penny. She roundly cursed me."

"Cursed you?" Dencombe murmured.

"For giving her up. I gave her up for *you*. I had to choose," his companion explained.

"You chose to let a fortune go?"

"1 chose to accept, whatever they might be, the consequences of my infatuation," smiled Doctor Hugh. Then, as a larger pleasantry: "A fortune be hanged! It's your own fault if I can't get your things out of my head."

The immediate tribute to his humour was a long, bewildered moan; after which, for many hours, many days, Dencombe lay motionless and absent. A response so absolute, such a glimpse of a definite result and such a sense of credit worked together in his mind and, producing a strange commotion, slowly altered and transfigured his despair. The sense of cold submersion left him—he seemed to float without an effort. The incident was extraordinary as evidence, and it shed an intenser light. At the last he signed to Doctor Hugh to listen, and, when he was down on his knees by the pillow, brought him very near.

"You've made me think it all a delusion."

"Not your glory, my friend," stammered the young man.

"Not my glory—what there is of it! It *is* glory—to have been tested, to have had our little quality and cast our little spell. The thing is to have made somebody care. You happen to be crazy, or course, but that doesn't affect the law."

"You're a great success!" said Doctor Hugh, putting into his young voice the ring of a marriage-bell.

Dencombe lay taking this in; then he gathered strength to speak once more. "A second chance—that's the delusion. There never was to be but one. We work in the dark—we do what we can—we give what we have. Our doubt is our passion and our passion is our task. The rest is the madness of art."

"If you've doubted, if you've despaired, you've always 'done' it," his visitor subtly argued.

"We've done something or other," Dencombe conceded.

"Something or other is everything. It's the feasible. It's *you*!"

"Comforter!" poor Dencombe ironically sighed.

"But it's true," insisted his friend.

"It's true. It's frustration that doesn't count."

"Frustration's only life," said Doctor Hugh.

"Yes, it's what passes." Poor Dencombe was barely audible, but he had marked with the words the virtual end of his first and only chance.